Diploids

ISBN: 978-1-63950-037-6   [Paperback Edition]
        978-1-63950-038-3   [eBook Edition]

Printed and bound in The United States of America.

Writers Apex

Gateway Towards Success

8063 MADISON AVE #1252
Indianapolis, IN 46227
+13176596889
www.writersapex.com

DIPLOIDS

CLEMENT MASLOFF

Although Lugeus was only two years older than his fourteen year-old brother, Alpheus, he acted towards him like a mature adult toward a subordinate child. The younger sibling felt this attitude with special force when the pair made a trek on foot to a summer fair in their district of Upper Provincia.

The forest the twosome passed on their way to the festival site wore the leafy green coloring of acer, rhus, fraxine, morus, quercus, tilia, and haw trees prevalent in their region.

Lugeus set a brisk, quick pace for his shorter, lighter brother. Both of them, blond and azure-eyed, had received several copper drachmae from their father. Even a poor cottager like the latter could afford to send his boys to the once-a-year celebration of the countryside's most pleasant and happiest season of the year.

But Alpheus was not free of commands and directions even on such a holiday.

"Lift your feet faster," barked Lugeus. "I want to arrive there early, not late."

"Stick close to me, because I don't want to have to hunt for you in the crowd."

"I will decide what you buy to eat, so don't try to feed yourself."

"Don't stray away, but keep close to me at all times."

On and on went the unending instructions, admonitions, and orders to Alpheus.

After a while, the latter's ears seemed to turn off and tune out on their own, as if saturated and overfilled. His mind wandered forward to the games and attractions he had witnessed year after year when the upland district assembled for its celebration of the aestival pause of summer.

Alpheus looked ahead with the expectation of the earlier joy and wonder he had experienced there. What new things was he going to see this year?

As they neared the cleared-off field with its attractions, many rural inhabitants were taking the same path through the buttonwood forest. A crowd became visible in front of and behind them.

Finally, the wooded area ended and the brightly colored tents stood before the pair. A growing throng was already present.

"Follow me as I circle around the outer edge of the fair," said Lugeus to his brother.

Several thousand celebrants had congregated from far and wide for the occasion. Their mood was a rollicking, festive one. The villagers and cottagers appeared determined to have themselves the best time they possibly could.

Along the outer meadow, mensals and tables had been set up for card games of slapjack, spoilfive, scarto, canfield, corncan, lansquenet, videruff, slam, gleek, piquet, cinch, and monte.

Daring country swain played at tip cat, knocking large wooden pieces into the air with all their strength. Running races went on without pause or end.

At numerous stalls, women sold maypops, soursops, cracknels, shandygaff, and freshly baked farl cakes. Adult men swigged local oenomel and malt. Mudcat and tench from nearby streams was offered for sale.

Costermongers who wandered the roads sold nugae and trifles available only once each year, at fair time. Furtive chiromancers read palms and told fortunes in the dark of their tents. A box full of marionettes performed on a traveling wagon. Giant tugs-of-war drew spectators to an open spot. An old barrel organ sent dissonant hurdy-gurdy melodies through the ever warmer air.

CLEMENT S. MASLOFF

The two brothers bought themselves almond macherones, followed by cups of apple shekar.

As they finished eating and drinking, they heard a loud cry from down the fairway path.

"The dancing ape is performing now!"

"Let's go at once before it finishes!"

"They say it looks like an old, bent-over little man."

"The crowd is crushing itself around the ape-owner's wagon."

Lugeus and his brother exchanged quick glances and the former decided instantly. "Let's go see what everyone is excited about," he said with authority to Alpheus.

The two immediately joined the throng drifting toward the scene of the ape show.

A sinuous, undulating music was sounding from a small reed melodeon played by a tiny, wizened oldster on the tail of a large wagon. Beside him was the gyrating figure of a stoop-backed ape, only four feet high.

Lugeus and Alpheus muscled their way gradually forward, till they stood close enough to see for themselves the wildly excited, abandoned dancing about of the dumb creature.

The two brothers stared with total fascination at a sight neither would have ever imagined. It was something utterly odd and strange, from an unknown distance away from their region.

By what name did this creature go? each asked himself.

They watched in awe as the animal raised its extremely long arms and waved them about to a rhythm from the melodeon playing loudly to its side.

The face was completely hairless, though simian in structure and contours. The ears were so small as to be almost invisible against the shaggy hair of a reddish-brown hue. A low, heavy brow hung down above lively chestnut eyes.

What was one to call this unusual creature? pondered Alpheus. What kind of ape was it?

At last, the little man in charge of the beast stopped playing music and rose from his stool.

No longer dancing, the animal sidled over to the man who was its master. As the latter faced the audience crowd, so did the ape. Loud applause broke out, growing louder as it continued.

Lugeus and Alpheus could not but join in the frenzied clapping of hands on all sides of them.

Smiling with joy, the human owner bowed to the captivated public, his hand clutching that of his performing pet. A slight squeeze signaled the latter to imitate the low bow of its master.

The short man in an old, discolored city suit then spoke to the assembled crowd.

"Thank you, fellow citizens. Both Pongo and I are grateful to you. For now, we both need some time to rest up, but a complete performance of our act will follow shortly. In the meantime, my assistant will pass among you with a cannikin in which voluntary contributions for maintaining Pongo can be made. We both thank you all."

Lugeus turned to his younger brother as the audience began to disperse.

"I am thirsty for some spicy milk posset they always have available down at the opposite end of the fair."

Alpheus had a ready reply to that. "It is curdled with strong ale that I am not old enough to drink yet. Father and mother would both be angry if word of my drinking strong posset ever reached them. No, I think it best to stay right here where I am and wait for the ape to do its funny dance once more. Is that alright with you, Lugeus?"

The latter gave him a wry smile. "Don't wander off anywhere. I'll be back to get you when the time comes for us to start home."

With that, the older brother set off to enjoy an alcoholic milk drink by himself.

Alpheus looked back at the small performance platform at one end of the wagon. The master and his Pongo had retreated into the closed sleeping cabin in the front of the vehicle.

Feeling how intense curiosity was seizing hold of him, the young man decided to have a closer look and perhaps ask the old man some questions about his simian charge.

The assistant, a stocky fellow with green eyes and flaxen hair, blocked the forward progress of Alpheus as he approached the big nag that pulled the show wagon.

"Wo! Where do you think you're going?" challenged the act's helper.

"I wanted to speak with your boss and ask him about his animal, that's all."

"He and Pongo are busy eating inside," grumbled the subordinate. "I can tell you anything that might be of interest. Just shoot."

"Well, what variety of ape is this creature called Pongo?"

"Don't you know? Can't you tell? He comes from faraway islands off the coast of Provincia. The native population calls him a Oran or Orang. For many years, people called these beasts a type of wild man from the jungle forests.

"Our Pongo, though, is a very smart animal. He is able to accomplish many surprising things. Did you notice how his brain sticks out from his forehead? No one dares call him stupid."

"I have no doubt at all that Pongo possess sharp intelligence for an ape," grinned Alpheus. "Would it be possible for me to have a private view of him, all by myself? I mean with you present, of course."

Before the assistant could reply, the master showed his face between the folds of the front curtain of the wagon's sleeping cabin.

"You say, young man, that you wish to see Pongo by yourself, in private? Can you furnish me ten drachmae for such a privilege, my son?"

Alpheus remembered how much remained in his coin pocket.

"I still have eight left from what I came here with, sir," he answered.

"That will have to do, then. Jump up the front step there and I will lead you to where dear Pongo is now fast asleep, resting from his work for the public."

With energy and enthusiasm, the country boy did just that.

"My name is Mr. Thalum," said the owner once Alpheus was standing in the prow of the wagon. "Come with me into the interior where you can have a good look at my oran."

The two stepped into the dim cabin where Pongo lay in a bed resembling a manger. But the ape was not asleep, for his darkly gleaming eyes took in the stranger standing beside his master.

"We have awakened the creature with the noise we made outside," whispered Thalum. "But that is even better, for now you can see the animal when it is fully conscious. Move closer, if you please. But do not try to touch the precious dear."

Alpheus inched nearer, till he stood at the edge of the wooden cradle holding the ape. The eyes of the latter followed the unknown intruder, peering into his azure-colored eyes.

All at once, the oran sprang into an upright position, surprising his unexpected visitor.

Pongo extended his right hand forward.

"He wishes for you to shake it," murmured Thalum in a low tone. "Go ahead, there is absolutely no danger at all to you, young fellow."

Alpheus did so, soon holding the hairy forepaw of the dancer. He could feel the clutching grip of the animal's fingers. How strong it was!

A weird guttural sound flowed out of the oran's throat as its mouth opened wide.

"He likes you," declared the master with a small grin. "Pongo judges you to be his friend. That is the reason he purrs that way, for he is a sensitive judge of human character."

Staring into the sparkling dark brown eyes of the ape, the country youth sensed an influence that contained a mysterious wisdom that was inborn and natural. What could it be? Why was it affecting him so?

An unforeseeable message beyond his comprehension was sent to and received by Alpheus.

The two beings of different species held each other's hand in a fast grip of amity. Both their minds felt an inscrutable link, arcane and invisible.

Thalum broke their connection with words of intervention. "You will have to go now, because the time is coming near for our second performance today. Pongo and I have many things we must get ready at once."

As Alpheus released the hand of the oran, its arm dropped and it let out a gutteral noise from deep inside itself.

The youth moved to the front of the cabin and parted the curtains hanging there.

Before jumping to the ground, he threw a rapid glance at the animal whose fingers he had held.

Was it a wink that Pongo sent in his direction?

It was impossible for Alpheus to determine whether he had actually seen what he believed he had.

Lugeus appeared at the edge of the audience crowd as the final show was about to begin.

"We must leave immediately if we are to reach home before nightfall," he said to his brother. "There is no time to lose. Come along with me at once."

What was Alpheus to do? He wished to stay and see Pongo dance again, for a third time. But it would worry his mother and father were he to be out of their area at night.

Without resistance, the younger brother fell in behind Lugeus.

Soon the pair were away from the site of the oran's performance. The music of the melodeon came to their ears, fading into the general noise of the fair. The distance from that particular show grew ever greater.

Into the buttonwood forest they moved as the first signs of dusk fell from the sky.

As he walked on, Alpheus kept returning to his most recent experience, that with the ape.

His memory clung to the manner in which the oran gazed at him. He could not recall ever before being the focus of such a persistent, penetrating look. No human being had in his few years of life made him feel such intense attention. There was something inexpressible and undefinable in the eyes of the ape.

As the sky swiftly darkened and the brothers approached home, Alpheus had an uncanny sense that there was going to be a major change in store for him. But he had no idea what it might consist of when it came.

He turned his head back as he walked toward the family cottage. Why did he have a feeling of being followed and watched?

Lugeus abruptly stopped and turned to his companion for the day. "You had better go to the ecurie and feed the horse," he grunted harshly. "That should have been done before we left for the fair, but we hurried off."

Without a word, Alpheus turned away and headed for the stable opposite the cottage.

Why does my brother enjoy ordering me around? he asked himself as he walked away.

The interior of the barn was becoming very dark and shadowy. Alpheus picked up a pitchfork and started moving hay to where the plough animal could reach it for a late supper.

As he worked with speed and diligence, the boy thought that he heard a noise at the barn door. Turning his head around, his eyes caught sight of an intruding figure.

Alpheus stopped his chore and moved to face the stranger who was moving closer to him.

A small, bent shape with a square head and glowing chestnut eyes stared at him, addressing the farm boy in a guarded, muffled whisper.

"I need your help. Is it possible for me to spend the night here in this barn?"

No immediate reply came from the startled, dumbstruck Alpheus. When he succeeded in opening his mouth, the voice was nearly gone.

"Who are you?" asked the youth. "What is your business in our barn?"

"I am but a fugitive in need of refuge. Please, do not allow me to perish tonight."

It took time for the confused, alarmed Alpheus to formulate a decision. "Stay in the barn, if that is necessary. You look hungry. Can I bring you some food to eat?"

"That would be fine. I will always be in your debt, my friend."

Without a word, Alpheus threw down the pitchfork in his hands and made his way past the stranger, out of the barn and toward the cottage where supper awaited him.

"How did you enjoy the fair?" asked the father, turning azure eyes on his younger son.

"It was exciting," mumbled Alpheus, peering down at his plate of rockahominy grits.

His mother, short and squat, with her straw hair fastened in a bun, sat down across from her lanky husband.

"What was the biggest attraction for the two of you?" she asked both sons simultaneously.

Lugeus was the one who replied first.

"I liked the athletic contests and the card games going on. But my little brother was fascinated with the dancing ape, I believe."

"Oh!" chirped the mistress of the farm. "I can remember once seeing such a creature when I was a small girl and father took us to the festival. Was this animal what is called a babuin?"

The father turned his eyes on Alpheus, as did all the rest of the family. "Yes," he noted. "I can recall seeing an ape they called a mandrillus one time."

Alpheus felt obliged to describe what he had seen himself.

"This one was an ape with red hair and a ridge above its eyes," he explained. "It goes by the name of oran. In the coastal islands where it lives, they call it an orang."

"I think my brother was entranced by the strange creature" mocked Lugeus. "I was afraid he was about to run off with the animal and its owner. They travel in an old cabin wagon. Who wants to live around the smells of an ape, though?"

Alpheus felt compelled to justify himself in any way possible.

"This oran, whose name is Pongo, is quite intelligent. Not only has he learned the patterns of various dances, but he can also adjust his movements to different melodies and tempos. It is an amazing show that was put on by the pet and its trainer."

"My brother is under the spell of a dancing ape!" sneered Lugeus. "Perhaps you should get him one to raise and take care of, father."

Small smiles and light laughter followed, but then everyone turned to finishing their supper.

Alpheus, remembering the promise he had given, watched for scraps of food and leftovers that might be taken to the fugitive hiding in the barn.

The parents were sleeping soundly in their bedroom. As the midnight hour arrived and passed, Alpheus lay awake in the attic loft of the cottage. He was waiting to hear loud snoring from his brother across from him. At last, with certainty that it was safe to move, he rose and slowly crept down from the upper storey. Down the ladder he cautiously climbed, into the dark, lightless kitchen. Memory told him where the larder box was. He noiselessly opened it and removed a long loaf of stale rye bread that was to be fed to the horse for breakfast the following morning.

Taking it in hand, Alpheus closed the box and stole out of the cottage without a sound.

To the barn and into it he walked in the starlight from the sky.

Would he have to wake up the stranger? wondered the youth bringing him nourishment.

As soon as Alpheus entered through the barn door, he found the straw-haired man standing near the opening, as if he had sensed the approach of his rescuer.

Without saying a word, the fugitive seized the bread out of the hand of Alpheus and started to devour it with speed and force. Only when it was completely gone did the unknown person speak.

"Thank you. I will be forever beholden to you.

"Let me first of all introduce myself. I go by the name of Naren. But you must tell no one, even those closest to you, of my presence here. I depend absolutely on your discretion. Will you protect me from being found and identified?"

"Yes, of course I will," answered the frightened, confused teenager. He was uncertain why it was he felt compelled to cooperate with the unusual person seeking his aid and protection.

The man who called himself Naren now gave an explanation of his plight that, at first, was difficult for the boy to understand.

"I have to wait for the district fair to end, the day after tomorrow. Only then can I be certain that my employer will not be able to locate me and drag me back into servitude. Only a little while, then I shall be able to surface in my other form.

"It looks as if it will be a difficult process. But I am determined to appear and act as a free human being, despite my nature of being folded into opposite forms. None of it will be easy for me."

He stopped and gazed intently at Alpheus, asking him a vitally important question.

"Are you understanding the kernel of what I am telling you about myself and my nature?"

The reply was a simple, truthful "No."

Naren then reached out his right arm, grasping the other by his wrist.

"I was born in possession of two opposite natures: one that of human and the other that of an anthropoid ape. Do you remember Pongo at the district fair? You watched the dancing with fascination, then paid to go into the wagon cabin and have a closer look. Do you know why it is I am aware of all that happened there?

"It is because my secondary form is that of the oran that you saw yesterday while at the fair.

"This now is my human form, but I remain cursed with double forms of myself. When I fall into my animal stage, I become Pongo, the Oran."

Alpheus sensed a painful dizziness in himself that grew the more he heard.

Was Naren some sort of madman? Or was he, as he claimed, a freak of nature?

"I do not at all understand what you say," confessed the confused lad.

"Do not worry, I shall explain more for you tomorrow," promised the weird guest. "Can you come here in the early morning hours of the day?"

"Yes," promised Alpheus. "I will bring you more to eat."

With that, he turned and exited, stealing back into the sleeping farm cottage.

There was no more sleep that night for the youngest member of the family, not a single wink.

How could what he had heard be true? Yes, he had listened to local legends about double-natured creatures with opposing forms. Children often spoke of vampiric and ghoulish monsters that hid themselves as human beings. His own father had once spoken of bifold beings said to dwell far away beyond the forests of Provincia.

Was Naren a deluded fool, a victim of fantasy of the mind?

Or was it a credible truth when he characterized himself as an anthropoid oran from the faraway islands of the sea? What should he believe or not believe?

Could a double being be there on the family farm? It took time for the idea to consolidate and solidify in his mind. Could Naren and Pongo be different forms of the same being?

As the solar daystar rose, illuminating the sky and the world below, the sleepless young fellow had to accept the conclusion that what Naren had revealed to him was true. It had to be accepted.

"You must not stay here in the stable barn longer," Alpheus warned his new acquaintance. "My father will soon be coming to fetch the horse for morning plowing in the bleuet field down by the stream. It will not be safe for you in that area or here."

Naren swallowed the last of the rockahominy that the boy had brought him to eat.

"Yes, I can understand what you are saying. It will be necessary to spend the day in the woods nearby, even though Mr.Thalum is probably still hunting for me."

"Won't he have to give up the chase when he fails to find Pongo?" asked Alpheus.

"No one can say for sure, because he is stubborn and obstinate."

"Does he know of your two different phases and forms?"

"I have tried to keep that secret, but I suspect that the bastard has guessed the truth about the condition of his oran."

"Was he a cruel master to Pongo?"

Naren nodded his head yes. "It became necessary to leave him."

"Forgive me for asking, but how does it feel to have two forms by nature?"

"It is not easy, nor always pleasant. Look at what my present situation is."

Alpheus dared to continue probing. "Do you enjoy control over the change of form, or does it happen by itself without choice or decision?"

The fugitive grew tense. "At first, in my early years, the leaps were always surprises. But in time I came to possess considerable power of will over these transfers back and forth."

"I see," said Alpheus, although that was perhaps only half-true.

In a short while, Naren ran off into the buttonwood trees in the distance.

As the family finished eating breakfast that morning, Lugeus turned to his younger brother.

"Guess what? Father decided I can take the little shooter and try to find small game in the forest. Who knows? I might get me a lepus or a sciurus if I'm lucky. But having a scout to help me would be a favorable boost. That is why I want you to accompany me."

Alpheus attempted to conceal the inner shock that he felt.

"I don't think I want to go out hunting. There are chores around the cottage that have to be carried out. They will keep me very busy."

"That can wait," insisted Lugeus with force in his voice. "This is more important, even father says." He gave his brother a cold, unflinching stare, nearly a glare.

What could Alpheus do, then?

He surrendered, realizing what might happen out among the trees.

Which form would his new friend be taking out in the woods? wondered Alpheus.

CLEMENT S. MASLOFF

The elder brother removed the antique fusil from its resting place above the fireplace in the front parlor. Then the pair left the cottage and started walking across the farm.

I must watch every move my brother makes, silently resolved Alpheus. I must look out for the possible presence of either Naren or Pongo. One or the other, whatever the form, might be endangered by shots aimed in error.

The hunter and his scout went into a thick stand of buttonwoods. They penetrated deeper and deeper into the forest where shadows outnumbered the few spots of light.

All of a sudden, Lugeus stopped. His brother was compelled to do the same.

The two glanced a second at each other, until the one holding the weapon aimed it and shot.

Alpheus waited in shock, peering toward the point where tree branches formed a solid wall.

There was something there, the younger brother realized. Lugeus had seen and aimed at some target. It was a low shape near the ground and had a reddish coloring. He recognized at once what it had to be.

His eyes turned on Lugeus. When he had fired the fusil, it had made a thundering sound in the previously silent forest. Alpheus continued to feel the echo in the cells of his body and brain.

How could such a thing have happened? he asked himself.

Alpheus saw that the animal had fallen to the ground, for his brother had a keen, accurate eye. He had no doubt but that Lugeus had brought down the fugitive ape, the oran that was the other self of the man who called himself Naren.

As if petrified, the body of Alpheus refused to move.

It was the brother with the shooter who stepped forward to examine and claim the prize. He bent down to touch the fur of the felled animal, then looked up and called out to his shocked, paralyzed younger brother.

"You will not believe what we have here. This is an ape, just like the one we saw doing its dance at the fair. What an amazing development that is. How can there be two such unusual beasts in the same region where they are not common or natural? Come over and have a look yourself."

But Alpheus refused to move. His eyes were focused on the corpse lying on the ground. Why go forward to see? he asked himself. I know what has been done. I saw how this form was killed by my brother. What is left that anyone can do? The deed is accomplished and finished. There is no going back. The future has been decided. Naren and Pongo are both no more. The oran was killed, but so was the friendly human being I talked with.

Neither phase now exists. There is nothing left alive of either one.

Alpheus heard his brother thinking aloud. "This was useless shooting, because no one can eat or make any use of a dead oran. It's best to bury it here as fast as possible. You and I cannot tell father or mother what has happened. Do you understand why? This has all been a mistake and we must get rid of all traces of the dead body."

The other nodded his head, then followed Lugeus back to the barn.

Instead of helping his brother dig a grave for the dead animal, Alpheus made the excuse that he felt ill and stayed in the stable where Naren and he had met.

Isolation became the haven of the fourteen year old.

He only spoke to his brother when specifically addressed, and only in the briefest possible terms. His attitude toward his parents became one of silence and passivity.

Alpheus fell into a stupor of depression and regret.

Why had he been unable to protect his double-formed friend? Why had he failed to take immediate action that could have resulted in a different outcome?

Alpheus placed final blame and responsibility onto himself. Was it too late to liberate his conscience from its heavy burden of guilt? Perhaps not, if a proper escape was now attempted by him. A desperate dream arose in his imagination.

He had to flee from he farm and a brother he could no longer tolerate.

If he ran off from home, as countless country lads had done over the centuries, his life would become a rough, hazardous adventure. He would never again see his mother or father. His mind would forever contain an empty gap. But then he considered what might have been had the man named Naren survived and gave him new knowledge and understanding.

No, Alpheus concluded, I have to leave. But where am I to seek my future? To what location do I go now?

While he ruminated in bed one sleepless night, an idea occurred. It struck him with the force of inevitability. The concept had a certainty to it.

Alpheus had often heard of the great metropolis of Provincia, the capital of Diaema. He could both lose and find himself there. But how was he to feed, house, and cloth himself as a new migrant?

There had to be ways to survive in the big city. And he would be far away from Lugeus and what his brother had done in the buttonwood forest that day.

Secretly he hid the clothes he would need in the barn, along with a small supply of food.

When the night of escape arrived, he was as ready as he could be.

With a gunny bag over his shoulder, he stole off into the summer woods.

From village to village, then to towns and boroughs, he tramped over trails and roads. In several weeks Alpheus reached the outskirts of Diaema. With unexpected luck, he found a job as a kitchen helper in a lower class eatery.

Alpheus became a part of the busy, energetic urban drama of the great metropolis.

II
The Harpines

Alpheus went out to swim in the bay of the Amphiscian Sea early on his first full day on Harpine Isle. He did not anticipate what might happen to him that early in the morning. In his ochreous trunks, he rose from the chilly but refreshing water and stepped onto the dry sand as dayspring brightened, not aware of any impending peril.

Tall, blond, and azure-eyed, he had a muscular body that possessed natural balance and grace. Though by no means an athlete, he could have easily passed for one. The swim at dawn had put him into a state of electrified vigor. But he stopped in his tracks when he saw something that startled every nerve and brain cell within him.

A willowy young woman of a stately, sculpturesque beauty stood a short distance before him. Where had she come from? His eyes had not caught sight of this magnificent vision while he had been in the water, but now her presence had become unavoidable.

Her physical form was both slim and curvaceous. He had never before seen any female exactly like this one, he was certain. A dark brunette with a frizette of tight natural curls, she wore a short lemon-colored dress that revealed slender, delicate legs. Alpheus was drawn to her velvety sloe eyes, staring at them as if mesmerized. It was she who spoke first.

"You must be the vacationer staying at the Harpine Hotel. And you only arrived late yesterday and are now having your first swim. Am I correct in my guesses?"

The man from the mainland smiled shyly and replied. "Indeed, that is the truth. Let me introduce myself. My name is Alpheus and I live in Diaema. I work as a botanic apothecary. My employment is with a large medicinal firm, one of the biggest. Yes, I came to Harpine for a good, well-earned rest. My plans center upon swimming in this glorious bay. Are you a permanent resident of the island?"

"I am that," she answered him. "I have never been anywhere else but here."

"That is nothing to be sad about. Nowhere have I seen such beauty as in this place of yours." He felt an instantaneous embarrassment. Would she think he was referring to her own charm and grace of body? That was what he suspected had entered the deep recesses of his mind.

"My name is Electra," she informed him with a radiant smile. It is a very old name on our isle, going back ages."

The two studied each other, concentrating on face and eyes, no longer gazing directly at torsos.

"I hope to see you again, Miss," muttered Alpheus with hope discernible in his voice.

She grinned with pleasure. "That will not be difficult. In fact, it is most likely. You see, it is my mother who is owner and manager of the Harpine Inn. Have you met her yet?"

"No, I don't believe that I have. It was the hotel famulus who registered me last night. A young gossom boy carried my bags to the room where I slept. I will certainly look forward to meeting your mother. What is she called?"

"Celaeno." She paused a few moments. "Have you eaten breakfast?"

"No, I haven't. My plan was to get in an early swim before the daystar rose. It has refreshed and invigorated me. I am now ravenous to have some food. Then I intend to explore your island, so full of marvelous wonders, I understand."

"Breakfast is just about to be served," she informed him with a small laugh. "We can have a table in the canteen and have our meal together, and I can introduce you to mother."

"I shall change and meet you there, then," said the bedazzled Alpheus.

Their breakfast consisted of samp porridge with freshly picked ficos mixed in it. The side dish held bergamot pears with muscoval sugar on them.

The two who had met on the beach said little as they ate. But as their meal ended a plump mature woman in an expensive black gown appeared. There was a commanding aura about this person who was evidently the mother of Electra. Her chestnut hair was unlike that of her daughter. But the iridescent violet eyes had the identical velvety quality.

The buxom older woman introduced herself to Alpheus.

"I am Celaeno, mother to Electra and her sister, as well as manager of this hotel. I am sorry I was not available to greet you when you arrived late yesterday. But now we see each other, and I can welcome you to the isle. We are anxious to meet all of your needs. Just tell us whatever is necessary for your comfort and enjoyment, and we shall endeavor to provide it. For instance, you may need a guide to get about the island and see its highlights. I know that Electra is willing to assist you in that, aren't you, my dear?"

"Of course, mother," replied the daughter without any hint of shyness. "It would make me most happy to do so for our guest."

She gave a sunny smile to the young man she had earlier watched swimming.

All at once, a sharply crackling voice sounded from behind Alpheus. He turned his head to see who was talking with such force.

"So this is the apothecary from Diaema! He looks quite fit and healthy to me. The fellow must be taking his own compounds and medicaments to have such strength and stamina. I watched him swimming in the bay before daystar rose. Why don't you introduce me to him, mother?"

Alpheus saw a small young woman resembling Electra move around their table and stand beside the mother. The latter made introductions in a low, soft tone.

"This is my elder daughter, Aello. She is older than her sister and is a great help to me in running the hotel. Here is the man from the capital who wrote to make his reservation. Electra has agreed just now to show him our isle. Isn't that marvelous, dear Aello?"

The latter was a smaller version of her younger sister, but for some reason not as fetching or attractive. Aello had the same brunette hair and velvety sloe eyes, but was not at all as curvaceous or statuesque. She lacked the grace, dignity, and self-control of Electra.

Suddenly Aello made a bold step toward the surprised visitor to the isle.

"I think it would be better if our friend had two guides rather than one. Therefore, I shall offer him my services as well. He can have both of us with him simultaneously. Or at different times each of us can be separate companions and guides. What do you think of my idea, mother?"

For a moment, the latter appeared to gasp for breath.

"It is not for me to decide," she succeeded in declaring. "What do you say to my older daughter's suggestion, Mr. Alpheus?"

The vacationer answered with diplomatic tact. "It cannot be for me alone to choose or decide. I shall allow these two charming girls of yours to agree between themselves as to that matter. However they arrange things will be acceptable to me. More than acceptable."

Celaeno looked at Aello with severity in her eyes.

"That is how it will be, then. Tell our dear guest as soon as the two of you have it settled."

Alpheus realized that he had little familiarity or experience with women. That did not mean that he lacked interest in them. Far from that. His professional education had absorbed so much of his time and energy that he had overlooked previous opportunities to get close to anyone of the other sex.

But now things were different. His condition had changed with his work and salary assured. His career seemed well settled. He could afford vacations like this excursion to Harpine Isle.

I have met two unusual sisters very quickly, he told himself resting on the bed in his room.

What does that mean for my future? Can I come to understand either one of them in the few days of my stay here? It all depended upon him and how he related to each of the pair.

Alpheus smiled at himself. He was treading in unknown territory and had to be watchful and awake. There might be some unpredictable adventure in store for him here. But he had no reason to be fearful. His decision was to try to be carefree and seek the lark of innocent joy.

Electra accompanied him by herself on his first trek by foot into the tropical woods.

Here the guide pointed out kingwood, satinwood, gumwood, and featherwood trees to him. She showed him the stumps of felled baobabs, cut down for their edible pulp.

A tribe of hanuman monkeys cavorted above them, laughing and jumping in the high branches. Songs of a bellbird and a zygodactyl floated down in a quiet part of the trail the two were on. All at once Alpheus saw something and stopped. He bent down and pointed to a purple-red flower with large black berries. "Do you know what that is, Electra? It is a nightshade known in the pharmacopeia as Atropos. The popular name for this poisonous plant is the belladonna. In small quantities it induces sleep, but beyond a certain dosage the berries kill. They are extremely lethal."

Electra seemed to look away, as if troubled. "Yes, I recognize it. Let us proceed on and then turn and go back to the hotel."

They walked a long time in silence, reaching the end of a long, thick bosk.

"Shall we rest here before returning?" asked the guide. "I can see that the walk is tiring you." She pointed to a large fiddlewood log lying near the border of the forest.

Alpheus sat down first, while Electra hovered for a time behind his back. Her eyes feasted on his neck and spine. With his own eyes pointed away so that she was not in his line of sight, her eyes of velvet were free to gaze with abandon on the patch of exposed flesh. Her mind measured his reserve of muscle and tissue.

The inner self of Electra became ensorcelled by his young body as she moved closer toward him.

All at once, a loud voice yelled out from some unknown location.

"Electra! Why are the two of you sitting and standing about like that? Don't you have the energy to return home? I came all the way out here to accompany the two of you. Come on, let's be on our way. We should not be wasting time. Mother is expecting us for afternoon repast. Everyone must be ready to march back now, on the double as they say."

The surprised and interrupted Electra sent her sister a look of sharp anger and disdain. Saying not a single word in reply, she jumped over the fiddlewood log and grabbed the arm of Alpheus, who had risen to his feet.

"We have little choice but to follow Aello back," she whispered to the young man from the mainland.

The three young people concentrated on eating the spicy burgout soup and budgerigar. Celaeno entered the private dining room as they finished their plates of baked parrot.

"I hope you enjoyed the native bird," she said, looking at Alpheus. "It has always been indigenous to our isle. We think of the tender flesh as a native specialty."

"I found it deliciously delightful," said the guest. "It is a rare, expensive delicacy in the city."

The hotel owner laughed. "I dare say there are edibles in Diaema that are scarce and infrequent for us." She glanced for an instant at her two daughters, first Electra and then Aello.

Alpheus began to think out loud. "I do not understand why the population of Harpine Isle is so small. The woods are full of valuable materials. Your plant life is rich and varied. Yet one sees few human inhabitants hereabouts. Just this morning I noted a wide herbal and medicinal inventory in the unique biota of your tropical forest. It was incredible."

He reached over the table and took a stock of wild smallage to munch on.

Celaeno moved closer to him. "You appear not familiar with our ancient legend about the harpines. Fear of them may have prevented some from elsewhere settling here, I fear."

"I read historical and geographic descriptions of the island before deciding to visit," admitted Alpheus. "In other regions of Provincia, those female body snatchers were called the harpies, but on this isle their name came to be that of harpines."

Electra decided to intervene.

"What do you know about such a strange subject as that? There are many fanciful, imaginative tales in circulation. Who can tell what may be true and what is pure fantasy?"

Alpheus turned his head so that he could focus his eyes on Electra.

"Some sources I have seen say that they began as wind spirits and that their original purpose was to steal the souls of all their victims. I remember some of the colorful names given to the harpines in legends: Stormwind, Swiftwind, and Swiftfoot. These spirits were eager to consume the bodies of children so that they could more easily get to the inner soul and swallow it. That was what they were ultimately after, to absorb and digest the psyche of the victim.

"Harpines fit into the category of supernatural anthropophagites. In other words, cannibals."

"You call them unnatural beings?" questioned Electra, aroused but also puzzled. "Why do you say that? Aren't the harpines corporeal rather than incorporeal?"

Alpheus looked deeply into her velvet sloe eyes as though searching for something. He was surprised that she used the present tense in reference to the ancient soul snatchers and flesh eaters. Unless she misspoke, did she believe that they continued to exist in her own time? That they were still about somewhere?

Suddenly Celaeno broke the prevailing silence. "It is time we enjoyed some dessert. I made my favorite orgeat today with fresh hesperidiums. I can bring the pot out in a jiffy. You will like its sweetness, Alpheus. I am sure that you will."

Aello interceded to praise and describe her mother's almond orange syrup. "It is unlimited in its sweetness, but does not overburden the organs of taste. That is how things should always be, of course. Excessive degrees of any particular quality can delight us, but can in time negate themselves. A small amount can be a good guarantee against overindulgence. Don't you agree, Alpheus?"

The tourist smiled at her. "That is how it often turns out, though few can foresee the dangers that result from overdoing a sense or taste. In my apothecary work I have become conscious of how a very small surplus can ruin the positive effects that would have been ensured by a smaller, but adequate, dosage.

"Perhaps that is how it is with many of the situations we have to face in life."

Celaeno directed a pleasant smile his way. "There is wisdom in what you say, young man. If only we all adhered to the necessary limits that exist in all sectors of the world we live in."

She looked at her two daughters before going to fetch the orgeat she had made.

The visitor put off a second excursion, the one he had promised the older sister, each afternoon that passed by. She grew increasingly insistent, until Alpheus was compelled to relent. "I shall take you on the southern coast of our isle," the small brunette told him as they departed from the hotel along a narrow pathway.

"We must watch out for grass anguines and forest aphidians," Aello warned as they walked through the tropical woods. At last they arrived at the placid shore of white sand. She pointed out to him the tiny, bright yellow dragonets swimming in the shallow water, along with spiny-rayed gobies of a rainbow of colors. The two of them watched as newts and efts came forth from the sea, onto the pristine

CLEMENT S. MASLOFF

sand. Alpheus spotted a giant green terrapin a short distance away, moving toward the water. An eel-like lamprey, its teeth protruding, was devouring a small gecko it had captured.

Aello gave her male companion an unexpected nudge in the small of his back.

"You can see the battle in nature everywhere here on the Isle of the Harpines. All of life is a constant, unending gobbling, chewing, ingesting, and swallowing. Did you know that before making your trip, Alpheus?"

She looked squarely into his eyes as they faced each other. He could see how the velvety pupils engulfed and overpowered her shrinking irises. Had this young man ever witnessed such a strange sight before? Was he capable of withstanding its power?

An uncanny sense of impending danger struck his startled mind. Aello spoke to him in a new, impersonal tone of voice unfamiliar to him.

"You must never fear me, my dear. It is Electra, not I, who threatens to harm your body. She is the hungry one, not I."

He could say nothing, gazing at her in helpless confusion as she continued.

"Why don't you kiss me, Alpheus? I will do the same for you, then."

As he gaped at her, she took a step closer, until her breast was less than an inch from his chest.

All at once, with open mouth she began to fall forward, until her face rested against his white summer shirt. He made out her hands coming upward as if to tear away the cloth covering his heart.

At that moment, a loud shout from the forest halted the assault about to hit him.

"Aello! Alpheus! It's time for you two to come back to the hotel. Supper is going to be early tonight, mother informed me. You must hurry back."

Both trekkers turned to the approaching figure of Electra.

Alpheus gave a sigh as he marched forward to meet the welcome intruder who had rescued him.

"We lost all track of time out here on the beach," he said to Electra. "The afternoon slipped by with us unaware of it. Thank you for your thoughtful effort in walking all this way. We both thank you."

He purposely ignored Aello as he joined her sister. The emotion that seized hold of him was revulsion. Talking only with the one who had summoned him, Alpheus allowed the embarrassed Aello to trail behind on their return to the hotel.

Celaeno realized there existed antagonistic rivalry between her daughters. The first to come to her in the kitchen that evening was Aello. As the mother turned a roasted entellus monkey on an open spit, she listened to the complaint of the disappointed sister.

"She intentionally interrupted me when I had him caught in a trance. Only a few seconds more, and his body would have been totally overpowered. What can her motive be for such behavior except a selfish hatred of me? She has always been the favored one in the matter of young male flesh. You tend to give her first crack at every man, How will I ever satisfy my deep hunger, mother? Am I to remain a starveling because of my sister's greed? Is that it?"

Turning toward her, Celaeno spoke with rough harshness to the complainer.

"Both of you are to blame for this unacceptable situation. When haven't the two of you quarreled and interfered with each other? You will not allow her to proceed toward Alpheus, while she blocks and prevents your satisfaction. What am I to do, if my pair of daughters are unable to solve the dispute on their own?

"Cannot this man be shared through division, half of him going to you and the other half to Electra? Wouldn't that be reasonable and fair? That is my advice, though it will be very difficult to carry out for you two."

Aello's anger at her mother's proposal exploded in a wild outcry.

"Difficult? I call such a scheme impossible. Why does Electra harbor animus toward me? Why such undisguised odium? Is it because I was first to be born? That I am senior to her?"

Hearing these words, Celaeno turned spectral pale.

"Do not talk like that. You only think that you are older. Your sister has the same idea about herself. She believes that she is the older one. The truth of the matter cannot be determined because of the years of amnemonic starvation that I underwent on this isle after the male population died out or disappeared. That was a horrendous period of my life. Two small girls and no masculine flesh for either me or them. Not till I started the hotel was there any reason for men to visit here. Today we enjoy a very limited number of fitting candidates. Are my two daughters to war over a single herbalist who is attractive to both of them?"

"But what should I do, mother?" pleaded Aello. "I must have him all to myself. There can be no equal sharing, no surrendering on my part."

The mother thought a moment. "Let me discuss the matter with Electra. Perhaps she will be more forthcoming than you are. I must convince her not to fight over the one male we now have."

Alpheus felt gravely ill, but was uncertain of the cause or the nature of his malady. Was there something malignant he had contracted? Aello had approached him in a frightening, sinister manner. But so, in a way, had her sister. Was there a kind of menacing danger in the pair of attractive siblings? he asked himself. The one person who could throw light on what he sensed to be bothering him was their mother. She might be willing to enlighten him about the eerie thoughts that were troubling his mind.

He decided to question the woman after supper one evening. First came the meal of entellus meat. All four of the participants shared a feeling of unease as they ate. Little was said among them. No one took the risk of opening delicate subjects that might prove disruptive.

"I know that we are all very tired," said Celaeno once supper was over. "My own plan is to retire early and get some rest. I want to be strong for tomorrow's demands and labors. What do we say to this idea of mine?"

The daughters and the guest agreed to her proposal. As the two sisters exited the room, Alpheus lagged behind, finally approaching the matriarch where she still sat, stolid and unmoving.

"May I talk with you before we all retire?" asked the apothecary.

"Certainly," she answered. "Sit down here beside me."

When he was comfortably seated, Alpheus got down to what was bothering him with his first words to her. "I am vastly troubled by a certain attitude of both your daughters, Madam. There is something that pains and mystifies me in their behavior towards me."

She stared at him with equanimity. "My girls are inexperienced with the opposite sex. Their knowledge of men is limited to the few guests we have had here in the hotel and what I myself teach them. The attitude that you say disturbs you is a combination of curiosity and shyness. You must be tolerant of their awkward behavior. Please have some mercy toward them, I beg you."

"They have met few outsiders, then?" said Alpheus, digesting her logic.

"Yes, that is the truth. They rarely mix with other residents of the isle. Allow me to reveal the reason to you. Their own ancestry is a cause of enmity. Yes, enmity. They are called hideous names behind their backs, as I was before their birth. The three of us live quite isolated from the other inhabitants. Hidden hatred has poisoned their lives, as it did to mine."

"I do not understand," confessed the guest. "What is the nature of the slander against the three of you?"

Her eyes looked downward and focused on the dining table's surface.

"That because of harpine ancestors, we possess harpine blood," she slowly declared.

Raising her head, the mother peered anxiously at Alpheus, waiting to gauge his reaction.

"That is a malicious sort of gossip," he finally replied. "Why don't the three of you leave this island for elsewhere? Why can't you flee such libel? There should be some escape from evil tongues."

"This isle is our home. Where else could we go?"

"I understand," he said, rising and leaving the room for his own.

Fast asleep that night, tired Alpheus did not see or hear the entrance of a ghostlike figure into his bedroom. Nor was he conscious of what it accomplished once it dispersed itself beside him on the bed he lay on. Only a moment after their climax did his mind arrive at a degree of awareness that something strange and unusual had transpired, that he had been the subject of an unseen event.

As if emerging out of a deep sopor, the botanic discovered that he had been undergoing a completed coupling without his mind being awake to the act of copulation. How could that be possible? he wondered. Turning his head to one side, it became possible for him to identify who had been his partner, for there was a body beside him, sound asleep.

It had not been imaginary, he had not been dreaming. He had not experienced some kind of lonely nocturnal emission.

There had occurred actual union with someone, because at his side slumbered the beauteous woman named Electra.

How could that have happened to the two of them? It made no sense to him, but then he remembered something: what he had once read, before visiting this island, about the nature of the being called a harpine.

Such an entity only chose a male mate once. She then became his eternal slave, in a state of total loyalty that approached worship. An unbreakable nexus of love would then connect the harpine to the object of her devotion. She would forever be the adoring servant of her beloved. And from their physical conjunction would issue one or more new females as her harpine daughters. That was how the species continued on. As long as the male mate lived, she would be his follower.

Alpheus glanced at her head, aghast at her grotesque teratoid face, that of a monster. Was this the true Electra? he asked himself with dread. She was so unsightly and repulsive in this form. A pasty pallor gave her face a yellow, ashen cast. Twisted and malformed, freakishly wrinkled and distorted. Was this the true visage of the beautiful Electra?

He was unable to fall asleep again that night. How was he to survive tied to a harpine for life?

The two of them had to settle many matters when she awoke, he instructed himself.

She stood facing him with the glorious face that he was familiar with. Leaning forward, Electra kissed his dry lips.

"I have to return to my room," she told him in a soft whisper. "You only fell asleep a minute or so ago. You must have more rest if we are to do anything today. I am planning a tour through the forest heights after you eat breakfast. We have a lot to decide about our future, dear Alpheus."

All through his morning meal of birdling ovules folded into omelettes, he avoided speaking to his new harpine partner. Instead, he concentrated on asking general questions of the mother of the two female siblings.

"Does anyone know what the population of this isle happens to be, Madam?"

"No. We have never experienced a census of any kind here. No one knows that."

"I take it that there are very few exports of any kind."

"Correct. The mainland has, unfortunately, little demand for anything from here."

"I have noticed in your tropical forest many plants familiar to me as a botanic. Take the zedoary, for example. We commonly use it as a stomachal to strengthen digestion or as a carminative to prevent flatulence. It belongs to an entire family of curcumas and zingeberis such as cardamom and maranta. I am quite knowledgeable about these ancient remedies. I have even spotted some santonica in the forest. Do you know what that is? A powerful vermifuge, a useful anthelmintic that expels intestinal worms. Isn't that something that can be exported?"

"That is most interesting," grinned Celaeno. "But how could we who live here on this island take advantage of our numerous herbals?"

Alpheus smiled back at the mother. "Let us imagine that I was to stay on the isle for an extended period, surveying what was growing in the wild. I know that soon I would have gardens of things like medicinal rhubarb and licorice jequerity. My employer in Diaema would allow me to purchase all that I might find in these woods."

"That is an amazing concept," said Celaeno. "Let me think about it and how I and my girls could help you achieve the goals you envision. But at least today, you must continue your explorations. Electra will be the one serving as your guide this morning. It will soon be time to start out."

Alpheus carried a memorandum pad given to him by Electra. He began to make notes on all the medicinal plants he spied in the woods of the isle. His hand pointed out the herbals he identified to his harpine lover.

"This is the euphrasy used to treat the eye. Some call it eyebright. And over there is jalapa, from whose roots I can make a purgative. Further on is a stramony plant, from which pharmacists concoct a strong sedative that always produces restful sleep."

He stopped to write down what he had seen, using a cone-tipped stylograph. His companion said nothing. They started forward again, proceeding slowly down the trail.

"See that goldenseal plant? From its roots we obtain a traditional stomach medicine, hydrastine. And over on the other side is a ipecac bush, from whose roots comes the emetine that will cause vomiting and emptying of the bowels. And the common dandelion provides us with taraxaeum, a diuretic.

He stopped, wrote, and then went on with Electra beside him.

"That one is asafetida which stops muscular spasms." He raised his arm and indicated a tree further on. "Do you know what that is called? It is the nux vomica, from the bark and seeds of which we extract the poisons strychnine and brucine. Those are deadly weapons in the wrong hands. But I know how to obtain them from the plants."

It was Electra who suddenly stopped in her tracks and turned to him, forcing him to do the same.

"You are well-versed in all the poisons in the forest?" she asked excitedly. He examined her face, staring into the velvet-black eyes. His mind raced ahead, anticipating what her thoughts would be. But before he could decide what to say, she spoke to him.

"This afternoon, my sister means to accompany you on a tour of the farthest reaches of the isle. Her appetite for flesh will have been raised high by all that has happened since you arrived. She intends to finish what was not completed before. Can you foresee the danger for you? No man can survive the kind of attack she plans to make. All the signs for that are present and visible."

He looked down at the empty page of his notepad, as if searching there for an answer.

"I need to leave the island quickly," he told her, "but that is not possible for me without you along too."

Electra stepped forward until she stood inches from him. Her head leaned toward him and she kissed him on the mouth.

An uncanny feeling took hold of all his body, mind, soul, and life.

Alpheus instinctively knew that he no longer belonged to himself. The harpine woman possessed him now, and would continue to do so in his future.

"I have decided that both of them have to die," she whispered. "At once, before the afternoon is over. I need an instantaneous poison that no one can recognize."

"Your mother, too?" gulped the botanic in shock.

"If only Aello is dead, my mother will chase after you for vengeance. I know that is what will happen. Both of them are impediments to our love for each other. Both of them must disappear, very soon, at the same time."

Alpheus fell into concentrated consideration of what he had to do.

Nature, in all its happy anarchy, went about its unending activity on Harpine Island.

Arboreal frogs jumped about in their aerial homes. Tall grasstrees, fringetrees, tupelos, and black gums soared toward the sky. Shrill shrieking of butcherbirds, dickcissels, killdees, and rallines rent the air. Orange-colored butterflies and red bloodroots flew about. Diving coots and scoters were visible about ponds and lagoons.

A thick shaugh of ocote pines and annatto trees provided shelter for nests of grayish brown mangabey monkeys with white eyelids. Rodent gerbils crept around in the shadows. Horned moloch lizards lay in wait for insect meals under a jargonelle tree.

And Alpheus provided Electra the compound of poison that killed her mother and sister.

He lacked her fundamental duality. His own mother and father, like their parents, did not possess the binary character of the harpines. Could he ever draw Electra from her diploid inheritance? Could he bridge the profound chasm between them?

Life together would always hold potential risks. His hope was that their connection was strong enough to conquer the problems in their genetic differences. In the meantime, they had to steel themselves for what ordinary human society would label a criminal solution.

Alpheus and Electra became convinced there was only one way out for them.

In a week's time, the two of them stood at the deck rail of a passenger bateau sailing away from Harpine Isle.

The large head of a gerenuk antelope was visible on the shore, then disappeared.

"They are now gone and we need never return," quietly said Electra to her chosen lover. "In time, we will forget they existed at all. The fire I set destroyed the hotel, along with all traces of those two."

Alpheus turned his head so that he could see her complete face, splendidly shining in the light.

"It was my mixture of island poisons that silenced them, though. No one, not even a harpine can survive belladonna, strychnine, aconite, and brucine, all at once. Those four deadly poisons were not noticed in the spiceberry tea that you brewed for them." He drew a very deep breath. "We will not be under any suspicion, will we?"

She gave him an angelic smile. "Only the two of us know what happened on the isle, my love. There is nothing pointing to how it was done. We are now free to fulfill our dreams. Your own pharmacy! I can finance an independent business with my inheritance from mother. In a couple of years, we can set up a chain of dispensaries. I will make you a leading apothecary, dear. All your ambitions will be fulfilled."

At that moment, the isle disappeared in the distance, falling below the watery horizon.

III
The Chatan

Diaema, the capital and metropolis of Provincia, was a city of cement, concrete, and betonic compounds. The offices, stores, monuments, and residences were mostly made of stone and rock in varied forms. Even the windows were of processed silicon sand.

Equine traffic of all kinds filled the busy streets and boulevards.

Stylish men and women rode proudly in luxurious coaches and hansoms drawn by chevalot horses.

Gas heating and night lights were nearly universal throughout the vast city.

Electricity was a rarely used form of energy, too costly to compete with its magnetic rival.

Government buildings, solid and formidible, took up most of the central district. Trade, merchandising, and business pursuits occupied the ring around this core.

The inhabitants of the city, both the minority of diploids with two forms and the majority with only one, were ambitous and energetic people. Identification of bifold individuals through their human shape was not at all an easy thing to do. Outside appearance was not a good sign of the sort of person one was, single or double.

Diploids preferred to conceal their secondary stage and appear in human form when in public. The cultural norm remained the outwardly human. That was the preferred way to be.

Alpheus and Electra accepted the need to suppress as much as possible Electra's harpine secondary nature. It was the customary way to live in Diaema.

Within a year, there was a second shop and a first child. The father took his wife by horse ambulance to the sanative hospital where midwives delivered a baby girl. Electra lay in a recovery hammock, the little one sleeping in an ajacent crib. The mother appeared surprisingly strong and awake for all her pains. She had a matter to discuss in private with her husband.

"I've decided what we should name her, Alpheus. My grandmother was very close to me and taught me many things before she died. There can be no better cognomen for our first child than Clotho. Isn't it beautiful?"

He immediately felt his head swim. Almost instinctively, opposition arose within him.

"That should not be determined too swiftly. There is plenty of time for a name, dear."

Electra seemed to sense a problem, one that would grow in the future.

"I can think of no substitute for Clotho. For me, it is impossible to conceive of some other name. No, this baby must become a Clotho. I will never call her anything but that. Nothing else will do. She shall always own that name in my mind."

The two looked at each other with a coolness that had never been there before.

Alpheus tried to change the subject to his expanding herbal business.

"Several people have applied with letters for the position I advertised for in the medical journals. It is impossible for me to continue without a managerial assistant with considerable experience in the trade. There has been a flood of candidates for the job. In the coming year, we shall be opening a third pharmacy. I need a competent helper by my side to help carry the heavy load of work."

"That is clearly the truth," said his wife in a vibrant voice. "We need an individual who has a strong interest in the nervine materials that calm and tranquilize the brains of the mentally ailing. That will be the area of coming advancement and development. The person you decide upon must stand together with us on the ground of botanical remedies."

Electra gave him a glowingly brilliant smile, then continued. "That is the key to becoming a successful business for us. If the strategy works, we will become a major firm on the medical stage."

"I intend to devote all my time and energy to our growth, my love. The prospect before us is breathtaking." He took her hand in his and held it gently.

"And tiny Clotho can grow up to become an important participant in our company, Alpheus. You and I must teach her all that we have learned from life."

No more opposition to the name she had chosen came from him. In a few minutes, he departed from his wife and the baby who came to be called Clotho.

Seated behind his deodar desk, Alpheus watched the brawny, lantern-jawed aspirant enter the office and sit down. This robust, virile young man was the one who went by the name of Tugau. He had short straw-colored hair and chatoyant eyes of bright copper. There was the look of a tiger or cat about him.

Alpheus began to question the candidate with personal inquiries.

"Tell me, what first brought you into the field of botanic medicine?"

The answer came as if it had previously been prepared and rehearsed by Tugau.

"My father owned a small plantation in the highlands near Diaema. He started to grow pharmaceutic herbs on the side. This expanded until it became his dominant concentration of work and effort. When he died, our farm had become a major supplier for urban practitioners. That has been so ever since: our farms produce herbal cures and remedies for all Provincia.

"I decided to become a botanic who directly treated patients. To accomplish that, I came to the city and spent years as apprentice in a number of dispensaries. That is the story of my life in this field , sir."

Alpheus studied him closely. "But why is it you wish to be my assistant manager?"

"My main interest lies in the area of nervine preparations used to treat cases of stress and anxiety. Mental disorder and nervous tension have to be considered major problems that need progress in healing with plants. I see your pharmacy as in the forefront of advancing medicine, sir. My ambition is to take part in the progress foreseeable ahead."

The older man smiled. "Your attitude is most encouraging. Are you familiar with the most commonly used herbal medicines for anxiety and depression?"

Tugau was able to think and answer speedily. "I have myself prepared rosemary and kola nut powder as antidepressants. For more serious mental anxiety, I have prescribed lemon balm and vervain. The nervously exhausted were given withania by me. When I faced a patient with severe mental illness, my reliance has been on water hysop and codonopsis. But I wish to explore beyond these common remedies. My dream is to go beyond what was achieved in the past. That is the hope that inspires me."

He paused to study Alpheus a moment, then went on. "There are scores of substances I would like to study with you in my spare time. I see no need to go beyond plant medicinals. Why take the risks involved with metals and minerals? Centuries of experience teach us that folk traditions of herbal treatment contain all the therapies that will ever be needed.

"For every illness, there is some leaf or plant, according to popular legend. So believed the countless generations before us. Why should anyone doubt the wisdom of the botanic tradition? The way of nature is the sole road to health and well-being."

Alpheus, all at once, made a momentous decision.

"My own thinking runs in the very same direction. I can, at this time, tell you that my choice for the job is made. Will you be my assistant and day-to-day manager, Tugau? I would be proud to have an idealist like you at my side."

"Of course, sir," said the other with surprise on his face.

"It is you, then. Come with me, I want to introduce you to my family. They are in the residential part of the building. Follow me there."

Electra had an internal hyperesthesia that made her extremely sensitive to the cardinal, though secret, traits of those she met for the first time.

At once she recognized a disturbing quality about the newly hired assistant pharmacist. But it was impossible for her, at the time, to define what was troublesome about Tugau.

The latter grinned warmly as Alpheus introduced his wife.

"Are you from the coastal highlands, Madam? There is something in your accent that tells me that you are. I myself come from the upper forest along the sea."

"No, I am an islander. There has been a great amount of cross-migation over the ages. It is hard to be too definitive about what region a person may come from only by accent and dialect. Our speech can be a misleading indicator of past population movements."

"What was your island of birth, may I ask?" he persisted.

"Isle of the Harpines," she softly declared.

Alpheus spoke at that point. "Where is Clotho? She will be glad to meet the person chosen to work at my side."

Electra turned to her husband. "I just saw her go to the fun room to play."

"Fine. I'll take Tugau there and show him our extraordinary five-year old."

Before the mother could say anything, the two males were making their way down the corridor to the special chamber where the daughter exercised her rich imagination in make-believe and play.

"Clotho is an exceptional child," boasted Alpheus as they reached the door to the room. "Her intelligence permitted us to teach her to read at four. You will be surprised at her precocious achievements. She is a wonder to behold."

As the proud father opened the door, the two saw the child sitting on a stool with a large folio volume open in its lap. She looked up and grinned. "Father!"

Once her velvety eyes spotted the stranger, her smile vanished.

"I want you to meet the man who is going to be my assistant, Clotho. Come over here and let me introduce you to Tugau. You will be seeing him often from now on."

The girl placed the folio, still open, on the floor and slowly stepped forward as if reluctant to do so. She avoided looking directly at the large man she did not know.

"Do not be fearful of me, little lady," murmured the stranger. "I shall soon be your good friend. We two can become like members of the same family. You like to read? What kind of books are our favorites?"

At first, Clotho spoke shyly, but then with increasing confidence in herself. "I like tales of high adventure from other times. Before the world we are in today. I enjoy learning about things we don't see ourselves. Faraway places are so interesting! I am especially thrilled when I read about animals. I try to remember all I can about each kind, so that if I meet one for the first time, I will know what it is and what it is called."

Smiling, Tugau looked at her with astonishment.

"That is amazing, Clotho. My own favorite literature also consists of stories about what is unknown to me. Could I lend you some of the books I've had since my own childhood? I grew up in the hilly high country and my early fascination was with the myths of that region. Would you enjoy seeing some of my early readings?"

She replied with a bashful nod of the head.

Alpheus then made a suggestion. "Let me show you the repository where I keep our herbal supplies," he proposed.

Soon Clotho was again alone in her private fun room. Her thoughts were a mixture of vague apprehension and hopeful joy. Could this brawny herbalist reveal new natural wonders to her? She was intrigued by his claim to have books with fabulous legends in them.

Tugau helped expand the fortunes of the Gallipot Company, making Alpheus happy. The market for both old and new medicinals grew ever greater. Feverfew and pereira bark were wanted for high fever. Ergot was used for high blood pressure. Soapstone and cullay treated dysentary. Papavarine cured muscle spasms, while hellebore was used for internal catharsis.

The curiosity of the new assistant led him to prescribe heliotrope as a sedative as well as rhodella as a calmative. It was Tugau who started using the herb called cat's claw as an anti-inflamatory.

After two years of unbroken success with the new man, Apheus invited him to move into the back area of the residence. What had been a storage area was converted into an apartment for the managing assistant. Tugau now took all his meals with the family. The barriers between him and the others vanished completely. Their relationships became close and informal.

Eight-year old Clotho, attending a girls' academy not far from home, devoted much of her spare time to reading the many volumes that Tugau brought with him. She learned about the dipsas, a snake whose bite made a victim eternally thirsty. Did any such creature ever exist in reality? she asked the assistant. He could not say yes or no to her, only an enigmatic "maybe". The young girl found that so funny that she laughed a long time at him.

She cringed at the stories about the chimera. Could any such animal be part lion, part snake, and part goat? How was that monstrosity possible? It would be called a trifold, with three different forms, he answered her. But primarily it was a she-goat with two other shapes it could change into at different times. That was how he cleverly explained it to Clotho.

She grew fascinated with the monsters of ancient legend.

Who had ever seen a griffin with the head and wings of an eagle and the body of a lion?

Tugau, alone with her in the fun room, answered with a wide grin. "Who can deny that a biform is more reasonable and possible than a triform or a multiform? Such a double being could be classified as diploid in nature."

The girl turned her curiosity to monsters of the sea. Could a hippocampus possess the head and forelegs of a horse but also have the tail of a dolphin? Clotho wanted desperately to know, but got no definite reply from her informal instructor on such subjects.

She was ten when she delved into the possibility of creatures half human and half wild animal. Could a person like herself have a bifold or diploid nature with two varied forms to it? She showed Tugau a book with an illustration of an entity with the head, arms, and torso of a man, but with the legs of a horse. He placed his right index finger on the drawing.

"Notice how the two forms here exist simultaneously. It would be a true diploid only if the creature was to go from its animal form to a fully human one, or from the completely human shape to one that was nothing but a horse. Do you see what I am getting at? At any one moment of time, it is either the one or the other, but not a mixture of the two opposites."

He noticed that she lowered her head as if despondent.

"There is some evidence that the centaurs that puzzle you so much were the originators of the botanic science that deals with medicinal herbs. There exits a rare herb called the centaury. Legend has it that a centaur discovered its value, thus taking the first step forward into our field of study. So, that means that your father and I, along with all herbalians, owe a debt to a double creature, but one different from most of the others. The centaur has two forms at the very same time, unlike what I term a genuine diploid."

She was unable to say another word, but only giggled.

After brief study of a half-man, half-bull called the bucentaur, Clotho concentrated on the riddle of the sphinx. She found that a human woman could be one part of a monster. The legendary being had a female head, face, and breasts, but the torso of a lion.

It destroyed anyone unable to answer the riddle it posed. The name of sphinx meant "the strangler" in ancient times, referring to the method it used on its victims. Only when a great human hero solved the riddle was the monster defeated. In shame, the sphinx strangled itself. Clotho found this tale so humorous that she was for a time unable to stop laughing, forcing Tugau to do the same.

"But we cannot call a sphinx a true diploid," he managed to tell her at the end.

By the age of twelve, these therianthropic combinations dominated the free time of the brilliant, precocious girl. She studied mermaids, mermen, and tritons of the sea, as well as the frightening satyrs of the forests. Could a supernatural spirit take a semi-human form? she asked Tugau. Goat legs, horns, and pointed ears were the marks of the evil, lecherous satyr, a danger to human women. It was a puzzle to Clotho that Tugau had to solve for her again, as he had done before.

In time, she came to enter freely the apartment of her father's assistant. Clotho took book after book to read from Tugau's collection. She was thirteen when she came upon an old folio that described and presented the legend of the lamia and the harpine.

The harpine! She recalled that her mother had come to the city of Diaema from the Isle of the Harpines. There might be some connection to that island in the book, she supposed. Clotho took it and immediately went on a hunt for what she wanted to know. In the former fun room, she started to peruse the folio. This work was the most absorbing she had ever read. The creature described was credible to her. Why could it not exist as an actuality?

The original Lamia was an island queen whose children were stolen from her by a jealous female rival. In revenge, the queen changed into a murderous monster with a woman's head, face, and breasts, but the body of a great snake. The word lamia came to signify an abyssmal mouth that devoured and swallowed its enemies alive. Legend had it that an entire race of such creatures arose, luring innocent children away from home and sucking out all their blood.

The illustrations of a lamia disgusted but mesmerized the curious thirteen-year old girl.

In the back of the folio she came upon description of the harpine. Her mother had never told her anything specific about that particular being for whom the island had been named.

Clotho delved into the fascinating material. Early harpines were body-snatchers who stole young boys and girls from their parents in order to eat them alive. The description was of hideously filthy winged horrors with a woman's head and trunk above the tail, legs, and talons of a monstrous bird of unbelievable size. It sought to get at the soul of men by eating off their physical bodies first. How horrifying! thought the young reader. But an unseen force drew her to read on. It was horrendous and frightening material, but profoundly interesting to her.

Turning a page of the folio, Clotho saw something she never expected. Her memory received a violent jolt. It seemed to her as if a bolt of stormy lightning had struck her. She had no explanation for what she experienced.

A drawing of a harpine, with both head and body visible, lay open before her. The face had a strange familiarity to it. Her mother's features, as well as some of her own, were recognizable. It all came to her in a flash. There was an uncanny resemblance of lines and markings. Electra was clearly visible in the monstrous face, and so was she herself.

What did that mean? How significant was the similarity of features? she wondered.

Clotho decided to read no more for a time. That was enough, it was more than enough.

All the experiments that the assistant conducted were carried out by himself.

He chewed coca leaves to measure their effect as an anesthetic, but also as a stimulant in large dosages. From poppyseed oil he extracted codeia and morphia to see what they would do to his thinking, both awake and asleep. His dreams became wildly uninhibited as these substances came to affect him.

The kava nut, piper methysticum, put Tugau into a long, deep stupor. The passion flower did not prove very strong. His experience with damiana was a joyeous one. Sources described its aphrodisial and thymoleptic characteristics. He felt both of these in his mind and body. Anxiety disappeared entirely, replaced by exuberance and excitement. But that was not what he was after.

His innermost drives compelled him to investigate further.

Tugau next chose to use datura on himself. His books warned that in large amounts it could lead to hallucinations that were close to madness. But he had no fear of trying out the thornapple leaves with that substance in them. What could datura do to harm him? he thought. It could relax all his muscles and release his mind for far flights of thinking. Gradually, he built up to a high enough dosage to reveal its full power.

He brought a vial of datura to his apartment and slowly digested it lying on his settle bed. Unusual dreams began that night. It was unprecedented both in violence and illumination. He had never had visions like that before.

The scene he experienced in his deep unconscious was one set in a tropical forest with thick dark trees on all sides, stretching upwards into a cerulean sky. From behind a yellow-green bush emerged an indestinct shape. Soon it could be identified as a giant feral cat. These had once inhabited many wooded areas of the highlands, but the numbers had been reduced through centuries of hunting them down.

Eternal eyes gazed out of the head, catching everything in all directions. Nothing was missed by this wild cat of the mountains. What category of felid did it belong to? he wondered.

Am I imagining that I dream, or am I actually experiencing a herbally generated reality? Does this feral cat see and notice me? Am I within the focus of its own consciousness?

Perhaps it is the cat that is dreaming, and it sees an imagined image of myself.

I am not the important one in this hallucination. No, it is the cat that is the central fact. Without the felid, there would not be this dream. The animal is not a mere phantasm. It is an existent being with greater reality to it than I have when asleep and dreaming. Maybe it exists in a truer way than I ever have. If that is so, then I am merely a thought of that untamed cat. That would mean that I only have my own life as the product of an animal's dream. It could awaken and I would no longer think, see, hear, or even live. Wouldn't that be something?

Instantly, it all came to an end and Tugau woke up from his troubled sleep.

He sat up and rubbed his eyes. An eerie happiness filled him. I shall have to analyze what I saw, or think that I saw.

This strange dream is going to change the rest of my life, something told him.

At the age of fourteen, Clotho graduated from the girl's academy.

Both of her parents grew concerned about her further education. Each of them questioned her about what she wanted. What were her plans and ambitions?

Alpheus talked with his daughter in the privacy of his apothecary office.

"What do you foresee for yourself, my dear?" he asked her after the two of them sat down on opposite sides of his work desk. "If you have decided upon your ambition for the future, then we can choose what educational institution to enrol you in. What do you think?"

She spoke immediately, without hesitation.

"I believe that botanic medicine interests me more than anything else can. That is the career that I dream of, father."

The latter was unable to conceal his happiness at hearing these words from her.

"Good," he grinned. "What you say warms my heart."

"And I think that the best training for me would be as a junior apprentice here at the Gallipot. I have already learned much through reading and watching. It would be simple and easy to begin work in remedy preparation. There are hundreds of volumes here that I can study in my spare time and in the evening. What do you say, father? I will not have to leave home at all. I can just continue studying right here."

Alpheus rose from his chair and approached her."I have no objections. It is an ingenious idea. But let me discuss it with your mother first. She must be allowed to give her opinion."

"That's right, father," said Clotho. She had no fear that her mother might object to the plan to become an apprentice in the pharmacy. The two of them were going to remain together along with her father. And Tugau, as well.

For over a year, Tugau had been experimenting on himself with ever stronger hallucingens. In every instance, he envisioned a wild forest cat that absorbed his own identity in itself. Was he melting into the dreamed animal? This riddle vexed him, month after month. Then, by chance, the foundation of a possible explanation came to him. It occurred at an outdoor book fair.

A short distance from the Gallipot stood a large open square where peddlers and merchants sold their wares. Tugau was out for a walk with the now sharply curious Clotho. She was first to spot the stacks of volumes on the stone surface of the public thoroughfare. "Let us stop here and have a look, Tugau," she said in a chirping tone. "We may be lucky and find some hidden treasure in the piles of folios."

The two went over to where a seller in dark country clothing stood overlooking his offerings. Clotho began examining the titles on front covers, putting back whatever seemed of no interest.

All of a sudden, she thrust one particular small book at her companion.

"Look at this, Tugau. It may ring some bell for you."

He took the slim volume and read the soiled title on the front cover.

"A Highland Bestiary" it succinctly said.

An instant decision resulted. "I'll purchase it for both of us," he told her. "We could both learn something from it."

Indeed, that afternoon Tugau poured through the book after the two of them returned home to the Gallipot. The section on mountain felids was where he concentrated attention. A short paragraph near the end was the place he discovered what he had been after for so long. It was what he had longed and hungered to find out.

"An ancient highland legend centered on wild torbie cats is that of a double called the chatan. It was for ages believed in many places that certain bloodlines of humans had the capability of passing out of dreams and existing as a wild torbie. Some such chatans evolved into lynxes, others into servels, ocelets, and margays. The felid stage of the biform was temporary, ending when the dream did."

Tugau looked away in wonder and amazement. Was that what was happening in his experiments with hallucogens? Did he happen to have the blood of chatans in him? Had the herbal compounds only sparked a potental already within him at birth? This mystery consumed him.

He knew that a small fraction of the population in Provincia had a diploid nature with two different forms. There was a human primus, but also a non-human secundus. Two forms of life but the same overall entity. There was no question in his mind that the double beings existed.

Was he one of them, with the bloodlines of the ancient chatan? Was there a feral cat hidden within himself? Could that be the meaning of his dreams?

It was clear to Tugau that he was not the first individual to undergo metamorphosis into a large torbie cat. There was evidence of the phenomenon in the distant past. Perhaps it had disappeared for a long time. But now, it appeared, the chatan was reborn. Perhaps this was due to his use of potent botanicals. His double identity grew into a firmly held opinion.

I must not allow Clotho to read this, he told himself. It took only a second for him to tear out the page with the alarming paragraph. If she looked into the folio, the absence of one sheet should not arouse her suspicion.

It was best she knew nothing of his diploid nature. More exploration of the chatan cat stage was needed before he dared talk of it to her.

Tugau resolved to import more mental herbals from other countries. What would their effects on his character as biformed be? It is not easy to be diploid, he said to himself.

Electra spoke candidly to her husband. She did not think it a good idea that her only child stay at home and learn the craft of botanics from Alpheus. It would be better for her to go outside for professional training. Clotho should not become a stay-at-home.

"Why must we shelter her from the inhabitants of Diaema?" argued the mother. "There will come a day when we will no longer be here to protect her. How will she be able to meet others her age unless she attends some school away from home."

Alpheus looked surprised. "You want to place her in a boarding school?"

"If there is no good alternative, then that must be the answer," replied his wife. "She must not become a prisoner in our home nest. It is not good to shelter the girl too much."

The pair looked blankly at each other for a while. Finally, Electra spoke."I have to talk frankly with her. What does she truly wish to become?"

The mother went to the reading and study room that her daughter had set up and furnished for herself. It had once been the fun and play room. Volumes collected over time filled shelves that Tugau had made for his young friend.

Dare Electra say all that she had for so long kept hidden from Clotho?

How does one tell an only child of her diploid essence and the possible hazards connected to that brutal fact? How does one speak of such a sensitive matter?

Opening the door, she found her daughter seated in a sofa chair with a book in her lap. Clotho looked up, saying "Mother, what is it?"

"I want to talk with you about...your future, my dear."

"Come in and sit down," said the reader, closing the volume and placing it on a small stand.

Once her mother was comfortably seated, Clotho took the initiative.

"I have chosen to stay at home as a beginning apprentice. Father has hinted to me that you are opposed to the idea. Is that why you came to see me?"

An understanding smile crossed th face of Electra. It was an indulgent, diplomatic one.

"I merely wish to reveal the reasons for my thinking that way. Isn't that the fair and right thing for me to do? There is no alternative to complete candor on my part. Up to now, certain facts have not been told to you. Very important facts. Your age and sensitivity prevented disclosure of these things by either me or your father. But at this particular crossroads in your life, it is best that the matter be presented in all its aspects. The repercusions for the future are enormous, my beloved."

Clotho pursed her lips on one side. "You refer to our harpine ancestry, mother?"

The latter reddened all over in astonishment. For a time she was unable to say anything.

"Let me tell you how I came to know the truth," said Clotho with a smile.

It took her only a minute or so to describe how she had read about bifold monsters of the distant past and come upon illustrations with the outline of the familiar family face, that of a harpine.

"That was enough to convince you what I am?"

"Yes, and what I am too, mother."

The two women gazed into each other's velvety eyes.

"I have inhibited and buried the danger within my mind," confessed Electra. "It was not at all easy to do. I could not have succeeded without the steadfast support of your father. He gave me the strength to resist the inner harpine drive that occurs from time to time, even at my age. I owe everything to the aid he gives me without fail.

"But it is you I worry about. How can you meet young men if you work and live at home? I want you to marry as soon as it is possible, with someone who can be informed about our family stain and is willing to cooperate with you in restraining the forces we are cursed with. Do you understand me?"

Into the mind of Clotho suddenly flashed the image of Tugau. It was a sharp and clear one.

He was older than herself, yet with the potential to comprehend her diploid nature.

All at once she knew that what she felt for him was the same as what existed between her father and mother. It had been there a long time, unnamed and unrecognized by their child.

Was it realistic for her to project forward into her adult years the attraction toward the highlander who had taught her so much about so many things?

For a considerable time, the daughter said nothing, perplexing Electra. But all of a sudden, Clotho's face and eyes glowed with enthusiasm.

"Yes, it is best I stay at home and deal with this thorny subject in conjunction with you and father. That is the only way that makes any sense to me. We have to be close together."

And Tugau will be nearby, ready to help me, she thought to herself.

⊕

The city park along the Diadema River was filled with bluewood and yellowwood trees in vernal leaf. Picnicking couples sat on blankets and sheets in the open areas. Tugau led his companion, Clotho, along winding trails forming a maze where only a few ever walked.

The vegetation here was thick and leafy. Many shades of green were evident. The high voices of birdlings and nestlings begged to be fed, carrying far from the branches where they waited for mothers to bring them the materials of life.

Whose idea was their excursion? Clotho had first mentioned that there was an opportunity to see nature in bloom during the three-day holiday around Galactic Day. Placid quiet in the park away from the traditional pyrotechnics of the occasion, promised Tugau. She agreed that it would be a pleasure to circle the park with him.

Tugau wore a highland balmacaan coat of rough cloth with raglan sleeves extending up to the collar. On his head rested a flat pork pie hat. She had on a green spring mantelot and a yellow sunbonnet. For a long time, neither of them said a word. They looked a stylish couple indeed.

As they slowly moved along, Tugau began to express his connected musings.

"Nature is wonderfully beautiful when ordered and organized, as here in Diadema Park. And I can see no risks or gambles, as up in the wilds. One cannot expect a surprise encounter with the beastly or feral in this setting. That is why I like it so much.

"The only brutes one is apt to meet are human ones. Yet few of the citizens realize how near they are to primeval animal lfe. They do not know how wild they could become in a secondary form, under the appropriate circumstances. For are we not merely animals that have human minds and souls? Talking, intelligent animals and nothing more. Am I right or not?"

The eyes of Clotho, turning more velvety, gazed ahead at the unpaved path. What did his thoughts make her imagine in her own mind? Her double nature as a harpine? The two sides of her being? She was both one, but also two in one.

What is the true character of someone like me? she worried. Can the two planes of existence be reconciled, or will there always occur an internal war of the two sides? How can it ever be resolved? What are the life possibilities for a diploid?

Tugau grew concerned about the silence of the young woman. "What are you thinking about so hard, Clotho?" he inquired.

She turned her head so that she could see him at a direct angle. "I was wondering about the same matter you were talking about just now. There were moments in my life when I felt a similar division happening to me."

"A division? Tell me what that was," he said with unexpected vehemence.

Tugau glanced at her a moment. Finding she was gazing at his face, he turned again to the path they were traversing. There was no one else but them about.

Clotho let out a pouring of dammed up emotions she had repressed a considerable time.

"I want to be one thing alone, good and worthy. But there is a feeling within me that I am a hypocrite and pretender, that there is a second, wicked character in me. Is that understandable? Does it make any sense at all?"

In an instant, he stopped walking forward. She did the same a second later. They turned and faced each other. Though they were both unaware whether anyone was near enough to observe them, they extended their arms out and embraced. His long arms took hold of her, and her shorter ones hugged him. This position lasted no more than a few moments. They experienced a solid caress of endearment. No kisses were exchanged. Only a single snuggle occurred. That was sufficient for both of them.

Then it was over simultaneously for both of them.

From the distant land of Jilin came a packet for the assistant pharmacist. A small vial of schisandra had been bought with which Tugau could carry out an experiment upon himself. In its native country, the dried fruit of this bush was in wide use by herbalists. A sexual tonic could be distilled from its berries, the one who had ordered understood. He had something else in mind, of course. It had for centuries been prescribed in Jilin for psychotic and neurotic cases. How would it affect his own dreams about the feral cat? he wondered. That was the question most in need of an answer for Tugau.

The next day, before he had tried the substance, a second box arrived. It came from the land of Kechua. He opened it at once, finding inside it the woody vines of the ayahua. At last he had in hand a rare bark from which he could obtain one of the most potent hallucinogens anywhere. It was said to be stronger than any material he had yet used on himself. How might it change his dream adventures? That was what he had to find out.

Tugau made a fateful decision: to combine the two imports with the damiana and datura that he had used and was familiar with. What would result from the mixture with the addition of schisandra and ayahua? He looked forward with zeal to the trance that this soup might produce in him.

He invented an abreviation for the combined formula of damiana, ayahua, datura, and schisandra: D.A.D.S. His hope was that this new concoction would cause a major change in his chatan dreams.

Taking the combination with him to his apartment, Tugau placed a large dose into his mouth as he lay on the sofa he had recently purchased. How soon would the hallucinating visions begin? he asked himself. When will I enter my chatan phase?

Sleep and then the dream came to him with surprising speed.

The now familiar corbie cat entered the field of his unconscious. He forgot who and what he was in the light of day. It was as if he were no longer the human being called Tugau.

The large feral cat had a brindled silver coat with light red patches on it. Its long, pink ringed tail made it very distinctive. It looked like an ancient, rare torbie from the highlands. This particular cat seemed nervous and driven by an overreaching curiosity. For several minutes it moved about the room, exploring the furniture, smelling at whatever it could. The giant chatan moved to the closed but unlocked door to the corridor and played with the knob. This was unprecedented. No cat had ever attempted to open a door, Tugau realized. Was it a sign of enhanced intelligence? he wondered. A period of pothering and fussing finally resulted in success in turning the knob sufficiently to release the door so it could be pushed slowly open. A final effort with its large head and the chatan was able to exit into the darkened hallway.

The cat was able to open a closed door!

As if by instinct, the animal found its way to the door of Clotho's room and stopped in front of it.

The beast obviously wanted to enter here, but was unable to handle the complex physics of such a feat. Frustration grew on its silver face and copper eyes as time passed. Again and again it pushed, struck, and scratched the wooden door. No success resulted from these persistent efforts.

But all at once, the door opened from the inside.

The noise of the clawing had awakened the lightly sleeping Clotho. She rose and went to see what was causing the sounds in the corridor.

Her dark, velvet eyes seemed hypnotized at sight of a gigantic cat out of some bestiary. Was this animal logically possible? How could it enter a secure structure like the one they were in? Was she awake or inside some terrible nightmare? Her confusion rose higher and higher. She realized that action by her was necessary. Clotho pushed on the door till it swung open all the way. Her mind could not calculate any further than that for the time being.

No one tried to move, neither the girl nor the big cat. Both were overwhelmed by sight of the other. Clotho had never been in the presence of such an enormous feline. And the latter seemed mesmerized at the sight of her. Why did it appear so tame and pacified near to her? It did not advance or attack. Not a move was made as the animal contemplated her. Why was that so?

Suddenly she extended her right hand, placing it directly on top of the head of the self-controlled creature. The latter stared at her with something cryptic in its eyes. A sign of recognition, an intimate message, it could have been either. There was no way for her to tell for certain.

She realized that a cat has extraordinary powers of concentration. They are by instinct masters of mental focus. It is difficult to distract their attention.

But there came an unforeseen moment when Clotho fainted and fell to the floor, her mind unconscious and no longer thinking complex thoughts.

She had gone into a deep swoon in which awakening was far away.

How did the chatan react and what did it do? It slinked away, back to the apartment of Tugau. No more outside roamimg for it that night. It had confronted a harpine, but did it realize that?

Turgau entered a full, deep sleep without dreams. He was recuperating from the adventure of his chatan secundus, his other self.

Alpheus found his daughter lying in the doorway of her room early next morning. Picking her up off the floor, he carried her in and deposited the unconscious young woman on her bed.

What had caused such a misfortune? There was no time for a detailed investigation. He left with a sense of distress, eager to get to the truth when she was awake again. But now he had hours of work to complete before he could question her. Was he able to wait that long? he wondered.

Tugau awoke with a combined feeling of both joy and foreboding. His mind was divided in reaction to last night's dream. The feral cat showed that it had the freedom to move out of his flat. But Clotho's encounter with the chatan had proved too much for her. His dream had captured, enveloped, and swallowed her into itself. It was now urgent that he talk to her and ask how much she remembered of the incident. How was he to explain his knowledge of the event in the hallway? That would be difficult to rationalize in any coherent way. He was afraid that he would have to tell her about his chatan double. Was the time right for that shocking revelation? Was he bold enough to come out with the truth?

Sooner or later, everything had to be candidly explained to her, he realized.

Tugau prepared for his day's work in the apothecary shop with his mind in ferment.

Electra sat on a stool beside the bed, waiting for her daughter to awaken.

When Clotho opened her eyes, the mother quickly excused herself and went to the kitchen to prepare a late breakfast for her. Alpheus had informed her of the fall and the need to monitor the girl's condition. Electra brought a bowl of hen soup for Clotho. Only when the latter was finished did the mother ask a direct question.

"How are you feeling now? Are you better?"

"I don't know, but I can say I feel weak. What happened to me last night?"

"Your father found you on the floor out in the corridor."

Clotho looked away as she recalled the giant cat that had terrified her.

"I remember I had a horrible nightmare. I saw a frightening sight, I believe."

That appeared to be enough for the mother listening to her. "You should rest in bed for today, Clotho. Do not get up at all until tomorrow. I can bring your meals here. Do not worry about what happened to you and what was in your dream. The falling was just an unfortunate accident. Your fear will disappear with time. I will cook some chicken galantine for supper tonight," she smiled.

Clotho turned her face away, knowing that the experience was one that would never vanish from her memory. It was an event that becomes a permanent relic of the mind. The torbie cat would never sink into oblivion for her. It was to remain clear and alive forever. It seemed to her that the large feline self wished to stay in her mind and never disappear from there. The imprint of the cat was one meant to be inerasable, never to grow faint.

Tugau did not come to her until late in the afternoon, after work. He knocked lightly, then opened the door, entered, closed the door and tiptoed to the bed where Cotho lay. Was she awake? Indeed, her eyes followed him across to her side. He asked how she felt now.

She stared in his face imploringly. "I can't say, because I don't really know yet."

What does she mean by that? he wondered anxiously.

"Did you hurt yourself? Your father told me he found you on the floor outside."

A grimace of inner pain crossed her face, but she did not answer him.

Tugau made an instant decision to reveal all of the truth that he knew. There was no other way out. If he could have avoided it, he would have jumped to grasp such a solution. But now his duty was one of total confession to her.

"My dear, you expressed the secret of your ancestry to me, but I failed to reveal the most important aspect about myself. What do you think that was? It closely resembles what you said to me at that time." He gazed down at her frightened face. "I, like you, was born a diploid. But my second form belongs to a different species entirely."

There, it was out. He had no path of retreat now, only a road forward.

She peered at him with confusion in her widening velvet eyes.

Tugau proceeded to identify himself as a chatan who had last night metamorphosized in a dream. His other self was the cat that he now discovered had confronted her. He tried to justify his previous silence on the subject. "This is the truth, believe me. I am biform, but in a different way from you. I can become a chatan wild cat. A dream is the means by which I move out of my human form into the other. Let me show you what scholars have written about ancient chatans in the highlands. I took a page out of one of the folios we bought at the outdoor market. Let me go and get it from my apartment so you can see it yourself."

He was gone only a few moments, returning with the page of text he had hidden in his apartment. Handing it to her, Tugau pulled up a stool and sat quietly as she read the paragraph about the chatan legend in the highlands.

When she was finished with it, Clotho gave the page back to him.

"It was you, then?" she whispered.

He nodded that she was right. "I enter a timeless dreamland and then come out of it in my second form. That is what happens with active diploids."

"What are the two of us going to do?" she moaned. "What is going to become of you and me if we are biforms? Are we both freaks?"

Tugau, misunderstanding her query somewhat, replied concerning the immediate future.

"I want to go out and explore the world in my secondary form. It can only be accomplished at night, with most of the population of the city asleep. Exploration could educate my cat into tameness and self-control. There is enormous curiosity in every felid that has to be satisfied. Will you agree to accompany my chatan when this happens, Clotho?"

She anwered him without a moment of hesitation. "Of course. When do we start?"

"In a few nights, when you recover your full strength, my dear."

"Very well," she promised. "I will ready myself for experimental exploration with you. There must be much that both of us can learn from such an adventure."

Clotho sneaked out of her room at midnight and opened Turgau's door for the large torbie cat. It recognized and followed her out the back door of the Gallipot building. The animal seemed tame and under control. Turgau had made an effort to prepare it for this. He wished the cat to hold itself in check within their relationship of primus and secundus.

Once outdoors, Clotho let her big, furry companion take the lead, following wherever it went. They hurried past a locked-up confectionery, a bakery, and a general cookery. The four-legged explorer stopped in front of a meat market. This was a point of profound interest for it. The brindled cat looked with visible signs of hunger through the shop window at the sausages and pieces of flesh for sale. Something has to be done for the chatan, decided Clotho. But it had to be safe and judicious, or it would cause alarm and much trouble for them.

An idea occurred to her. She herself would break into the butcher shop and appropiate by stealth the food her companion craved. That made sense to her. She could accomplish what was impossible for the cat that Turgau had turned into to do.

As quietly as possible, Clotho tried in turn the front, side, and back doors of the building. They were all locked fast. How about the windows, though? She succeeded in locating one in the back that she jimmied open with her hands. The chatan immediately jumped through it, into a paradise of carnal delight.

The carcasses of steers, oxen, cows, hogs, pigs, sheep, and deer hung on hooks. Beef, veal, pork, mutton, lamb, and venison meat were available free. Ribs, flanks, rump, round, chuck, brisket, shank, shoulder, foreshank, loin, breast, plate, hind shank, hocks, and every conceivable cut of meat was offered the night raider. The big cat stayed inside the shop a long period. When the torbie at last emerged through the opened window, its face had all the signs of stomach satiety. Rest and digestion loomed ahead for the animal.

Clotho could only imagine what beastly gorging and gluttony had just occurred. She looked at the now heavier cat with disgust. It had fulfilled an instinctive character it could not itself change. She led the surfeited creature back to the Gallipot where they both belonged and were safe.

Electra prepared a festive celebration for her daughter's sixteenth birthday. A dozen neighborhood teenagers were invited. Clotho ignored them, all her attention focused on Turgau, seated at the opposite end of the long table covered with food. Timbales filled with custard, jelly rolls, cream puffs, mince pies, frumenty, and buckets of ice cream kept the young guests busy. There was little opportunity for any talk.

Occasionally, Clotho glanced across at her closest friend. The one she had learned to love.

What did the future hold for them, two diploids, he an active one and she still inactive?

Alpheus, sitting in the middle of the table opposite his daughter, rose to congratulate her.

"I offer a toast of iced cake in your honor, dear child. You have always been the pride of your mother and me. You are considerate of everyone around you. Helpful, generous, and honest. We, all of us here today, send our best wishes for the years ahead. May they be happy ones for you. In token of our deep love for you, let me toast you on this sunny day. Congratulation, dear."

With that, the gathering came to a swift, nearly abrupt, end.

Clotho soon went to her room to rest, but a knock on the door informed the celebrant that it was the one person she knew would soon be present. Without a word, Tugau slipped in and approached her. He only spoke after they had embraced, kissed, and then separated.

"I have decided to ask you something," he murmured softly. "Will you consent to marry me? If you do, I intend to go at once to your parents for their approval. That is my plan for the two of us."

She stared blankly at him, mute as her mind revolved. Her mouth continued to gape. For a time, it was impossible for her to say anything, whether rational or not.

A powerful argument took hold of her and she expressed it to him. "There is so much that must be settled first. Where can we live? What will you and I do? These quesions have to be answered. We have to know what awaits us."

Turgau shook his head. "There will be no practical problems. We continue here, working as we do now, but living together. You will continue your apprenticeship."

Clotho grimaced. "We two are really like four persons," she objected. "You are a diploid and I am likewise. That makes our situation a complicated one, my love."

"But we love each other. That is enough for us to thrive on," he objected. "If the ties between us are the strong union we believe it to be, then both halves of each of us has been melded into the single unit that we have become. We are already the mates we shall formally become with marriage. There will be no difference except the public acknowledgement."

Clotho suddenly looked away toward the bed she slept on.

"Let us go on, for now, as we have from the start. There is no need to change right now. When the moment for something different arrives, we will both know it."

One evening in Clotho's seventeenth year she went with the growing, greater corbie to the necropolis of Diaema, where the dead lied. For the young lovers of the city, that was a favorite place of tryst. Snuggling couples hid themselves behind gravestones, marmoreal monuments, and enormous mausoleums. The leafy tilleul trees provided thick shadows in which movements were unseen. As if by agreement, sheltered groups of lovers said nothing to each other.

Noise was unwelcome here. Silence prevailed as if no living person was in the grassy cemetery.

No cat the size of this gigantic one had ever entered the grounds before. First one, then another couple was disturbed and distracted by the arrival of Clotho and her furry companion. No one could really identify what the creeping intruder beside the young female figure was. But its odd presence produced cold shivers. There was something terrifying about the indefinite form, whatever it might be.

Strange rustling began among the interrupted trysters. First one couple, then several others, left the burial grounds. Uncertain of the degree of danger to them, many decided for safety in departure. Why stay where the unknown lurked and wandered about?

Sensing this exodus, Clotho slowed her steps, causing the same by the chathan. She had not anticipated this uneasy situation. The necropolis was not a quiet retreat that evening.

The chatan itself began to seek a way out of the cemetery. Clotho realized the need for a change in plans. Soon the pair were in an adjacent pome orchard of apple, quince, and pear trees. They soon were beyond the city's borders. They had surrendered the necropolis to other beings, it appeared.

Clotho was assigned by her father to assist Tugau in the nervine section of the pharmacy, in order to gain experience with calmatives. She and her lover were thrown together both at work and after hours. A new joy pervaded her whole day and evening hours.

"Are you trying out on yourself some of the remedies you make?" he asked one late afternoon in his flat as the two of them sat and rested.

"Why do you ask?" she said in surprise.

"Because you seem so positively enthusiastic of late, that's why," he slyly grinned.

"I am trying out some of the mild becalmers, those that I know have no drastic side effects. I am glad that you can see the difference they make. Much of the stress and agitation I once felt has vanished like a fog. There is now new strength in me. And things should be going our way once I rise above the level of an apprentice. That will be soon, only a month from now. I can hardly wait."

He looked down at the floor. "You still will say no to marriage, though?"

She looked him squarely in the eye. "We have a lot of time ahead of us for that. Rushing forward does not make sense to me. Neither of us has a simple nature like those who are not diploid."

He frowned darkly. "I believe enough time has gone by. We each know the other. We should at least inform your parents of our plans. I am growing impatient to make public what we already feel toward each other. What is wrong with that, Clotho? It will be a better condition for both of us."

She furrowed her smooth young brow into a frown.

"I must have a sense of the correctness of that hour when I inform my parents. The marriage will have to be an accepable change for them, not only for me."

"Why such pessimism?" he asked in desperation. "I don't see why we can't tell them immediately."

"It would not be easy to do. They have their own plans for my future, Tugau."

"But so do I. They have no right to veto what both of us decide has to be. We both wish to wed, don't we? Why, then, not become one in law?"

"It is not that simple. Both of us are already more than a one. How can we foresee what will come of our combining?"

He shook his head. 'We would not be the first pair of differing diploids to join together. I see no reason to be fearful of the diversity involved."

Before they realized it, they were clutching each other in a shared embrace.

Electra roasted a huge porker stuffed with pancreatic and thymic sweetbreads. Tugau and Clotho were unusually silent throughout the supper on Harvest Holiday. Only Apheus did much talking during the meal his wife had prepared for the important celebration.

When the parents were alone after the feast, Electra expressed her worries to her husband.

"I have to speak to you about something that troubles me of late."

Still sitting at the long table, Alpheus looked up in surprise. "What are you talking about?" he inquired, aroused by her words.

"I am deeply concerned about your assistant, Turgau."

"What about him?" said the pharmacist, rising out of his chair and facing his wife. "What has he done?"

"I can't say for sure, but recently there are signs that he has become much too familiar with Clotho. You and I have to discuss the matter. Perhaps you can talk to him. Is there a problem here? It may eventually cause much trouble for us, I fear. Now is the time to act to avert any harm to Clotho."

Electra began pacing up and down the dining room as she pondered what to say.

"Have you become blind, Alpheus? There may be something here that demands serious attention before it is too late. We cannot ignore the need to deal with the matter."

As her meaning dawned on him, agitation arose in the mind of the father.

"You can't suspect them of carrying on, can you?" he asked.

"It is a possibility, isn't it?" she replied with a question of her own.

The two stared at each other for a time.

"How can we find out?" said Alpheus. "And what can we do if our fears are proven correct?"

"I have been thinking hard, besides watching them carefully," revealed Electra. "This is what I noticed: they never talk between themselves much when we are present. What does that indicate?

Are they trying to throw us off by giving no cause for any suspicion? Only when they are alone, it appears, do they talk at all to each other. Before us, they are like strangers. Do you see what I am getting at? Why are they trying to act so indifferently to one another in front of us?"

"You believe there could be conscious deception involved?" demanded Alpheus.

"I am being forced to that conclusion by their concerted silence," she told her husband.

"It is, then, a conscious indifference they are showing before us?"

"Yes, a joint effort to throw observers off the track," said Electra with confidence. "It is clever."

"I may have to fire him in the end," declared the botanic with a moan. "Though I have great repect for his abilities, he could prove unthrustworthy, if what you suspect is true. What you have told me is greatly troubling."

Electra placed her hand on his forearm. "For the present, we have to be guarded and cautious. Both of us must watch them to learn what it is they do together." She paused for a moment. "We have to be the protectors of our daughter. No one else can or will."

He nodded yes to her.

Rain, drizzle, and thick mists kept the two lovers indoors day after day. Sneaking to the room of the other became a habit for them. Neither realized how far they had lowered their guard. The fact that Electra lurked about, following their movements, they came to ignore. The two concentrated exclusively on each other, no one else.

One foggy morning, Cloltho entered the apartment of Tugau in a troubled mood.

"What is it?" he asked. "Is there something bothering you?"

She wrinkled her smooth brow. "I am not feeling too well. This has been so for the last week. It is hard to describe, because I don't know what it is."

He stepped closer to her. "Where does it hurt? Is the pain constant?"

"My head bothered me, so I took a becalmer."

"Did it help?"

"Only for a short while. It could be serious." Her hand went to her abdomen. "It is starting to ache in this region, too. I have increasing pain. Never has my body ever suffered thus before."

The two exchanged looks of significance they both understood.

"Could it be..." he started but stopped in mid-sentence. "I can get you the strongest possible nervines. We can try some piper methysticum, and if it doesn't help, then go on to codopepsis. I promise to rid you of this, my love. I know I can accomplish that."

She opened her mouth to reveal another change in her, but stopped in time. Why alarm Tugau in case she was mistaken? She would wait a few days to be certain it was true. suspicion was not enough on the matter of carrying a child.

Clotho left the flat for the pharmacy library. She found a folio on the physiology of female pregnancy, placed it in a notebook, and took the book back to her room. There was much for her to learn on the subject.

Why have I grown so distant from my mother? Has love for Tugau caused a division and separation from her? So mused the daughter as she entered the kitchen where Electra was busy preparing food.

Before informing her beloved, she had to ask her mother for advice. How would Electra act, as counselor or punisher? she wondered.

Clotho walked in almost on tiptoes. Electra was chopping ascalonic onions on a thick board. She looked up and stopped her labor.

"I want to ask you something important, mother," began Clotho.

Looking at her closely, the mother knew that something was wrong. "Are you ill, child?" she asked.

"I may have conceived within me," blurted out the daughter. "I am not certain."

With gaping mouth and widening eyes, Electra studied her from head to toe.

"How can that be?" screamed the mother with full voice. "How could that happen to you?" She paused, her face reddening with anger. "It must have been Turgau, no one else."

Clotho turned her face away, to the other side. Her mother asked a question weighing on her experienced mind.

"You wish to carry it to delivery now that it is quickening in you?"

"Of course," answered the daughter. "But how can I do that? It will not be possible to keep the secret from father. Do I have to run away from home?"

Electra took Clotho's two hands in her own and held them.

"I must be the one to tell my husband the truth. That will be my responsibility. And it will have to be done quickly, very soon."

She asked Clotho to sit down on a kitchen chair, then felt her body in various places. The forehead, neck, chest, and the stomach felt her gentle touch.

Electra looked her squarely in the eye. "I believe you are correct, my child. You will now experience nine months of gestation. Then will come the painful labor of giving birth. Do not be afraid, I will stay with you and help when there is need. You shall not be alone."

"But father will feel outrage at Tugau and me..."

"Have no fear, I can handle him," the mother promised, realizing that Tugau might be compelled to leave. But she dared not tell that to her daughter, not at that time. There was enough at the present moment to be concerned about.

"I wish you to get as much rest as possible, my dear," smiled Electra. "It will, before long, become necessary for you to leave your tasks in the pharmacy. That cannot go on as before. Have you told Tugau what to expect?"

"From how he talks, I believe that he knows. But I need to communicate more details to him. It was you and father I dreaded to tell. Your advice is saving me from unnecessary heartbreak."

"Thank you," said Electra in a mellow tone. "Now, I have work to finish here in the kitchen. Life must continue without needless interruption. Go to your room and lay down at once. I will bring you some anthemis tea to drink. It will help strengthen you.

Clotho lay thinking, unable to fall asleep. One idea came to occupy her thought. Was the child a boy or a girl? Whom would it look like? Would it resemble her or Tugau more? She considered the possibilities and the odds for or against each one.

A girl had the threat of a harpine inheritance from grandmother Electra. But a male child carried the risk of turning out to be a chatan. Two diploid strains had been combined. What kind of person would be the result?

Would her grown-up son wander the streets at night as a wild chatan? Was there the risk of a man-eating monster if the girl became a harpine? The child she carried would be an experiment. No one at present was capable of predicting the results.

The child's education would have to be strictly supervised at home in order to guide its development. Her responsibilites would be grave ones.

Hours passed by as she planned the methods of civilizing the expected diploid son or daughter.

Someone slowly opened the door to her room and entered as she lay resting and thinking. Clotho turned her head and saw that it was Tugau. He stepped near cautiously in case she was asleep.

"I'm fully awake, darling," she whispered as he bent down just over her.

They kissed each other, and she informed him she had not worked that day. "I felt a little ill. And mother advised me to rest and made me herbal tea to drink."

"I am so sorry," he said. "Didn't the nervines I prepared help you any?"

She smiled but did not answer him.

"We have to talk. Let me get up, I've been resting here long enough."

Soon Clotho was standing on her feet. Tugau helped her to a soft chair, he taking a stool by her side. "Is there anything I can get for you?" asked the highlander.

"Not now, thank you. I have something important to announce to you."

He gave her a powerful look that told her that he knew what it was she planned to say. "About the pregnancy you will be going through?"

Clotho experienced a jolt, almost of relief. "I imagined in the back of my mind that you picked up the marks and signs. It is quite certain now."

"Certain?"

"I had my mother examine me so that we could be absolutely sure."

"Your mother!"

"Yes. There was no other woman I dared to trust."

"Trust? She will disclose what she knows to your father. No doubt about that."

"It couldn't be helped. She had to know what was going to happen to me. Isn't it best that she act as my intermedary with father? She will appeal to his moral character in the name of the unborn grandchild of his. I think it was the best way to proceed, through my mother. Is there any alternative? Best that he find out as early as possible. Now is the right time, not later."

The face of Tugau had turned pale. His lips quivered with emotion.

"What if he explodes in wrath? What if he decides to confront us? The consequences may be painful. What is going to happen next, Clotho?"

She did not answer him because she could not.

How long should I wait to break the news to Alpheus? pondered his wife all day.

He will be returning to the residence to eat supper before too long. Her cooking for the day was done. No better opportunity than now would come, before he left his office for the home dining room. So, she closed the roasting oven and headed for the pharmacy where he would soon be finished working.

She found him writing accounts up at his noixwood desk. He looked up at her, a grin on his face. "You arrived just in time to walk me to supper, just in time."

Electra moved close to where he sat. "I came to tell you something important, my dear."

He looked at her with surprise. What are you talking about? asked his azure eyes.

"It concerns our entire family, because it centers on Clotho. There is something about her that I must reveal to you. It will not be easy to do. I can foresee a fiery response from you to what I am about to say. You must permit me to speak without interruption."

Alpheus looked confused. "What are you talking about?" he muttered in a low voice. His face had turned deep red. The storm is gathering and ready to break, realized his wife as she continued on.

"Our daughter is in a beginning maternal state. Before too long, we shall become grandparents."

Alpheus neither moved nor said anything. His mind was overwhelmed.

Electra felt obligated to answer a question she knew was now his. "I am certain that her partner is in our household. There can be only one possibility. I think you will agree with me about who was responsible. There is no other close male to her."

"Where is she now?" he suddenly demanded.

"She has been in her room all afternoon. I made some tea to rest her nerves and lower her stress. We must treat her with gentleness, Alpheus."

The latter brought his fist down vehemently on the noix desk. "I know that Tugau left the pharmacy for his apartment, so we can find him here in the residence. That is where he is now."

"You must not argue with him, my love," she pleaded. "It would bring harm to everyone. At most, fire him and expel him from living with us any longer. Only that far do you have the right to go. Think of Clotho and her welfare."

Fury flashed out of his eyes, over his entire face. His wife could see the sparks of emotion about to ignite. She was helpless to hold him back.

"Don't tell me what I do or don't have the right to do," he coldly spat out. "I am the one who has to set the matter straight. The responsibility is on me. I am the father. There has to be a settling of our accounts. We have admitted an evil interloper to our home. It is my duty to exact justice. No one else can do it."

"Alpheus, do nothing you will regret," she shouted with emotion.

He brushed by her swiftly, exiting his office, then the pharmacy.

Electra stood petrified. She had thoroughly failed. Her body shook with fear over what might happen next.

I can only deal with him if I am armed with sufficient force, decided Alpheus. A father's obligations cannot be compared to those of anyone else. He convinced himself that he bore a heavy duty to avenge his honor.

The decisive moment had arrived. Several futures depended upon him. He had to act with solid determination. In a instant, he flung the door open and ran into the assistant's apartment.

As if he had been sent a premonition, Alpheus saw exactly what he had anticipated.

CLEMENT S. MASLOFF

The head of Clotho peered out from the coveret over her body. But there was also someone else also looking at him from the bed. He realized who was lying beside her.

The flow of events might have been different if Tugau had not spoken to try to justify what the intruding one saw for himself. "We are all but formally wed, sir..."

There was no time for him to continue or finish, for that was when the first shot was fired from a pepper-box gun. The avenger only realized what he had done after he had pulled back the trigger. No reversal could have been possible.

A gasping filled the room, then a second cartridge went off.

Electra reached the site of slaughter only seconds after the firing ended.

As if awakening from a nightmare, Alpheus dropped the pistol to the floor.

You killed both of them!" cried out his wife. "Both your daughter and her child! Now what? Now what?"

By the time the yellow-coated constables arrived, the young woman was beyond help. Only her lover wheezed for breath now. An officer placed Apheus under arrest and confiscated his pepper-box. He was led away to a cell in the city lock-up.

Tugau was placed in a horse wagon and rushed to a chirurgery for immediate surgery. Specialists had to try to remove the pistol shot in his torso.

Electra was alone when the corpse of Clotho was hauled away. She asked to ride with the unconscious victim of the shootings. Flesh surgeons would try to save his life.

Was he going to survive? she asked herself.

What she had gone through had no order or reason to it. Things had merely occurred. She had no good answers to what caused all the death she had witnessed.

Did her diploid ancestry have anything to do with the fate of Clotho and those around her? she asked herself, but could find no explanation.

Were there invisible factors hidden in ancestry behind this tragedy? How could anyone ever know? mused Electra with a shiver of dread.

IV
The Sylphines

The removal of the bullet from the abdomen of the victim was a delicate operation. Tugau was placed under a strong soporific that desensitized his entire body. The chirugeon who cut into him was Dr. Ongle, the director of the Therapeutic Center.

Upon awakening from the unconscious ordeal, the first person that Tugau saw from his resting hammock was this skilled, successful surgeon. He was a short, somewhat frail, sickly looking man with a sharply hooked nose. Both his hair and eyes were the color of chestnuts. The medico had to identify himself to the patient he had opened up and saved.

"Good morning, Mr. Tugau. Let me introduce myself. I was the surgeon in the removal of the shot lodged inside you. My name is Ongle and I am director of the Center. Tell me this: do you feel any kind of pain at the moment? It is very important to me that you have no discomfort or suffering, so I wish you to be perfectly candid about your condition. Please tell me the truth."

"I am having no distress of any sort," calmly replied the patient.

"That is a good sign. In fact, it is remarkable."

At that point, a willowy woman in an orange uniform stepped into the cubicle where Tugau had his hammock.

"This is the nurse assigned to look after you," said the doctor. "She is Attendant Megaera and will supervise your everyday care and needs."

Tugau saw a tall, slim young female who seemed to be an insubstantial apparition of some kind. A rare allurement radiated from her face and attractive torso. Her hair was a whitish flaxen shade, the eyes a bright, shining blue close to azure.

The patient doubted he had ever viewed such a beauty before. The charm of her thin shape threw a spell over him, making him forget his beloved Clotho for a time. He entered an unintended state of trance.

Tugau suddenly recalled his dead partner and looked off to the side. You must keep your self-control, said an interior voice.

Dr. Ongle excused himself and left the cubicle.

"Can I get you anything?" asked the attendant. Her voice was soft and pleasant to his ears.

"Yes, I want some saxifrage tea. I feel a sudden thirst for it."

"I'll get it for you at once, sir."

"Thank you," graciously said the patient, leaning back in his hammock.

Tugau began to understand how the ruination and death of Clotho had come about. It was not their love for one another that had destroyed her. It was a factor much more subtle and hidden, an influence neither of them had foreseen. But it had led both of them into an abyss that killed Clotho.

Blindly, he had convinced his beloved into accepting the role of companion of his chatan secundus. It was now evident to him that this had dragged her into his own interior diploid drama. She had become an actor in a chain of tragedy that she could not stand up against. The result was death and destruction of her still undeveloped harpine diploid nature. She lost her life as victim of his own biformal character by getting entangled in its complex web.

He had learned a sad lesson of the hazards involved when different strains of diploids become intimately involved with each other.

A sealed envelope arrived addressed to Tugau. He raised himself in bed so he was able to read it in comfort. The letter was from Electra and originated on the Isle of the Harpines, where she had withdrawn to live.

"I am here on my native island because there is nowhere else I could go for peace and solace. The death of my daughter and the imprisonment of my husband has been too much for me to bear in Diaema. My hope is to find an easing of my pain on this isle. I shall never return to the mainland or the place of my life's tragedy. Best wishes for your recovery."

Tugau insisted on rising to his feet as soon as he had enough strength to do so. Megaera brought him a walker support to lean on when she helped him out of his hammock. It took him several moments to establish equilibrium. Then he started to step forward, faster and faster.

"Good!" smiled the nurse. "I've never seen a patient with so much ambition. Don't try too much at once, though. Try to moderate your pace. It can't be done all at once. Slow and steady will get you there. That's the formula. I've never seen any patient with your drive to recover."

Tugau completed several circles about his cubicle, then along the nearest corridor. Megaera brought him a squab to rest on. His labored breathing became calm and normal.

"Your accent is a unique one, Megaera," he told her one day. "From what region did you come to Diadema?"

"The Zenithal Mountains," she informed him. "I am not the only person here from that area. Dr. Ongle was born there too and moved here to study and practice surgery"

"That's interesting. I've read that poverty in your mountains drives many to emigrate to lower altitudes where there are greater opportunities for them."

A shadow fell over her face, which he noticed. "Yes, that's true," was her only comment.

Tugau said no more about where she came from.

When the doctor visited him the next day, the patient posed a question to him.

"I'm hoping to leave the Therapeutic Center before too long, sir. When do you think it can be?"

Ongle waited a little before answering. "I have learned that the gallipot is now closed down and that your old job has disappeared. The bills and expenses that have accumulated for your care will be enormous. So, I have been thinking over a possible future that could benefit you a lot."

The patient in the hammock perked up. "What is it?" he asked with excited curiosity.

"As this institution expands the need for a skilled botanic like you grows. Would you agree to stay here as our single herbal specialist? Up to now, each therapist and chirug has had to compound his own medicaments with the help of assistants. That is extremely laborious for all our staff. I can arrange for you to have a free apartment in our staff quarters. The job will enable you to pay off your debts to our Center quickly and efficiently. What do you say to the proposal I've made?"

Stunned and overjoyed, Tugau still hesitated. "I don't know. Give me time to decide, please. I have to think it over for a while."

"Certainly," grinned the other."But please make your choice before leaving us."

Megaera introduced Tugau to three other nurse attendants, all of them from the Zenithals. The amazing similarity among them took his breath away. All were tall and lithe, with unusual beauty and personal charm. Their names were Sterope, Merope, and Alcyone. The last one, Alcyone, revealed to him that she was their leader, the head of their trio of nurses from the mountains. All three spoke with a Zenithal region accent.

The patient was walking ever greater distances outdoors. But he had to announce his decision on staying on at the Therapy Center soon. Time for leaving the hospital neared.

Late one afternoon, Megaera entered his cubicle to take his temperature. Once she removed the meter from his mouth, she surprised him with some whispered advice. "All of us nurses believe that you should accept the doctor's offer and remain as our botanic. You are a person everyone can get along with. The work will be rewarding and very interesting for you. Stay and see."

Did she wink one eye? Tugau was uncertain if he had seen that happen. He acted as if it hadn't. That seemed best to him at the time.

"It appears to me that few natural herbals are used by anyone here. What would I be doing? There will be little use for one with my skills and background."

Unexpectedly, she laughed. "Why are you talking that way? Are you supposing that you will be underworked here? Is that your idea of what lies ahead for you?"

He thought a moment. "Perhaps I can do much to advance the use of plant materials. You are right, Megaera. I will think it over tonight and give an answer to Dr. Ongle tomorrow morning."

"If I were you, I 'd accept it," she told the patient.

Soon after finishing his breakfast of poached ovules Tugau saw the director of the Therapeutic Center walk into his cubicle. The two greeted each other, then Ongle asked the overhanging question. "Are you going to be with us permanently, my friend?"

The affirming nod in reply exhilarated the surgeon. "Good. We can get you going at once. How would you like beginning an inventory of all our medicinal stocks right away, this morning?"

"Fine," beamed Tugau. "I'm ready to start at once." He seemed to have had that idea in mind from the first time it was presented to him.

The botanic put on a working smock brought him by Megaera. "Good luck," said the nurse. "All of us wish you the best of fortune in your work with us."

He thanked her with joy on his face. A new stage had opened for him. But disappointment struck immediately. Tugau was shocked by what he discovered in the chamber where medicines were stored. He entered by himself, using a key card that Dr. Ongle had sent to him.

Minerals and compounds based on soil compounds, mostly salts, were the bulk of what was there. He sighed sadly. Only a few herbals were available. That was not his expectation. What did Ongle want him to do? he wondered.

The opportunity to ask that question came swiftly when the director appeared in the depository room as Tugau was examining its contents.

"What do you think of my treasury?" inquired his employer. "There are so many substances that exist, but we have been unable to put them to use with efficiency. My day is dominated with surgery. I need someone like you to set this storehouse in order and oversee its distribution among patients and former patients."

Former patients?"

"Yes. They all need continuous therapy, treatment, and monitoring. Why should our care end with release? We continue to look out for our ex-patients. In reality, they never become fully disconnected from us. My prescriptions for them tend to be life-long in nature. I never write an end to any case I deal with."

Tugau searched for what to say. "I find that amazing. But I have to ask myself why you want a botanic working on such a collection of materials as you have in here. From what I can tell, these are mostly non-organics, not plant products."

The surgeon grinned as if some secret had been uncovered. "Yes, that is true. Leading herbalists have criticized the Therapeutic Center for the unique emphasis on mineral-based treatment given here. But what better way to counter such arguments than to hire someone with your background and experience? I want you to bring your knowledge into practical application for the health of our patients. There will be no limitations on your botanic work here."

Tugau felt bold enough to declare his personal goals. "There must be no restriction of me in distributing herbal remedies. I hope that everyone recognizes that one condition of mine."

He gave Ongle a hardened, stony look.

"That is the way I want it to be too," calmly agreed the doctor. "Yes, that is how you shall be functioning, exactly as you say."

Turau abruptly turned away. "I mean to make a complete, total inventory of all that is in here. Then, I will have a catalogue printed up for everyone involved."

The canteen where employees of the Therapeutic Center ate their meals was a distance from the entrance of the main structure, necessitating constant exercise walking back and forth. Had that been a conscious decision of the management to help maintain the health of the hospital staff? wondered Tugau, eating at a tiny table next to a wide window facing the Center. As he finished his salmagundi salad of cardoon, he happened to look out at the main building. There were four tall, thin figures coming out of the entrance door. He recognized them at once as being Megaera and her three friends, Sterope. Merope, and Alcyone. Stepping vigorously, they all appeared to be hurrying toward the canteen in order to make good use of their break in work time.

He stared as if his sight was glued to the comely foursome. They grew more visible as they came nearer their destination, the lunch room where he himself was eating.

The sound of patrons of the place passing by him drew his attention for only a moment or so, creating a temporary distraction that was soon over. He turned his eyes to the small group moving closer toward the canteen.

But now, to his astonishment, there were only three of them.

He identified Alcyone, Merope, and Sterope. But there was no Megaera among them.

How could that be? Four had turned into three. Was he seeing with error? Had Megaera walked off somewhere on her own?

He had looked away only for a moment. How could so much have occurred in so short a time? His view was wide on both sides of the central cement walkway. She would not have gone far by now on the yellowish grass. Where was the willowy nurse who had taken such good care of him?

Tugau considered the idea that he had been mistaken from the beginning. Perhaps he had counted four bodies when there had actually been only three. Had he seen an optical illusion? Was this enigma all in his mind? he asked himself.

The botanic bit his lip. Was he involved in wishful perception? Did he really wish to talk with Megaera and imagined she was coming to be with him? There were several plausible explanations, yet none of them had the ring of verifiability. The entire experience was inexplicable.

He decided to ask the three about the missing nurse and where they last saw her. What they told him might throw light on the puzzle.

Tugau rose, paid his bill, and walked out before the group reached the canteen. He met and greeted them a little way from the entrance door. Then he got to what was bothering him.

"Isn't Megaera eating lunch with you today?" he innocently asked.

Alcyone spoke for the group. "She went to the air terminal to await the globoid arriving from the Zenithals. Her baby brother is flying here. Megaera obtained permission to meet him."

"Is that why she is missing? Did any of you see her go away on a trolley car?"

A reply came from Merope, standing in the middle.

"She left by herself, on her own. That was all, no big deal."

Tugau smiled, said goodbye, and walked on, bewildered and baffled.

Tugau was flabbergasted as he studied the content's of the medicine depository. He found large quantities of vitriol acid, colcothar iron, antimony, lead, arsenic, mercury, and laudanum. These substances were far from what he was accustomed to.

The use of opium-containing laudanum at the Center especially disturbed him.

CLEMENT S. MASLOFF

At his next meeting with the director in the latter's office, Tugau brought up his growing fears about patient safety with the heavy use of metals and metallics. "I am worried as to whether our patients are well protected when they take such mineral and metallic materials into them. Are they sufficiently warned of the possible toxic effects? I fear that some may be overdosing after leaving the Center without direct supervision. They cannot know the dangers they are facing."

Ongle made a furtive grimace that contained anger in it.

"I don't understand what you are complaining about. Look at any prescription that I write. There are always strict instructions on how much is to be taken, when, and warnings about negative signs to watch out for. All patients on these compounds are fully informed as to the risks they take. No one is treated without their complete knowledge and awareness. You exaggerate, Tugau."

The botanic refused to give in. "I imply nothing, I merely state the truth: many of these materials are deleterious without proper supervision and tight control. That should be evident to anyone who studys what we have stored in the repository." He paused a moment for breath,then went on. "There is doubt in my mind whether such compounds are really effective in a curative sense."

The face of the director became totally sanguine, yet he succeeded in disguising his outrage.

"I should have prepared you better for the work you are doing. For many years, my approach here has been one of simple iatro-chemistry. Do you recognize what that refers to?"

"That is when a physician uses materials extracted from the soil, whether rock, mineral, or metal ore. But only a minority of medics in Provincia use those substances. For generations, our dominant therapies have been botanical. Plants and herbs are the source of most medicaments today, not what we find buried under the surface."

"Are you familiar with the ancient medical practices in the Zenithal Mountains? We had centuries of development of folk remedies extracted from the ground. There were specialized persons with knowledge handed down over eons of time. They are still called spagyrists."

Tugau fought for breath. "The old alchemists? They continue to treat the sick?"

"They possess extraordinary knowledge and wisdom, though laughed at and denigrated in other parts of Provincia. There is much that they could teach all of us, even the botanics in our cities."

Glaring stares were exchanged back and forth. All at once, the facial color of Ongle returned to normal. He had thought up a proposal to present.

"Some time ago, I wrote a paper on this very matter, but never had it published. I would like to have you read it. My view of therapy with soil compounds is outlined in the work. Can I give it to you?"

Tugau answered with caution.

"Without obligating myself on anything, I will go though it, sir."

Of all the people of the Therapeutic Center, only the director had a cottage all to himself. The rest of the staff occupied a residential hall with small apartments. Tugau was assigned to a vacancy at the end closest to the structure holding the patients in recuperation from surgery. He made himself at home there.

The women who were nursing attendants were at the other end of the same building, facing toward the open countryside. Tugau rarely saw the trio that he knew. He sat down in the evening and read his employer's treatise. The first chapter dealt with parallel and similitude between the macromonde of the great world and the micromonde of a human being. It described analogies between the large and the small, then went into the intuitive knowledge that is possible because of the fundamental resemblances between the great and the small.

All at once, a loud noise sounded through the flat, coming from the corridor. The clanging din soon turned into violent shouting. What could it be? Tugau sprang to his feet, ran to the door, and quickly opened it wide to look down the hallway. What was causing the commotion?

He saw Megaera standing next to a towering male, each one of them shouting at the other. Sterope, Merope, and Alcyone stood immediately around their fellow nurse, as if trying to protect her from what was happening.

As he hurried down the hall toward the group, Tugau began to make out what the disputants were saying to each other.

"Don't try to fool me," yelled the young man. "I know treachery when I see it."

First the co-workers of Megaera, then she herself, turned toward the botanic. Last of all, the male stranger turned to see what the others were looking at.

Tugau stopped a short distance from them. He stared at the group, they stared back.

The first person to address him was Megaera.

"This is my brother, recently arrived from the mountains. His name is Xuthus." She turned her head and spoke to her sibling. "This man is the new pharmacist that Ongle discovered among the patients. He is busy cataloguing the medicine repository."

The two men looked daggers at each other.

Silence continued uneasily for a short time, until Alcyone spoke. "I'm going back to my room," she muttered. "Everybody else can do as they please."

Once the process began, two more of the group did the same. Soon only the brother, sister, and the herbalist remained in the corridor, facing each other.

Suddenly Megaera made a proposal. "Why do we stay out here, Xuthus? Let's go to my room and have a talk with Tugau." She then looked directly at the latter. "What do you say? Will you come in with us."

The nurse went to her door and opened it. She waved at Tugau to indicate he should be the one to go in next. Once he was inside, she signaled her brother to enter. Then she stepped in, closing the door behind her.

A cold wall of mutual disdain separated the two men. Megaera pointed to a stool, commanding her brother by gestures to sit down there. She then turned to Tugau and said "You can take the big chair." She herself sat down on a plain xyloid seat and started to speak.

"I shall be the one who makes the introductions between the two of you. Tugau, here is my brother, just arrived from the Zenithal Mountains. He was the youngest child in our family, and I have always attempted to look out for him. We call him Xuthus, an ancient name among us." She paused a few seconds as if waiting for something to happen.

"Xuthus, this is the new pharmacist of the Therapeutic Center. He was, until recently, one of our patients. In fact, I was his attendant nurse. Now he has recovered from his surgery. The director hired him, his first major duty being to catalogue all our medicinal stores of curative compounds and substances. It is a big and important job that he has."

Her brother gave the herbalist a glare of unconcealed suspicion. "So, you serve Dr. Ongle. That is interesting. As his pharmacist, you are the person in charge of all his supplies. Am I correct?"

The man's sister intervened. "He was trained as a botanic. That means that Tugau is not a spagyrist of metallic minerals, as were the pharmacists in the Zenithals."

Xuthus gave the stranger a sharp, questioning look. "I can conclude that you have control over the supply of laudanum, can't I?"

Megaera, now standing between the pair, all at once turned upon her brother.

"I believe that you are tired from your long journey, Xuthus. Why don't you go into the bedroom and lie down? You will see and talk to our friend again, once you are rested up. Please do as I suggest."

Meekly, Xuthus obeyed the command from his sibling.

Once he was out of the room, Megaera came close to Tugau.

"I apologize for his strange behavior. Back home, he was under medical treatment when he was a child. His therapist was Dr. Ongle. My brother's problems are deep ones. He spoke of laudanum because it has become an addictive passion for him. You see, it began as a prescribed medicament for his violent fits of depression. His entire existence is now focused upon getting hold of and taking that material based on opium. What a tragedy!"

"It is a very potent compound," noted Tugau.

"I know. It is laudanum that brings him to Diadema. That and a thirst for vengeance on Ongle, the one who put him in the prison you see that he dwells in."

"It is the director he blames?"

Megaera nodded yes.

Her visitor decided to excuse himself and leave at once.

"The key to everything in the universe is chemistry. God was the original alchemist. The Divine Chemist created everything that exists through his calcination, congealing, distillation, and sublimation of everything left from the original chaos. All that we see about us grew out of the original material protyle. That was the primal source of all the chemical elements.

"The chemist in his laboratory can decipher and read the mysteries of creation through research. Everything can be analyzed by the explorer called a chemist. The three primary elements were salt, sulphur, and mercury. Everything that burns is made of sulphur. Whatever can be sublimated is mercury. All that then remains is a salt.

"There is nothing anywhere in the infinitum that is not also in man. The physician must first understand all of nature in the world before he can understand his patient. All illness and disease comes from the constituent elements of the universe and their effects on human beings. Cures can only come from these same influences outside the patient. That is the key to unlocking the secrets of nature and obtaining medicines that can cure."

Tugau was breathless from reading the director's treatise on metals and minerals.

How different this was from what he had learned at the botanic Gallipot under Alpheus!

Megaera came to the dispensary for a private talk with the pharmacist. He invited her to sit down beside his work desk. She began with an apology for what had happened the previous evening.

"I must ask for your forgiveness. My brother behaved badly. It had to do with what he feels about his dependence on laudanum."

" Can't he find therapy for it?" inquired Tugau.

"He doesn't trust anyone. Not since his experience with Dr. Ongle."

"Did the director make some horrible mistake in treatment?"

She nodded that his guess was right.

"My brother was just a teenager when he first went for therapy. Ongle diagnosed it as a case of cycloid depression. Xuthus was told that he suffered from a chemical insufficiency in natural minerals. The laudanum he began with was meant to rebalance his inner metallic minerals. My brother was supposed to achieve a new, higher equilibrium between his sulphur and his mercury through the influence of medicinal drugs, but it never happened. Instead, the new problem arose."

"Xuthus placed the blame for that on Dr. Ongle," said Tugau. "Is that fair?"

"A share of the guilt definitely falls on the doctor, but by no means all of it. My brother exacerbated the difficulty with his emotional reaction. He took to the laudanum with a passion at first because it symbolized his revenge on the oppressive forces weighing him down. That is what I believe happened to him."

"What oppressive forces are you referring to, Megaera?"

She seemed to hesitate. "Our family was one of those shunned and discriminated against."

"I don't understand, so please explain."

"Our neighbors called us a sylphine family, and we were that. My brother was not strong enough to live with and accept the name. That led to his depressive state of mind."

"I still do not fully comprehend," said the pharmacist.

"Sylphines in the Zenithals are a people who are possessed of air spirits. They are believed to be capable of wingless flight though sheer willpower. With colossal effort, they hurl themselves in all directions. Dr. Ongle is said to have similar origins. That is probably why he hired me, as well as Sterope, Merope, and Alcyone. Otherwise, it would have been hard for any of us to find jobs as nurses up in the mountains. That is the main reason we came to Diaema. It is the factor that brought my brother too, as well as revenge on Ongle."

Tugau thought he felt his head spin. "You people, then, form a sort of cult that believes it is descended from air sylphines?"

She did not answer directly.

"It is very different in the mountains than it is here. The majority there have untrue ideas about us. They call us terrible names and are abusive. That does not happen here in Diaema and the Therapeutic Center. We are under the protection of Dr. Ongle here."

Tugau thought a moment. "It appears to me that attitudes of hatred aggravated the problems of your brother. Maybe he lacked the mental strength to withstand the pressure."

Megaera gave him a sad smile. "You have sharp perception and sensitivity," she said quietly.

"I would like to get to know your brother better."

"He plans to rent a room near the Center. We will be seeing him around here from now on. You will have opportunities to talk with him."

Tugau soon returned to his rooms, his mind in a whirl. Had he become involved with a type of diploid he was unfamiliar with? What would it mean for him? How should he orient himself in the unforeseen situation he had fallen into?

The night that followed was when Tugau finished reading the treatise of the director. He marveled at the audacity of the conclusions reached. He had never before come across these radically original concepts anywhere.

"The agents of all illnesses and diseases are poisonous emanations from metals, salts, minerals, and distant astral bodies like the stars. These causes are specific, not general in nature. Abnormal quantities of salt, sulphur, or mercury in the body results in perilous disqualibria and sickness.

"A human being has an internal arch located in the abdomen that controls the flows of salt, sulphur, and mercury within the body. Its function is to regulate all body processes. When it goes off the track, imbalances result. If the arch does its job properly at all times, a person could live indefinitely, without a termination by death. If physicians knew enough about body chemistry, they could create a human embryo that would then grow up into an adult. The latter would never die, if the right balance of the three elements could be reached. Life would be unending."

Tugau finished reading the work with many questions in his mind. He had met many unfamiliar phrases and ideas: seminal seeds from God, ultimate essences, sidereal bodies, astral corpses, aniada and grodinia germs, and hidden lusters. What did they mean? What was their practical impact on health and illness?

Tired and confused, he returned the volume to the office of the director. The latter invited him in for a review of the work. "What do you think of my treatise?" asked Dr. Ongle, smiling like a cat.

Tugau groped for an adequate reply that would not irritate or disconcert his superior. "I have never read anything as provocative in my life. The viewpoint is totally new to me and I have to think through the many new concepts I came across. How did you write such a work, sir?"

The face of Ongle turned icy cold.

"In the Zenithals, there are many similar explanations of sickness. We form a community with shared ideas held in common. The whole group thinks like me."

A sudden revelation occurred in the mind of the botanic. "Are you speaking of the sylphines of the Zenithal Mountains?"

Dr. Ongle appeared to undergo a jouncing jolt.

"How did you learn about sylphines?" he gruffly demanded. "Has someone here spoken of them to you?"

The pharmacist realized he had to prevaricate in order not to expose Megaera to her employer's wrath. "I knew of that group before I came to the Center. It is difficult to remember exactly where I found references to them, but I have a tiny bit of information about sylphines. Who they are, though, remains a mystery to me. Do you mean to tell me that their ideas are like those in your treatise?"

Looking away, the director did not reply directly. "There is much that I dare not say to you yet. Let me say this much: I was born into a circle of sylphines, as my parents were before me. My position with them grew into one of leadership. I still remain an important, pivotal figure here in Diaema. There are several others like me working at the Therapeutic Center. I try to look out for their interest and protect them from outside threats."

"Threats?" asked Tugau.

Ongle gazed directly into the herbalist's chatoyant eyes.

"There are certain enemies of ours in the Zenithals. I have long feared that they will follow us here. They go by the name of Gnomi and have a history in the mining industry. Have you heard of them?"

"No."

The director considered for a couple of seconds.

"I can loan you a history of the Zenithal Mountains. You can learn a lot about the feud between the sylphines and the gnomi from what it says."

Dr. Ongle went back to his office and took a thick volume from a shelf.

Tugau, busy with his inventory of the stores available in the safe room, heard the outer door of the substance repository open. He came out to see a skeletal figure of imposing height standing in the anteroom. It was clear at once to the botanic who it was: the disoriented brother of Megaera, the young man named Xuthus.

"Good morning," said Tugau, "Is there anything I can do for you?"

The answer was a jarring one. "Get me some laudanum, please. I beg that of you."

"Do you have a doctor's prescription? That is required by law."

The mountainer's expression changed from that of a pleader to one of threatening pressure.

"You do not understand my critical need. There is no time for a note to be written. Give it to me now and I promise to return with the writ you require."

"I'm afraid that nothing like that is possible. Why don't you find a doctor here at the Center and ask him for a prescript for that substance?"

Anger colored the face of the tall addict a crimson hue.

"Don't you remember me from last evening? I am the brother of Megaera. We were talking when you came in and interrupted our heated discourse. The subject that concerned us was what I am here for now. My need for laudanum is a result of the malpractice of Dr. Ongle back home in the Zenithal Mountains. He is a treacherous dissembler. I know, for it was I who uncovered the truth of how he treated his patients with chemicals. That is why he enslaved me with large doses of laudanum and gained absolute power over my mind. He had, at that time, unquestioned authority over what I could say or do. But I revolted against subservience to him and unmasked him as a mountebank and bamboozler. He never forgave me for that." Xuthus paused for breath, looking directly at Tugau with a knowing grin. "Ongle claims that he leads the sylphines, but that boast of his is a fraud. Only I know what, in reality, he is and whom he serves."

"What do you mean?" asked the pharmacist.

"Do you know what a mountain gromus is?"

"Of course I do," lied Tugau, determined to learn the truth by claiming to have knowledge he did not.

"Look at how short the doctor is. Notice how dwarfish his frame and bones are. He cannot qualify as one of the tall sylphines. We are big and large-boned, though slim and reedlike. No, Ongle cannot be what he says he is. He is a traitor and a spy, an enemy to all true sylphines."

The botanic pondered briefly, then presented a proposal to his visitor.

"If I gave you a minuscule amount of laudanum, just enough to tide you over for a few hours, would you agree to see me later to determine how to proceed with your condition? I will need to know where you are staying in order to find you."

The intruder accepted with surprising alacrity.

Tugau went back into the store vault to obtain what the addict needed. He took a pinch of tincture of opium and poured it into a vial. When he returned to the anteroom, Xuthus greedily snatched it out of his hand and rushed away without a word. He had done what he thought he needed to quiet the fires in him.

After an hour of cataloguing, Tugau found himself unable to proceed further. Curiosity compelled him to take the history of the Zenithals and skim through it, on the lookout for anything about the sylphines or gnomi. At last, after a long hunt, he discovered what he was after.

"The aboriginal tribes living in our mountain region believed that the entire universe consisted of four fundamental material elements: fire, air, water, and soil. And there were four corresponding divisions in the mountain population, each one associated with one of those material principles. These tribes saw each element as inhabited by a special being with supernatural powers. The four divisions of human beings were identified with these invisible immaterial beings living in the elements. Salamanders were spirits that dwelled in fire. Undine creatures were the ones in water. Gnomi lived underground in earth, rock, and soil. Each of the types of spirit possessed special powers. The gnomus, for example, was capable of moving through solid earth or rock like a fish swimming though water. Female undines were so beautiful they could steal a man's soul if he mated with one of them and gave her child. Such legends continue to exist in isolated villages and hamlets of the Zenithal Mountains."

Tugau sat back and put down the book. He thought through what he had just read.

The sylphines and gnomi were primal enemies. Xuthus, whether disturbed or not in mind, had ingested the inter-group conflict and hatred so thoroughly that he had to identify his foe, Dr. Ongle, with the enemy diploid of the subterrane. The sylphines had ruled the air, while the gnomi were rulers underground.

What is the truth about Dr. Ongle? he wondered. Is he the one or the other? Or something else?

What did he have to do in order to uncover the true situation of these strange diploids?

The answer appeared to his mind in a brilliant flash.

Investigation in the form of a small felid chatan could be effective because no one pays attention to a stray cat. He would forget the larger shape from his past and become a small tom or a tabby. As a little animal that posed no threat to anyone he should have entre wherever he wished to go and listen.

Tugau decided to transform himself into the other half of his diploid nature, as a small shape.

Another idea occurred as well. Suppose all the sylphines were able to move between two forms: the human and the airborne one. What if Megaera, for example, were both human and a spirit of the air?

He would have to keep that possibility always in mind as he dealt with the group of sylphines.

The concept worked flawlessly.

He transformed into a small catling, black with a white-spotted face. A pretty kitten that was no threat to anyone or anything. How was this animal to enter and leave buildings and rooms in them? It could not open doors larger than itself. But there was one possible way, Tugau cleverly thought of. What if the transfer process from one form to the other were speeded up and kept completely hidden from the eyes of others? If the cat faced a closed door, the creature would transform itself back into its human shape. Once he had solved the problem by throwing open the obstacle, then the chatan could immediately turn into its feline form again. Quick transmutation into the human status then back into the body of a cat. Speed and timeliness were essential.

Can I work such a scheme with satisfaction he asked himself.

Tugau first tried experiments inside his apartment with the bathroom door as the barrier.

It worked perfectly. There was no disruption or delay in the movement back and forth between the two forms.

The best site for his espionage was the flat of Megaera. Glancing at his wrist timer, Tugau realized that all the nurses were still at work. It was an opportune moment to enter her apartment in felid form, hide somewhere under the furniture, and wait for the return of Megaera with the others. He suspected that the other sylphine nurses might come to the flat along with her, ready to discuss matters of great interest to him.

From the timber of the voices, the black and white young feline under the living room sofa identified the presence of Megaera and Alcyone when the pair entered from the hallway. They were discussing surgical operations that Dr. Ongle had performed that day. Alcyone was taking a critical view of his results as a chirugeon.

"The little doctor cuts, slices, and carves like a meat butcher at a slaughterhouse. I am always surprised that more of his patents don't end up in their final form of flesh."

Megaera then spoke in a thoughtful tone. "It was a joy to me when he took me off the surgical team and put me fulltime in the recovery ward. I don't have to watch blood splattering on all sides."

"Some day the fiend will make a big mistake that becomes public and ends with his prosecution and punishment under the law. I can hardly wait till that happens to him. Why do we stay here and work for such a person, Megaera?"

"We started in innocence and ignorance, and now it is not possible to escape his power in the field of medicine and surgery. We have become the prisoners of Dr. Ongle and work under him. It is as if he has doomed us to remain here forever. We cannot find a way to flee, not yet."

Alcyone changed the subject to get away from the topic of the director.

"What are you going to do tonight, Megaera?"

"My brother left me a note saying that he wants to meet with me."

"Where will that be?"

"Down on the walkway alongside the canal. By the big monument and the fountains."

"At this hour the two of you will be alone and undisturbed."

Not at all, thought the chatan. I intend to be there with the two of you.

The monument was dedicated to an unremembered early ruler of Provincia, the Overman of that land. Yellow tinted water flowed over and over through surrounding fountains. The only light was that from the star-filled sky. A hollow silence prevailed.

The chatan, first to arrive, hid beneath the marble rim of a fountain. It was sure that no one would suspect its presence. But anything said would be audible to its ears.

Out of nowhere, a bass voice sounded. Xuthus had arrived and found his sister already there.

"Megaera, I had to talk to you. It is necessary that we straighten out the differences we have. I tell you the truth: I came here to destroy the man who made me what I am today. As long as Ongle is alive, I can never be free of the addiction that he drove me into. That is the reason I am in Diaema. My aim is to kill him."

"You traveled here through the air?"

"I flew in a globus. There was no alternative for me."

"None of us have done so for generations. It is too terribly dangerous and exhausting."

"No matter. I am here now and I must avenge what Ongle did to me."

"But was what resulted intentional or a mistake in his judgment? It might have been accidental, Xuthus."

"I have to believe that the doctor was aware of the risks of what he was doing to me. His motives have become clear to me. I have uncovered his true nature. He is not at all what he claims to be, a sylphine. Behind his outer disguise lurks the evil character of a gnomus. It was to prevent anyone else from learning this secret from me that he overdosed my mind and body with laudanum. That was the motive for his crime. The purpose was to take complete control over what I might say and reveal. His secret had to be concealed at any cost."

"Do not attempt anything you will later regret, Xuthus. Remember, the addiction you suffer will not end with the death of the doctor who caused it. The problem will still be there."

"I have to get back to my room," said her brother. "That pharmacist has my address and said he was coming to see me this evening. He may already be there. I must be present to receive him and whatever he brings with him."

"I must see you again, to keep you from turning into what you are not destined to become."

"No promises are possible, Megaera. I will talk to you soon. We shall all be free of that monster in one way or another in a short while. Trust me."

In a few seconds, both siblings were gone. Tugau changed himself from his feline form and hurried off for his meeting with the sylphine brother.

It was late, only an hour until midnight. Would Xuthus still be up, waiting for the promised laudanum? There was no way for Tugau to evade his commitment.

He knocked at the door of the rented flat and the brother of Megaera let him in. "You brought what I need?" asked Xuthus with his first words.

The botanic nodded yes and handed him a small paper package. "I have a day's supply inside for you."

Xuthus grabbed it from him and then rushed back into the kitchen to ingest in private. Tugau continued standing and waiting by the closed door. His mind was busy devising a scheme to hold back the addicted one from violent action against the director. Was that possible at this stage?

Tugau decided to attempt a diversionary tactic. When Xuthus returned, he was ready to maneuver.

"How do you feel now?" he asked the sylphine young man.

"Much better. I have to thank you for that."

"Perhaps now is the time to talk with you about a plan I have."

A plan?" inquired Xuthus with curiosity.

"To remove Ongle from his position at the Therapeutic Center. The idea occurred to me that he cannot continue in a high position if he loses his license to practice surgery and medicine. We must present a strong case against him to the Medical Board of Diadema. They have to be told of his crimes against patients like you. What if I prove that he is a danger to the sanity of those he deals with? In simple terms, he makes them crazy or demented. Take your sad case, for example.

"Even you must admit that your life has been anything but normal. He planted a strange idea in your mind, that you are a diploid with two different forms. That you have both a human and a non-human nature. He made you think that you are a sylphine who can fly high in the air."

"But...but..." stuttered Xuthus in confusion.

"I will take you as a witness before the Medical Board of the city. No doubt, I will find others who can testify how he harmed their mental balance. You are not going to be the only accuser."

"I am willing to help you, sir," offered the one from the Zenithals, surprising the other.

"Call me Tugau," said the pharmacist with an instant grin.

The two shook hands and the visitor left. He had accomplished more than he had expected or considered possible that night.

Director Ongle had a note delivered to Tugau. He was to report to his superior's office as soon as possible. Without delay, the new employee complied.

"Sit down, please," said the surgeon. When the summoned botanic was seated, Dr. Ongle asked an unexpected, unforeseeable question.

"What direction do you think medical treatment is going to take in the future?"

Completely astonished, Tugau had to grope for an answer. It would not do to antagonize, disgruntle, or insult this man who exercised so much authority over him, who could determine his future.

"It is hard to say specifically, sir. I feel there will be more preventive measures taken. People will be taught to eat healthier diets. Surgeries will be perfected and done earlier in an illness. Everything will be stepped up in time. There will be less waiting for things to happen.

"I also believe that means will exist to prevent imbalances in the equilibrium of elemental salts, sulphur, and mercury. As soon as any sign appears indicating the onset of sickness is near, balance will be strengthened and restored. There will be instruments for telling whether a patient needs more or less of a basic element. And they will be supplied in time to produce a cure.

"That is how I foresee the course of medicine progressing. What do you think we will see, sir?"

Dr. Ongle seemed disturbed by the reversal of roles. "I believe you have a good grasp of what is coming, Tugau. You surprise me with your width of vision. I agree with what you said about the future of elemental balancing. Your ideas are correct.

"In that specific area lies the reason I called you here this morning. I am planning to affiliate our Center with one of the leading mineral refining outfits in the Zenithal Mountains. They will produce certain compounds and we here will use them as medicaments. I intend to widen their use in Diaema and elsewhere through our example. This promises to be a major step in medical treatment. The initial actions will cover mercuric therapy and applications."

Tugau felt troubled and perplexed. "Use of mercury will become dominant over plants and herbs?"

"In a word, yes," answered the director. "You will have to put aside your training in botanics."

"But what will my function be in the new system that is to be?" asked the disconcerted pharmacist.

"Your knowledge of chemistry will still be of value. There can be continued use of plants, but it will sink in time as spagyric science is applied. I believe you are capable of adjustments, Tugau. Your immediate task is to take charge of procurement of supplies. I am sending you to make contact with mining and smelting concerns in the Zenithal Mountains. You are to test for the purity of what we purchase there. Do you happen to know the name for mercuric ore?"

"Of course. It is called cinnabar. The color of the ore is a brilliant vermillion."

"You are going to see a lot of it in days to come, my friend," predicted Ongle with a slight grin.

Tugau decided that action had to be taken against the director at once, before the day arrived for him to leave for the Zenithals on his odious mission. That evening he went to see Megaera about the plan to bring malpractice accusations against Ongle. It now had immediate urgency.

"You see why the charges must be presented at once?" he told the nurse whose patient he had been. "He is planning to flood the Center with mercuric chemicals. Our obligation to medicine is to oppose and stop his polluting of everyone's health with metals."

She thought a second. "My brother can be a major witness against him. But there will also be corroboration by Sterope. Merope, and Alcyone. I myself have direct knowledge of what he does. We had to work for him, there was no alternative for women from the Zenithals. The Medical Board will hear the truth from us."

Tugau made an instant decision. "I shall find the chairman of that Board tonight. His name and address were easy for me to find. It is unconventional, but necessary. It allows me to make an informal verbal presentation. I intend to go alone and speak in private."

The residence of Dr. Cupax, chairman of the Medical Board of Diaema, was at the end of a cul-de-sac with many trees on both sides of it. Through the deserted streets under a cloudy, starless sky strode Tugau, his steps slow and noiseless. He glanced at the numbers on each house, searching for one in particular. At last, the right one came up near the end. He climbed up a steep series of stone steps to a large wychwood door. With trepidation he gave the brass knocker several light raps.

A domestic maid in uniform opened the door and asked him what he wanted.

"I have important business with the doctor," said Tugau in a breathless voice. "Please tell him it is urgent that I talk with him. The matter is vital to the future health of all Provincia."

The servant blinked in confusion. "What is your name, sir?"

He gave it and the woman went away, leaving the door open.

Tugau looked into the brilliantly illuminated entrance way. How much money does this medico earn annually? he wondered. It must be an ample amount to allow him to afford this. Will he be willing to hear a complaint against another leader in his field?

All at once, a small man in a tuxedo appeared and spoke at once. "You wish to see me about something you believe a health danger?"

"I am a qualified botanic and I have credible evidence of malpractice by a physician. Everything that I charge can be proven with witnesses."

Ink black eyes stared at the night visitor with incredulity.

"Come in," said Dr. Cupax in a commanding voice. "Let's discuss this in my study."

The two made their way to a folio-lined room. The doctor went behind a tecona desk while Tugau took a planewood chair in front of it.

"Tell me your story, please," muttered Cupax severely.

It took surprisingly little time to describe the misdeeds of Ongle. When Tugau was finished, the medical official had questions he asked.

"According to what you say, these dangerous mercuries come from the Zenithal mountains and that is where the young man who became addicted to laudanum was treated there by Dr. Ongle. Isn't that so?"

"Yes. Now the patient has come to Diaema with those symptoms created through malpractice. He can be made available easily."

Dr, Cupax furrowed his brow as he considered his judgment of the matter. "I shall have to look into the question of jurisdiction. I doubt that we have the authority to consider actions that occurred far away, in the Zenithals. A case treated there has to be decided there, not here.

"As to mercury compounds, they are legally used in Diaema and often have positive effects on heart disease and hardening of the arteries. Scarlet fever and even syphilis can be alleviated with some of the mercuric compounds. I myself have prescribed calomel for digestive and alimentary problems. It is impossible to generalize about an entire system of medicinals."

"What are you telling me, Doctor?" loudly protested Tugau. "Do I understand what you are implying?"

All at once, Cupax broke out in an obviously assumed smile. "It will be a difficult charge for you to substantiate and for my board to assume jurisdiction over. Even with witnesses, such cases are extremely difficult to prove. I must confess that what you told me is baffling. There are many holes in the accusations you make.

"I will take the matter up with the four other board members a month from now. If there is agreement, we will call you at the Therapeutic Center and have you scheduled for some future time. These cases are very slow, I know. But we have to be thorough at every step of the procedure.

"Everything depends on the decision of my colleagues. The conclusion, as you see, is not in my hands. Do you understand what I am saying?"

Tugau scowled cynically and asked a final question. "When will I know what the Board intends to do with this complaint, sir?"

"In two or three months at the earliest," frowned Cupax.

The chagrined botanic shot to his feet. He recognized defeat when he faced it. This was for sure a blind alley for him and his comrades. He should have known better than to seek official assistance.

He said good night and stalked out of the study, then the residence of Dr. Cupax. The sense of defeat set all of him aflame with emotion.

It could not wait. He had to inform Megaera of his failure that very evening. Despite the late hour, Tugau went to her door and lightly knocked.

It took a little time before she appeared, wearing a velvet night cymar.

"I hope that I didn't awaken you from sleep," he apologized. "But this is so critical that you had to hear it at once. Can I come in and give you a report on what happened?"

Without a word, she opened the door wide and let him enter. Then she closed the door.

Both stood facing each other for a moment.

"I failed awfully. Nothing went right. Cupax is a petty, small-minded imbecile. He plans to delay any answer to my complaint, claiming long discussions with his colleagues lie ahead. The faker says that the Medical Board lacks jurisdiction over mercuric dangers that originate in the Zenithals. He completely frustrated me and all I said to him. I have never had such a disappointment with a medical authority as tonight."

"What can we do now?" desperately asked Megaera. "Is Ongle the victor and we the defeated?"

"We cannot surrender to him," gently murmured Tugau. "We must maintain our sense of justice."

"What can I do with Xuthus? He could go over the edge in his craving for vengeance. Or he might turn and harm himself. If only I could make him leave Diaema."

The last statement by her brought a sudden thought to life in his mind.

"An idea just struck me. Ongle intends to send me to the Zenithals to purchase mercurics and test them for purity. What if I arranged to travel there with your brother? He would be of enormous help to me in gathering evidence of criminality by the director and those in league with him.

"I might be able, with your aid, to convince Xuthus that it is vital that he accompany and assist me. Do you think he is persuadable, especially by you?

"My hope is based on what I have heard from all of you about Ongle's connections to the gnomi. What if I can prove that he is associated with those underground diploids? What if I can find proof of criminal fraud in the medical claims based on spagyric minerals and metals?"

"Indeed," she nodded. "You may have a way of saving Xuthus and prosecuting Ongle through such a trip as you are thinking of. You promise to keep your eye on my brother?"

"Of course. I will not leave him alone at any time. We will always stay together while there."

"I can get up before dawn and go to see him," she promised. "He will listen and heed my advice."

Tugau then did something he had not anticipated. He surprised Megaera by taking hold and embracing her tightly. She had no prior warning of this, but did not resist. It became instantly welcome to her.

As he broke away to leave, she started to miss his close presence and the feel of his body.

Megaera had a hard time finding sleep that night after what had just happened to her.

The sister convinced her brother to give his consent to the request from Tugau. The latter received detailed orders from Director Ongle: where to go in the Zenithal Mountains, whom to meet with, what terms to agree to and sign, how to evaluate metallic and mineral sources. Preparations for the journey were put in place.

Tugau went out to the Diaema Air Terminal to purchase tickets. He paid for the fare of Xuthus out of his own pocket, charging the Therapeutic Center for his own. The fastest time was with the express airship, a globoid that made only limited stops on its way to the Zenithals. When this was finished, he took a trolley to the apartment of Xuthus to talk over plans, preparations, and arrangements.

It was a surprise how enthused the young man had become over the prospects ahead to ensure the defeat of Dr. Ongle. The sylphine was returning to the region of his earlier tragedy, but with the hope of overcoming his past. The projected trip filled him with ebullient zeal and new energy.

"Yes," he told Tugau, "we two will perform wonderous things once we are there. My recollections and your leadership can be a potent combination. We two will entrap that demonic quack in his net of crime and lying. He shall suffer all the punishment he deserves. And I know how it can be done, my dear fellow."

The botanic smiled hopefully. "Tonight we take leave of your sister and her fellow nurses," he soothingly declared. "Early tomorrow comes our departure by globoid balloon for the distant mountains where we will determine our futures."

Alcyone brought a molasses pie she had baked, Merope an apple empanada, and Sterope a honey gateau. It was Megaera who provided citrusade punch and posset.

A guarded atmosphere prevailed, since no one was certain what lay ahead for the two making the journey to the Zenithal Mountains. Every person present ate and drank. Each of them wore a mask to conceal any fears or doubts about the outcome. No one laughed too much. This was not the time to carry on.

The first to leave were Merope, Sterope, and Alcyone.

When Xuthus took the trash that remained out to the building's refuse bin, Tugau was alone for the first time that evening with Megaera.

Only after embracing and exchanging kisses did one of them speak.

"I shall miss you terribly," whispered the nurse.

Tugau looked deeply into her sky blue eyes. "If we are fortunate, this will not take us long. If we arn't, it doesn't really matter, does it?"

No more was said, because no more talk was necessary.

Xuthus soon returned from outside. His sister said farewell with a hug and a kiss. She shook hands with Tugau and left for her own apartment.

The herbalist slept on a sofa in the flat of Xuthus that night. His luggage was there, ready for transport.

Their course set, the two males set forth in a horsecab before dawn the next morning.

They each attempted to encourage the other, lifting up their hopes for victory. Their battle would be reborn in the mountainous region where the sylphines had lost their long struggle against their enemies, the gnomi.

V
The Gnomi

The brightest achievement in the history of the sylphines was the development of the lighter-than-air globoid balloon, the primary means of general aviation in Provincia.

Seeing the rise of chimney smoke first gave mountainers the idea of using gas for aerostatic levitation. The earliest globoid was a sericus balloon with xyloid paper set aflame to move the vehicle upward. With time, experimenters took the risk of ascending in a large basket attached to the spherical bag.

The globoid came to enjoy practical applications for travel and transportation. It was able to draw together scattered sites over enormous distances, weaving into a network many routes over which journeys above the weather clouds became a possibility.

An enormous step forward came when hydrogen gas began to be used for lifting power. Higher altitudes and longer range resulted. Silk fabric was rubberized, giving it both strength and elasticity. Valves on the balloon surface allowed release of gas for lowering the airship. Gondola cars permitted the carrying of large groups of passengers.

An internal air cell, the ballonet, made possible the exact control of altitude. Wind velocity, temperature, and variations in air pressure became accurately measured on special instruments. A science of lighter-than-air navigation was established, with sylphines in the forefront as the pioneers. A group of these diploids invented an air injector that could control the composition of the balloon gas using a small steam engine.

Xuthus shared his personal memories of airship enthusiasm with his fellow passenger, Tugau, on their slow flight from Diaema to the Zenithal Mountains. He spoke nostalgically of how he had built model globoids and looked ahead to the day of his first air voyage.

"It was unparalleled in joyeous excitement," he told his new friend. "As with so many others like me, it was the grand event of my youth. I doubt that anything else will ever rival the thrill it gave me. That experience was incomparable."

Tugau was unable to suppress a warm laugh. "Don't be concerned about that. I believe that life holds a lot of other big adventures for you, Xuthus," he predicted with a wide grin.

The sylphine went on to describe avionic experiences with hang gliders and aerial albatrosses. "I have piloted rotatory planes with their rotor blades driven by compressed air piped out to their tips. The hot air engine has been a great boon to the sylphines who have gone beyond individual flight with shoulder wings attached to them. The hydrogen airships such as the one we are on now are flown mainly by pilots who are sylphines by birth.

"My own study of pneumodynamics and aeromechanics has allowed me to handle bat-wing skimmers, skitters, and skirrers. Every variety of glider is in my personal flying repartoire, along with many types of airships and rotatories."

Tugau looked out the side window at the mountain peaks in the distance with rising expectations. What were they going to hold for his companion and himself?

The long cordillera of the Zenithals has its highest elevations in the range called the Apicals. Here, in the valley of the Vallonia river, stands the commune of Aldea, neither town nor city but something in between the two. Too small for the latter, too large for the former. This was the community from which Dr. Ongle came. It was the final destination of the two travelers.

With snow peaks towering above, they left the globoid that had landed for a mountain barouche that resembled a sleigh, then a two-wheeled cart drawn by a single horse. Both of them were bone-tired upon arrival in Aldea. They took two rooms at the station inn and instantly fell asleep.

After a mountain breakfast of hot flapjacks and breadroot jelly, Xuthus led his partner on a brief tour of Aldea. The pair had taken a friendly liking to each other during their long journey by air. Where should they start their walk? The tall young skeletal sylphine decided they should first make a trek to the old refinery, two miles beyond the limits of inhabited Aldea.

"The factory is empty now, as it has been for most of my life. Work will begin again, though, when a new demand for mercuric medicines arises and grows."

They made their way along a one lane path that was only a little beyond a trail.

"People don't come out here much any more," said Xuthus. "There is no reason for doing it. Unless Ongle succeeds with his long-range scheme, that is." His face seemed to darken and turn stiff.

The roof of the facility was under a blanket of pure white snow. Rusted smoke stacks speared upward into a cloudless sky. A scene of emptiness and squalor lay about the factory that now produced nothing at all. Rubbish, trash, and garbage had been dumped about the old, unrepaired structure of brick, wood, and metal.

Tugau thought of a question to ask his guide.

"Did sylphines have jobs here when the mill was in operation?"

Xuthus turned his face away and upward as if contemplating the high peak of the mountain for which the range was named, Mt. Apical.

"The owners and the supervisors were all gnomi. No one except those diploids ruled and decided everything. Only a few worthless positions were left to us, perhaps because no gnomus was willing to take any of them." He thought a moment or so. "Perhaps that has always been the trouble with me. Nothing is left for me to do except what no one else wants, what everyone above me rejects and refuses to do. Could that be the secret factor behind my cycloidal illness: that individuals like me are left with the social slots that nobody that is anyone would willingly assume.

"The gnomi, for the most part, have become reluctant to take on their normal human form of average height and size.

"Their preference is for making their gnomic phase as permanent as it can be. They tend not to use their alternate form as human beings, because they are happier as small dwarves.

"At least that is what my own experience with them has taught me."

Tugau turned to him and grinned from the heart. Why are those with troubled minds and spirits so perceptive? he asked himself.

"Let's reeturn to Aldea," he suggested to his friend, the wounded sylphine.

Roast upland leporine with mountain colewort in matzoon yogurt was recommended to Tugau by Xuthus at the station inn for their noon meal. The herbalist enjoyed his first taste of Zenithal rabbit, which he had never eaten before. He spoke about their mission when both of them were finished.

"I must find the person whose name was given me by Ongle as the best contact agent for obtaining supplies of mercury compounds. He is a private mining engineer, so he should not be too difficult to locate."

After they left the restaurant area, Tugau asked at the front desk of the inn for a directory of Aldea.

"Directory? What directory? We have no such thing. It is unknown to those who live here. Would you be hunting for someone in particular?"

"Yes. The man's name is Digui. His business is mine engineering."

"Are you certain he is located here in Aldea? I have never heard of anyone with that name. But it is possible that I am ignorant of such an individual. So, let me advise you to stop in and visit our weekly news gazette. The editor may be able to tell you if the person exists here."

Tugau thanked the clerk, then returned to the tavern table where Xuthus sat drinking a cup of candleberry tea. He told his partner that he was going to find the office of the news journal and ask if they had any information on the engineer.

The two agreed to meet later here in the eatery of the station inn.

Asking several passersby, Tugau finally found the office of Aldea Publishing. He asked the front receptionist whether he could see the editor.

"He's busy working in his office, the first one on the right," she said with a friendly smile.

Finding the door to the room open, Tugau looked inside. A short, pudgy bald man in shirtsleeves was typing at a huge keyboard connected to an electrographic transmitter-receiver. He stopped when he caught sight of the stranger in the doorway. "Can I help you?" he inquired.

The visitor stepped into the private office and workroom, introducing himself.

"I am having a hard time locating a man who is an engineer in the mining field," said Tugau.

"What is the name you seek?"

"Engineer Digui."

Tugau perceived a minute change in the editor's facial expression. There had been a slight but visible nervous reaction at mention of the name, no doubt about that.

"Yes, I believe there was once such a man in Aldea. That was when I first came here, years ago. Let me think. Oh, yes, now I recall. It happened years ago, when the refinery was still operating and the mines of this region were booming. That was the era of major economic expansion up on Apical Mountain. As a result, the person called Digui was involved in the greatest scandal of that time, an affair that rocked all the Zenithals."

"A scandal?" reacted the outsider in surprise.

"The mining scandal. Have you never heard of it? There were half a dozen separate mines at work on Apical at that time. Then began the tragedies. Not one, not two, but six of them. Collapse of supports in tunnels, disasters in the vertical shafts, on and on. One of my first assignments was a lengthy feature story on the safety hazards involved up at the mines. I believe that our commune of Aldea has still not completely recovered from these six catastrophes.

The mines that remained were shut down in the name of saving the lives of the miners who were endangered."

"But where does this engineer come in?" demanded Tugau.

The editor grinned like a tomcat. "I was getting to that. The Chief Engineer over all of Apical Mountain was Digui. The cataclysmic crisis brought him down along with all the executives and managers of the firms in the mining business. Owners went bankrupt, workers were thrown out of the mines and smelters. The final plunge down was the closing of the local refinery here near Aldea. What Digui did then was to go and live a life of isolation high up under the summit of Mt. Apical. As far as I know, the man still abides there as a hermit, in isolation from organized, normal society. No one has spoken with him in years. He is much older and no one knows how his health happens to be."

"You are saying that Digui is a solitary recluse?"

Tugau had found the editor's characterization unbelievable at first from what he had learned when Ongle discussed the engineer who was to act as his contact on the subject of mercuric ores.

"You can only meet this odd creature if you climb up the steep mountain slopes," said the newsman.

"Thank you," replied the disappointed searcher. He turned about and made his way back to the station inn where the sylphine awaited him.

As Xuthus listened to what the editor had related to Tugau, the mountainer chortled with laughter. "Either the journalist is ignorant or else he is pulling your leg."

"What do you mean?" said the herbalist.

"I grew up in Aldea and can say that what you heard was an untrue tale. The engineer called Digui was never an anchorite without contacts or relationships. Perhaps he dealt little with people from the commune, but the inhabitants of the mountain hamlets were familiar with him. Mercury mines are small operations, and Digui supervised both their construction and maintenance for these upland communities. That is how he came to be so closely tied to the gnomi and their underground excavations. I believe that the engineer is not too far up the mountain. Certainly not anywhere near the peak."

"Could we locate him, Xuthus, if we went up there?"

His companion looked Tugau in the eye.

"Certainly, if you are willing to try the trails on Apical."

"I am," professed the botanic. "Yes, I am."

"Then, early tomorrow we can begin a climb up to Hameau. That is a hamlet near one of the mines that collapsed years ago, before my time. It is one of the easiest sites to reach on foot. I often climbed up to Hameau when I was a boy. We can get our bearing up there, ask questions about the engineer, and learn what we can."

Tugau readily agreed to the plan. The two of them started to get ready for the ascent of the mountain. At a nearby clothing store, they purchased anoraqs to wear on Mt. Apical, Tugau paying for them. At a footware store, they obtained strong, high cothurnes and snowshoes that fit them comfortably.

The pair returned to the station inn with what they had bought, tired from their shopping efforts

A late supper of chevrotain deer meat with rutabagas filled both of them to satiety and beyond.

"A good night's sleep will prepare us for the steep climb," were the last words that Tugau heard from Xuthus before turning in that evening.

There was a fantastic quality to daybreak in the Zenithals, discovered the pharmacist. The roseate aurora was present long before the daystar, hidden behind towering peaks, grew visible. Xanthic gold, fulvous yellow-red, and blood crimson merged and produced peach, apricot, and deep saffron hues. The colors of the morning light were a mesmerizing spectacle.

Tugau felt intoxicated by the glory of the mountain dawn, never having observed anything like it before.

The pair, bundled and shoed, left Aldea hardly seen by anyone. Only street cleaners with shovels, not noticing the two strangers, passed them by. If one were seeking aloneness and privacy, this area at dawn was the place to be, realized Tugau.

The street became a narrow road, then a path. Collections of houses disappeared.

Xuthus halted when they came to a trail heading straight upward and to the left. He pointed with his hand and they turned in that direction. On and on they trudged. At first they were both conscious of the time passing, but then they lost all sense of duration. A dreamy fog seemed to fall over the minds of the travelers. Their sense of self and purpose faltered.

The light above them lost much of its color. A cloudless day bore down on the two climbers. All about the trail lay the albescent snow, growing whiter and brighter by the second. No time to rest, and no time to stop and talk. The hamlet where Digui might be lay ahead. Both trekkers felt the urgency of their aim. There was not a moment to lose by stopping to admire the panorama of the deep snow on the mountain.

It was only when Xuthus, in the lead, reached the top of a high ridge that he halted to turn around. Breathless with exertion, he uttered only two simple words.

"Down below."

They started a speedy descent toward their destination, the hamlet of Hameau.

Tugau had his first view of the place in seconds. A single lane with a few houses huddled together on each side, that was all there was. Wood from a nearby pinetum burned in the separate furnaces of the buildings, sending smoke plumes skyward. Nothing here seemed of any interest or importance. There was no one about outdoors. Should they knock somewhere and ask about the engineer? Xuthus was on the verge of doing that when what appeared to be a young boy came into view from behind a small, low cottage. No, it was not a child at all, but a diminutive man who approached them through a winter garden of evergreens. Both travelers watched as he waved a hand at them.

"Hello, hello. Can I be of aid to you, sirs? Are you looking for someone, or only passing through our hamlet?"

Xuthus made a direct, succint reply. "We seek Engineer Digui."

"Turn around. You have already passed his place. The first house on the opposite side of the lane. That is where he makes his home these many years. I cannot tell you whether he can be found there at this hour. You must make inquiry on your own, sirs."

The midget turned around and walked away.

As the two went to the indicated building and approached the front door, it opened on its own. Their coming had been seen and noted. The journey was about to end, it appeared.

A lanky, bony figure of unusual height stood in the doorway. Niveous hair resembling snow, ash-white skin, and milky blue eyes made him a model of the sylphine mountainer. There could be no question what he was.

But how was it that he had associated himself with gnomic miners if he were not one of them?

Tugau decided to speak first. "We are representatives of the director of the Therapeutic Center in the city of Diaema. There are certain matters we wish to discuss with Mining Engineer Digui. That is why we are here in Hameau, to see him."

"Come in," said the towering one. "I have been expecting both of you."

The three men sat about a round table in the cookery chamber of the small house. An aged dwarf of a housekeeper brought them big mugs of spruce beer to drink.

"She makes it herself," explained the engineer."Her cottage is at the other end of this lane. All the widows of our hamlet seem to reside in that section."

The three of them drank in silence for a short time.

"How is the dear Dr. Ongle?" asked Digui at last.

"Quite well, the last that I saw of him," replied Tugau as the agent of the director.

The engineer stared at Xuthus for a few seconds.

"Have we ever met before? It seems to me as if we have."

"No," answered the sylphine visitor. "I would have remembered if we had."

The owner of the house then turned his head toward the more talkative Tugau.

"How are you connected to Ongle and his hospital?"

The herbalist grinned in a friendly manner. "I am the one in charge of our repository of medicines. I recently made a full inventory of our supplies at the behest of the director. All pharmaceutical supplies, both mineral and botanical, fall within my division. That is why this important mission was assigned to me."

"And your assistant here?" Digui turned and stared again at Xuthus.

"He works for me in my dispensory," lied Tugau. "Since he is from the Zenthal Mountains, he was sent along with me to assist on the mission. I trust him entirely."

"I see," sighed the engineer, again facing the pharmacist. "Are you well versed in all areas of spagyrics?"

"Yes. Dr. Ongle also thinks so. Otherwise, I would not have been dispatched to see you, sir."

"You two are welcome to stay in my home with me. My housekeeper will see to your needs. There will be plenty of time for us to converse on everything that matters to our work together."

Thus did the engineer put an end to their first exchange.

While Xuthus returned to Aldea to fetch the luggage of the pair, Tugau used the opportunity to show Digui the list of mercurics that the director of the Therapeutic Center wished to include in the first big purchase. He read and described its content to the engineer, both of them sitting in the room used as an office.

"Colomel will have wide use and application as a purgative. 'Gray powder' in a weak solution can be used for childhood illnesses. 'Blue pills' will be compounded for the diseases of adults. 'Blue ointment' is to be applied to illnesses of the skin. And the most powerful antiseptic known shall be produced in the form of what is known as 'yellow wash' and 'white ointment.' These all can be mixed in Diaema, at the Center itself, once sufficient supplies of hydrargyrum and quicksilver are shipped there from the Zenithals. That is our immediate problem: can enough cinnabar be excavated and then refined for our immediate needs in the capital?" said Tugau, gazing with fixed eyes at the mining expert.

Digui surprised his guest by cracking a wry grimace. "My foremen and their workers have only been going through the motions of mining on this mountain we are on. Believe me, if the demand for mercury products were higher, we would be in better condition up here in the hamlets of Apricol. But, as is visible to everyone, the mining industry has suffered decades of stagnation and decline. I foresee enormous opportunity for us when the use of mercurics in medical treatment becomes as widespread in the lowlands of Provincia as up here in the Zenithals. Yes, I think the Dr. Ongle's commerce with us can be the beginning of a rebirth of mining in the region. At least that is the hope that your arrival here inspires, my good man."

"Will it be difficult to satisfy our requirements?" asked Tugau.

"It will depend on the underground crews. I may have to hire more hands in order to send you shipments in a timely way. That is why the foreman who superintends the diggers must be consulted at once. Tomorrow we can meet with him. His name is Quimera."

"I look forward to meeting him," muttered the pharmacist, thinking ahead.

"You shall find him most interesting," smiled the engineer. "He is a veteran of the mines who can tell you much about underground conditions and future prospects down there."

Tugau and Xuthus slept long and soundly that night, arising with eager anticipation the following morning. The daystar flooded the mountain with sharp, warming rays. A simple breakfast of hordeal porridge made by the housekeeper was eaten quickly.

"Quimera sent word he will be here early," said the mining engineer to his two visitors. "I expect to see him any minute now."

At that precise moment, a loud knock announced that the foreman had arrived.

Digui rose and went out of the kitchen to let him in. Soon he returned, followed by an homuncular dwarf of a man in a dark, colorless coat of pelage. Introductions were made and the owner of the house took a seat at the table. The little mine superintendent continued standing. Perhaps it was uncomfortable for him to sit because of his size that made him unsuited to average chairs.

Tugau and his partner studied the strange figure. His face was a cartogram of lines and wrinkles. There was an unnatural glow in his bronzelike eyes. The two travelers glanced at each other for a moment. They both recognized a gnomus when they saw one. Each of them knew what the other was seeing in the foreman.

"What do you think, Quimera?" said Digui. "Can we increase production of cinnabar to the level of the years before the Great Catastrophe hit?"

The tiny one raised a hand and scratched the stubble on his chin.

"My boys can only try," he grumbled in a gravelly voice. "And I can only drive them as hard as I judge wise and sensible."

Deadly silence fell over the kitchen cookery.

So that is how a gnomus talks, mused Tugau to himself.

It was Digui who broke the uneasy quiet.

"Quimera's ancestors for untold eons worked underground," he told his two guests. "His people have come to feel that they own Aprical Mountain. They know its inner penetralia with perfection. I am constantly surprised at the extent of their intuitive knowledge of the mines and how to exploit them. The art of mining is unlike any other one. The world beneath us is all to itself."

The foreman made an undecipherable grimace. "We have always tried to do our best, sir," he said, somewhat slurring his words.

At the same time, Digui made an important decision. "Why don't you take our visitors down into Cavus Primus?" He turned to Tugau and explained. "It is the oldest cavern mined in this mountain and nearly exhausted long ago. Only a little usable ore remains in that hole."

Both newcomers agreed to the proposal and soon left with Quimera for the location. Digui told them that he had paper work to finish and preferred to stay in the house. He left them in care of the stranger they both considered a gnomus.

What were the sylphine and the chatan to learn from one of the Zenithal gnomi?

The trio traversed the snow blanket in silence, the superintendent in the lead.

Tugau was last, viewing the other two from behind.

I know the diploid identity of both my companions, he thought to himself.

My chatan nature is unknown to Xuthus, for I have never told him of it. What about the dwarf, though? Can he figure out the double nature of either one of us?

There is no way for us to know for sure how much Quimera is able to perceive or understand.

Xuthus is assuming that our dualities are invisible to the little gnomus guiding us. Our safety and success may depend on maintaining that screen of ignorance, reasoned Tugau.

The dwarf led them through the aditus of the mine, into a black cavern. He held a large oil lantern in his right hand. The three proceeded up an inclined winze to a newer level of the mine. Quimera pointed to a series of empty stopes from which the ore had long ago been removed. They climbed up onto a wooden stull from which the tiny miners had once labored with small picks. Words began to flow from the lips of the gnomus.

"This was the earliest vein containing hydrargyrum mined by our forefathers in Hameau. It was a rich one and made the stirpes and families around here quite rich and prosperous. Never again have we enjoyed such well-being. Today, as you shall see, our lives are miserable and impoverished. But Engineer Digui is suddenly showing a newly joyeous attitude. I sensed it as soon as I entered his house this morning. Now he talks about the rebirth of mercury mining in the days to come. That is wonderful to hear. I shall tell all my workers what I now know. Tell me the truth: is there reason for them to be optimistic about what is going to happen?"

"Certainly," confirmed Tugau. "There is going to be growing demand for the compounds produced from cinnabar. It is the field of medical healing that will give us an explosion of demand for all of the mercurics."

"After all these years can such a miracle come true?"

"I am present in Hameau to see that it happens," said the pharmacist, completely conscious of the fact that his tongue was telling a bald lie. In the inner chambers of his mind, he knew that nothing in nature was more dangerous to people than a compound based on this substance.

A question came to the foreman from Xuthus on the other side of the gnomus.

"Where will you get the huge amounts of cinnabar that will be needed? You told us that this cavern is completely exhausted."

The dwarf turned to him with a cunning expression on his face.

"This is not our only mine. No, there are many more of them."

Tugau now intervened. "They will be adequate for a great flood of orders and sales?"

Quimera turned and addressed the pharmacist directly. "The refining and combining will be faster and more efficent than before," he said with a sly smile on his wrinkled face.

The herbalist, rubbing his chin, asked no more questions. There was at the moment no way of finding out what the gnomus was hinting at.

Dr. Ongle had learned the art of eavesdropping in the Zenithals, but had avoided practicing it in the city of Diaema. But now the odd behavior of Megaera and her circle of nurses began to alarm him. Why had they become so cooperative and unusually obedient to him? Were the four trying to conceal something they were up to? I can see through their game, the director told himself. It would be useful to snoop on them in the manner he knew of old from the mountains.

On an early evening, the females had quit day work and left the Therapeutic Center. Returning to their flats from the nearby eatery, they stayed outside the entrance of the apartment building to converse among themselves in private. The four of them formed a small circle on the dark veranda. Alcyone suddenly asked a question of Megaera.

"Any word by mail from your brother or his friend? Have they arrived safely?"

"No letter, and I do not expect anything until there is some important business to announce to us. That could take considerable time, I think."

The voice of Merope then became audible.

"Xuthus and the other may be in great danger for all we know. The mines of the Zenithals are full of monstrous creatures, the gnomi who destroy others like us. I have heard horrible stories about what they do to anyone who opposes them. We can do nothing to help your brother and the other, for we are far away."

Megaera tried to console her. "I have trust in Tugau. He will look out for my brother and protect him. In a short time, we should receive some word. When their work there is finished, the two of them will return here. They will have triumphed over the director's insane scheme."

Sterope now presented a question.

"What about the sickness of Xuthus? Will he have enough of the laudanum he needs in order to keep his equilibrium? I fear for his condition should he run out of the substance he has become enslaved to. He is risking a lot by making that journey."

"Tugau took a goodly supply of it from the repository," replied Megaera. "It should last until the pair return to Diaema. I hope, of course, that is soon."

The others said nothing, for they harbored the identical wish.

As if on a signal, the four women shuffled into the building. The empty veranda presented itself to the lurking gnomus. Transmogrifying into its daylight form, the doctor ambled slowly back to his cottage with much on his mind.

What should I do? If I take a sudden vacation, that will liberate me to travel back to the Zenithal Mountains and attempt to rescue the imperiled situation there.

Yes, I must go there, to where these troublemakers are threatening my plans.

Tugau had a difficult time falling asleep that night.

His thoughts concentrated on the horrid situation in medicine should the program of Dr. Ongle succeed. Dangerous mercuric treatments would grow common, even generally prevalent. There would be a sharp decline in the use of botanics, the safest branch of therapeutics. And who would dominate the new direction in health care? The gnomic excavators and refiners in the Zenithals. He could predict that Engineer Digui would be at the head of an army of dwarf miners. Life would be turned upside down everywhere in Provincia. The gnomi would become the elite among all the varieties of diploids.

He thought of the plight of the sylphines he knew. What place would there be for Megaera and the other nurses in the new system under Ongle? There would be gnomic control based on inorganics. Where would a chatan like him be in that changed landscape of medicine?

His mind focused on the question of the relationship between the several strands and species of biformed diploids in such circumstances. His thoughts settled upon the person in the middle, the mining engineer. A sylphine who served the interests of the gnomi. A confederate of Dr. Ongle.

What might move him out of his present orbit? Was it possible to disaffect and estrange him from his alliance with the gnomi? Can his character and behavior be changed?

Tugau pondered how he might alienate his host from his function of supplier of mercurics for the enemy. Did such a strategy exist for him?

Translocation was a capability that the doctor, like most gnomi, rarely made use of. The effort sapped off all metal energy. It was a risky, exhausting exercise for even the strongest dwarf. The possibility remained potential rather than actively applied for most of the time in the majority of that type of diploid.

Dr. Ongle now faced the need for rapid transilience to the Zenithal Mountains. He had to investigate and deal with the pharmacist who was betraying him. What were his relations with the sylphine he had treated, the one named Xuthus? That had to be illuminated and resolved on the spot. There was no other way to accomplish anything in his own interest.

Ongle had not moved through hard ground in years. How adept was he in that kinetic operations after so much time? All that night the director did little sleeping. He lay awake in bed, recalling the principles of body translation he had learned in his youth. He had the disadvantage that his torso was larger and heavier than that of the average gnomic dwarf, therefore more difficult to transport. His nerves grew very tense as he prepared for the act. It would not be an easy feat to accomplish. His all would be required.

     CLEMENT S. MASLOFF

He decided that the most favorable time for movement was at dawn, when atmospheric and geological conditions were at there best. The air and the ground would be in magnetic balance, making his effort more effective. Yes, dawn was optimal for what he planned to carry out.

Conditions of mountain weather necessitated putting on as much winter clothing as possible. Bundled up, Ongle sat on his bed, waiting for the most auspicious moment for the leap through material space.

At last, the eastern sky started to brighten. Day was rapidly nearing.

The medico rose, then lowered himself downward until he lay prone on the floor.

Ongle concentrated the full force of his mind on the target, the desired destination. Since he had no idea where Tugau and Xuthus were at that moment, he had to translate himself to a central point from which it was possible to search them out.

Aldea. The pair he sought had to have passed through that municipality before heading into the higher elevation. So, his line of movement had to be ended in Aldea. From there he would hunt for them, following their trail wherever it led.

With no time to lose, he set his mind on the central square of that commune. In his imagination, he saw the snow-covered cobblestones of the streets. The hard stone surfaces of the buildings gleamed with rays of beginning daylight. The air was bitter cold, but the surroundings seemed familiar in his memory. It was a location that he knew well.

Before he realized it, the gnomic traveler had shifted from the bedroom of his cottage in Diaema to the central plaza in Aldea. The frigid temperature caused him to shiver. Lying on the cobble pavement, his bones ached with the coldness from below. It was a familiar pain that he felt in every cell of his body.

There was no one about to notice him as he lifted himself quickly to his feet. Looking around, he was able to conclude that no one had witnessed what had just happened.

The motion through the ground had been a success. Now to business and finding the pair he was after.

Sitting opposite Digui at the breakfast table, Tugau studied his milky eyes for a hint of his essential sylphine nature. What could possibly move him to change the way he served Dr. Ongle and the interests of the gnomi?

Finishing his stack of gaufre waffles, the engineer began to muse aloud.

"I am very familiar with the history of medicine in these mountains and can advise you on many remedies not on the list provided you by Director Ongle.

"For instance, there is an ancient antiseptic that combines mercury and cyanide. It is called mercuric gauze or cyanide gauze, because it is applied using a light cloth. And there is a bichloride of mercury that produces a strong disinfectant. These are products that might come to have applications in lowland medical practice, the way they do here in the mountains. There exist many substances that can be mercurialized. For instance, many compounds of thion. That is the name that sulphur is called by the miners who extract it from Apical Mountain. Several of the thionics are already being combined with quicksilver."

Tugau decided to try to make use of what the engineer had just said.

"You are a knowledgeable individual who can help our Therapeutic Center a great deal. It would certainly beneficial if you could speak directly, person-to-person, with our director, Dr. Ongle. What if that were arranged by us? A personal communication with the head of the institution about to embark into the field of mercuric primacy in medicine? That could be of enormous personal advantage to you."

The tall mining expert thought a moment. "What are you proposing I do?"

Tugau had to come up with a reasonable answer fast.

CLEMENT S. MASLOFF

"There is electrographic connection between Aldea and Diaema. It is an expensive means of sending messages, so that the general public is not too familiar with its use. But I saw such an apparatus in Aldea when I was searching for your present location. If we were to cover all the costs, I am certain it might be made available to us for private use. Such communication would be almost instantaneous."

"Where was it that you noticed it?" eagerly inquired Digui, suddenly excited.

"In the editorial office of Aldea Publishing. They use electrograph to send and receive news items and reports. I am sure that the commune police have a similar device connecting them to Diaema and other cities. But the one I saw at the news weekly appears the most convenient and available. What do you say to my idea?"

"Yes, it has possibilities," added Xuthus, perceiving the direction his comrade was taking. How better to set the engineer at odds with the director than this?

"If you wish," said Tugui, addressing Digui directly, "I can go down to Aldea and make arrangements with the publisher who edits the journal. I am certain that the man will be amenable. The project could be a profitable one for him. Why should he refuse to cooperate with someone like you, from the area?"

"Good," beamed the engineer. "When do you aim to make a descent?"

"Today may be best," answered the pharmacist, glancing at Xuthus as if to send a signal that he must stay in Hameau to keep an eye on Digui and the gnomic miners. Only one of them was to climb down to Aldea.

Thus it happened that Tugau descended to Aldea as Ongle searched about for him there.

The director found out that Tugau was no longer staying at the station inn. Had he already located the middleman, Engineer Digui? That seemed to be a reasonable conclusion. But where was Digui living? Ongle ended up going to Aldea Publishing. He discovered that he was not the first hunter to appear there looking for the mining specialist.

"There were two men only yesterday seeking the address of the engineer," declared the editor at a dactylograph machine. "I told them what I now say to you: Mr. Digui lives up on Apical Mountain, in the hamlet called Hameau. That is where you can find him, if you happen to be a good climber."

"I grew up here in the Zenithals," muttered the surgeon out of the corner of his mouth.

As he left the office and went out to the cobbled street, he reached an instant decision that he was not going to take the time and trouble to ascend on foot.

No, this was too important to suffer delay by the scaling of Apical.

It was far better to ride up the way that he had traveled from Diaema. A short jump through the ground to Hameau would do it. He would appear there speedily to confront his former patient and the traitorous botanic. Never trust a herbalist, he said to himself. Never trust any patient either, he added. They will both betray you if given motive and opportunity.

In a minute the angry doctor was far enough into the snow fields to fall down onto the ground and concentrate his mental energy on propelling himself through the rocky mountain soil. The translation would not be as far as the earlier one. It should be easier to accomplish because of the short distance involved.

No one was anywhere about to see how this strange person disappeared, or to wonder where he had gone to.

Tugui entered the office of Aldea Publishing out of breath from his laborious descent. The editor looked up from his electrograph board with a look of dismay.

"You again? Whom are you tracing down now?"

"It is something entirely different. I have a request to make. First of all, I believe that you have a magneto-electric link to Diaema. Am I correct on that?"

"Of course. What do you think this keyboard is connected to? I have links to all the major news services and periodicals in Diaema and all the other big cities. That is the only way the news and public information can be exchanged rapidly between different places."

The pharmacist smiled with success. "Good. I was sure you had that connection. Now, here is my request. Can I utilize your line for an exchange with my employer in Diaema? I am willing to pay for that privilege. It will not be exploited for a day or so. Someone else will come and take my place at this end. The use will be permanent. Can your line be made available to me and others?"

The editor gave him a scorching look.

"What are you and that other character up to? Are the two of you trying to play some trick on me?"

"Who is this other person you are referring to, sir?" asked a confused Tugau.

The journalist exploded. "The one who came here a short while ago searching for the address of the same engineer that you were tracing. A little man with brown, chestnut eyes."

Gears seemed to click in the mind of the other.

"Did this person have a hooked nose?"

"Exactly. I thought he might be an associate of yours. He was after the same individual."

"Did you tell him that the mining engineer is now in Hameau?"

"I did. Why not?"

"Did you mention that I had also asked about him?"

"No. Why should I have done so? He didn't ask me anything like that."

"When was the fellow here in your office?"

The editor glanced at a walltimer. "Around half an hour or so ago."

"Did you see in what direction he went after leaving?"

"No." There was a moment of pause. "When do you wish to use the electrograph?"

"I have to change my plans and cancel that request I made. Thank you for your time. I hope that I have not caused you any trouble."

With that, Tugau rushed out of Aldea Publishing. He had to return to the mountain hamlet as fast as he could climb. There was no way he could foresee what problems the presence of Ogle might cause up at that height.

The auditory powers of Xuthus were superior after his ingestion of a large dose of laudanum.

He discovered that if he lay down with his ear directly on the quercine floor, he could make out all the words spoken in the living room of the hamlet house.

Digui's voice dominated, whereas Quimera did little beyond obediently listening to what the engineer said to him.

"It will come to pass, a complete change in the balance of forces between gnomi and sylphines. The weapon will be the revolution in medicine stemming from the victory of mercurialism. How many people are aware of the genetic weakness of all sylphines to swallowing any substance with a lot of mercury in it? Over just a few generations, the sylphines will suffer so much mortality that they will decline in numbers and importance everywhere. It is a secret known to only a few, and must forever remain so. But it is our invisible weapon against the air spirits. These medicaments can provide the gnomi what they have hungered for all these eons: the end of these enemies who sail the air."

"Yet are you a true gnomus, sir? Why are you so involved in our cause when you resemble greatly the form of our ancient foes, the sylphines? I fail to understand you."

"My maternal grandmother was of true gnomic ancestry. I have never felt welcome among sylphines, nor did I ever identify with them. In a way, my body looks very much as if it were sylphine. as you can see for yourself. But my mind and personality have always taken a gnomic cast. That is how I think and feel. It has shaped my whole life.

"I resent my physical form. I hate the diploid creatures I seem to resemble. My mission in life is to advance the position of my hidden self, the gnomic me. It must always be superior over the part of me I see as my enemy. My dream is the overturning of all sylphine qualities in myself as well as others. No one is a greater enemy of air people than I myself am. My hatred of them is inborn. It is what drives me to take a lot of my actions."

At that moment, a loud knocking at the front door interrupted the two men downstairs. Neither of them said anything.

Xuthus pressed his ear, but was unable to pick up what was being said at the door.

Then he heard a new voice, recognizing it at once as belonging to Dr. Ongle.

The sylphine shook with emotion. How could this be? How did the director unexpectedly appear at this inopportune moment? Xuthus felt great fear of what might potentially happen next.

A new situation demanded immediate change of plans, he realized.

It was now impossible for him to stay in the house. Yet he was trapped in an upstairs bedroom.

The sound of footsteps on the stairs meant they were coming up from the living room to deal with him. What was left for him to attempt to do?

Xuthus ran with speed and force toward the window at the front of the house. He knew that the fall would be perilous and shattering. He foresaw the probability of smashing and fracturing. It was going to be very painful in its results.

With no alternative, the sylphine jumped through the glass, suddenly exiting from the house into the air. But what he had expected did not happen.

Instead of the cataclysmic disaster he found himself floating down to the snow like an air-filled balloon.

Of course, the air is the natural medium for every sylphine. He was doing what he had not even tried since his childhood. His flying capability had not vanished, but continued to exist in him.

But now, out of necessity, he had rediscovered what he had been born with.

No catastrophic collision into the ground occurred, but a smooth, measured descent with moderation.

Xuthus landed squarely on his two feet on the one lane of Hameau. He started to run away from the house on foot. Escape was now an actual possibility. He reached for it with all his energy.

What was the trio of Digui, Ongle, and Quimera to do?

Their foe had gotten away. There was no way for them to chase him. He was too fast a runner in the snow.

The engineer related to Ongle the attempt that Tugau was making to contact him in Diaema by electrographic means. "He will be climbing back up to Hameau in the next several hours," said the tall sylphine-looking conspirator. "We have a chance of capturing him when he returns here."

"But what about the mad dog that jumped from the window?" asked Ongle.

Digui turned to the dwarf foreman and spoke. "I want you to mobilize all your mine crews to catch the escaped one. They must reach him before he reaches Aldea. It would then be too late."

Quimera hastily left the house, heading for the buildings where the other gnomi miners lived.

The doctor just arrived from afar seemed to take command of the engineer and the situation.

"We are at the decisive moment of battle," he coolly declared. "Either we destroy these two adversaries, or else they ruin our plans and bury us. Both of them must be taken and killed."

"Killed?" excitedly asked the mining engineer.

"What other solution is available to us?"

The question required no reply. Their course was unchangeably set now.

Xuthus was the first one to make a sighting. As soon as he saw the shape moving up the mountain trail he called out to it. "Up here! I'm up here!"

Then he charged down the snowy path at the safest clip possible for him.

Tugau was surprised as the other embraced him. "What is it?" he demanded to know.

"Ongle is in Hameau. Why he now came here I do not know, but he is present. I had to leap from a second storey window to get out of the house in one piece. They suspect both of us. I overheard what Dr. Ongle was saying. We will both be their targets now. The game we were playing is ended. Which way is best for us to take, that is what we have to decide."

The pharmacist had to think only a single moment for an answer.

"Back to Aldea. That is our only hope. People will be around, surrounding us. They can provide us a measure of protection without knowing it. But we will have to make quick time in order to evade any posse following after us."

"Posse?"

"Think of the numerous gnomi who could be sent out to capture us. Once we reach Aldea, it will be our task to avoid being nabbed and taken back to the mountain, or worse."

They began walking down the trail, Tugau in the lead. Moving at a vigorous pace, the pair descended swiftly. The outskirts of the commune came into sight before long.

"Let's stop for a short rest," said the herbalist, turnng his head back. "We've earned it."

As they stood there without moving, Xuthus looked up at the slopes of Apical. There was the sight of small figures visible high up, near Hameau.

The sylphine pointed with his right arm. "The gnomi are chasing after us. What do we do? Perhaps there is a coach leaving soon for the south. Let us hope we can take it."

"They could still follow and stop the vehicle, capturing us in open country beyond Aldea. No, we have to find some refuge within the limits of the municipality."

"But who will grant it to us?"

Tugau thought for a second. "We could try to get constabulary protection. There is no alternative for us that I can see. We have to find some friendly sylphine magistrate who agrees to take us under his wing. But there is in all probability more than one official judge for the courts. We have to identify and locate the one individual most favorable to our plight. I can think of one person who might aid us in finding such a magistrate."

Xuthus looked puzzled. "Who is that?"

"The journal editor," answered the other.

Although the editor was about to close up the publishing office, Tugau insisted that he had a newsworthy story to relate to him. The little man relented, taking the two into his office in order to hear what this was all about. When the three of them were seated, the botanic started his tale from the beginning down in Diaema.

The fantastic project of Ongle to produce a flood of mercurics, the plight of Xuthus as a poisoned and addicted patient, the dispatch of the pharmacist to the Zenithals to arrange the production of a supply of medical substances, the travel of the pair to Aldea, their visit to the engineer in Hameau, and the sudden arrival of Dr. Ongle: all this was related with speed by Tugau.

Xuthus took over the narrative and described his experience in the mountain hamlet: the unmasking of what the two in the office were up to, then the chase to catch them.

"We do not know how safe we are in your commune, sir," added Tugau. "Is it possible for us to find shelter with the local constabulary? Surely they have sufficient arms to defend us from being kidnapped or harmed by the gang sent after us. This is my point: is there a magistrate who would be inclined to issue a writ or command of physical protection? My friend and I are in grave need of your advice. Our lives depend upon what you counsel us to do."

All of a sudden, a loud noise came from the direction of the street.

The editor rose from behind his desk and went out of the room. The visitors decided to follow him. Through the window in the anteroom the three saw a small group of tiny men milling about, entering shops, then exiting.

It was clear that mountain gnomi were hunting for the fugitives from Hameau. Without any official public authority, they were taking the law in their own dwarfish hands. There was no moderation or doubt in the behavior of any of them.

"Come with me," suddenly muttered the editor. "We can go out unnoticed. The rear door is the safest. There is a narrow alley there. No one will see us passing by."

"Where can my friend and I go in Aldea?" asked the desperate Tugau.

"To my brother-in-law, the police magistrate here. He, like me, is a gnomus by heredity. But we are of the town variety, not like those mountain barbarians. Hurry, for there is no time to lose. I have to get you away before it is too late."

The police justiciary was a combative bantam nearly as short as the editor.

His office was across the street from the constabulary centrum, the main citadel of civic order in Aldea. In the private chamber of the high magistrate, the editor made the introductions, then allowed

Turgau to present the history of the conflict with Ongle, Digui, and the dwarf miners. By the time he was finished, the daystar had set and night had fallen over the Zenithals.

"Please excuse me briefly," said the judge in a low, soft tone. "I need to find out what the situation in the streets is. By law, there is a curfew forbidding roving bands like this one. Let me learn what the conditions outside are at the moment."

The three left in the high, wainscotted room sat without speaking. What was the judge going to decide? Would they succeed in getting away?

At last, the small man returned with a sheet of flimsy in his hand.

"Things were close to getting out of hand, so I issued a prescriptive edict ordering all non-residents out of Aldea. The streets must be cleared and the miners return home. The curfew will be in effect until dawn tomorrow."

He paused a moment before continuing, his eyes on the two fugitives.

"It is shameful, what those criminals on Apical tried to do. I have signed warrants for Mining Engineer Digui and Dr. Ongle in the name of the courts of this commune. The day that one of them enters our boundaries, arrests shall occur.

"I am especially chagrined at the behavior of these gnomic miners. Their foreman appears culpable for personal crimes against you two. We who live in this town realize we have to live in peace with all our fellow citizens, regardless of their ancestry or group identity. Any attempt, such as you report, to poison or harm another genetic group, is despicable. Every honorable person, regardless of origin, must be outraged upon learning of this nefarious medical conspiracy. I will not stand for it, and neither will any of my colleagues on the bench. Early tomorrow I shall petition our regional high court to grant arrest warrants for the leaders of the evil plot to kill off all the sylphines."

"Thank you, sir," Tugau managed to say slowly.

The diminutive judge stared with compassion at the pair still in danger.

"Let me tell you what I plan to accomplish tonight. When the post coach leaves for the south at midnight, you shall both be stowed aboard it. The driver and his police guard are armed. They always have been. In a little while, a team of constables will take the two of you to the mail building. It is only one street away from here. The doors of the coach are always securely locked. There can be no way that these renegades learn that you two have left Aldea along with the post."

"We are forever in your debt, Your Honor," solemnly said Xuthus.

The magistrate smiled at him. "Doing what is one's duty entails no obligations or debts. It is what we are put here to carry out."

He excused himself and departed.

The editor then left after shaking hands with both travelers.

Tugau and Xuthus sat in silence, waiting for the next leg of their adventure in the Zenithals.

The postal coach left precisely on time, arousing no suspicions about anything. The pair of occupants inside sat among boxes containing letters and packages. They took short naps as the horse-powered vehicle followed valley roads into increasingly flat land. Both realized when they were finally in the safer territory of central Provincia. By dawn, they were barreling toward Daema with maximum speed.

Late in the afternoon of the next day, Xuthus voiced a fear he felt inside.

"Ongle must have traveled to the mountains by location transference. That is always the final alternative for gnomi like him. What if he now decides to return to Diaema the same way?"

Tugau thought on that for a while.

"My fear is that we may have to fight him at the Therapeutic Center," whispered the pharmacist.

At that very instant of time, the doctor was preparing to make a leap through the ground across Provincia, to Diaema and the hospital he managed.

"Why must you go back?" argued Digui. "Isn't your place here with us?"

"I believe that they succeeded in getting away. No one spying for us in Aldea can find a trace of those two. Somehow, they escaped our posse. If that is so, my place is where they are surely headed. I must get to Diaema at once."

The daystar set in the west. It was the moment for transilience. Putting on his heavy winter coat and hat, the doctor went out onto the hamlet street with the engineer. Quimera had swept a bare area free of snow on the surface of the lane. He stood on one side of the cleared ground, waiting for the underground traveler to begin his journey.

Dr. Ongle lay down between the two standing figures. Light was disappearing as the daystar fell into darkness. Full night could be sensed nearby in the offing, almost arrived.

Digui and Quimera, standing with heads tilted down toward the shape lying on the ground, now became witnesses to an unexpected surprise.

Perhaps the conditions were not adequate. Maybe the doctor had exhausted his instinctive inheritance through excessive recent use. There were a multitude of possible explanations for the malfunction that occurred. More energy, greater concentration of force was called for. These had to be present and available to succeed.

All at once, everyone knew that something was wrong.

No invisibility came to Ongle. No melting into the ground, no disappearance occurred.

This was evident as the surgeon tried to move again, and again, and again. There was a serious problem and no one knew its cause.

Not the expected, only the unexpected happened to Ongle.

In a fraction of a second, the body on the ground became pulverized into powder. Trituration into dust was instantaneous.

Billions of infinitissimal granules was all that remained of the conspirator in mercurics. He no longer existed in any organic form, but was atomized. Nothing else was left.

-

Tugui and Xuthus were astonished that they had no need to face Dr. Ongle again in Diaema. They could only speculate why and how he had vanished with nothing remaining.

"How strange the outcome of our journey to the Zenithals!" mused Tugau one morning in the pharmacy he once again was in charge of. "The director, since there is no sign of him anywhere in Provincia, has had to be replaced. Thankfully, we are under a person who is a botanic at heart. No more gnomic dominance at the Therapeutic Center."

"Everything has come out rightly and justly," smiled Xuthus, who was now free of laudanum. "What happened up in the Zenithals has liberated and renewed my entire existence."

VI
The Testudinals

Tugau and Megaera decided that their honeymoon vacation would be to a place neither of them had been to before. The choice was Cape Ness, a sleepy promontory jutting into Tortue Bay. A public carroch carried them from Diadema to the southern coast of Provincia and this quiet location. Their hotel, the Thyone, was a pleasant, comfortable stucco building of long ago where the same families returned year after year. As soon as they arrived and settled in, the newly wed couple made an initial tour of the cape peninsula.

A small amusement park contained a roller coaster, a merry-go-round, shooting galleries, gaming arcades, and children's rides of all sorts. Megaera proposed that they have a snack at the outdoor cafe overlooking the shore of sand. From a veranda with tables, the two looked out at a beach full of bathers in the coastal waters of the bay. Noises of carefree laughter floated up to them from there. The mood proved contagious. Both of them felt suddenly rhapsodic.

Megaera, after a study of the short menu, ordered a crevette fritter containing Cape Ness shrimp. Tugau decided to try the deviled peigne clam. He asked their waiter, a short young man in immaculate white uniform, whether most of the sea food served there came from the region they were in.

"Yes, sir," answered the server. "We enjoy an abundance of marine food caught nearby. These waters are rich with an abundant variety of species."

The honeymooners were soon consuming sea creatures with fresh, piquant tastes to them. Both were delighted with the unfamiliar tastes provided.

After finishing, the pair wandered the coastal walkway, beginning at the amusement center. As they went further away from the built-up areas, they began discussing their plans for the rest of the vacation.

"I think we should sail out beyond the bay," opined Megaera. "It would be interesting to see how the fishermen called piscators hereabout catch the fish and water food that comes from here."

"A good idea!" beamed her husband. "That sounds good to me, too. We would observe a lot of sights that are new and interesting."

So it was that next morning the two looked for a tour boat for hire. It was on a public pier near the Thyone that they found a lanky boater with his small bachot tied to a berth. Tugau started a conversation with the man in charge. First, he learned that his name was Yote. Yes, he was willing to take them around the bay and even beyond it. His fee sounded reasonable and economical.

"Thirty sesterces, that is all," pleaded the boater. "What can be cheaper than an excursion with Yote?" chuckled the tall, skinny youth.

The twosome agreed and jumped down into the sailboat. Soon the vessel was leaving the pier. A fresh, bracing breeze was blowing over the waters. Megaera, feeling its force and power, laughed and smiled. Tugau, following her example, did the same. This was going to be a day of pure fun and pleasure, they both understood.

Yote provided them a continuous narrative, describing the various sights and features of attraction as the boat moved parallel to the coastline. Soon they were beyond the outer cape, in the open sea itself. The breezes were light and soothing to them both.

But then the craft entered a tiny cove with white cottages along its curve of shore. There was something vaguely different about this isolated locality.

"This is where I live, on a fishing inlet. But my neighbors are much busier with what comes up on the beach by itself. Each dawning sees an army of creatures out there ready to be gathered. Our village goes by the name of Echinus. Would you like to tie up and spend an hour or so there?"

There was a bright spark in the boatman's tawny eye.

Megaera replied for her husband and herself. "That sounds quite interesting. Let's have a look at the little community on the coastline."

Yote proved to be an individual of encyclopedic knowledge concerning the shore catches of the seafood hunters of Echinus. An orphan at an early age, he had been raised by his grandfather, an aged man who continued to trap and gather the crustaceans of the cove.

Their guide took them to the shanty of the oldster named Uint, where this relative was sorting out the morning's catch for sale to local middlemen later in the day.

Thin and tall, the old man resembled his grandson in everything but age and whitened hair.

Old Uint, standing straight and proudly, was happy to fill in details of his relative's extended exposition on the local fish and seafood industry.

"A few of us persist in going out into deeper water for the gobies, sagax, and arengula. But why make so much effort for those small, worthless fishies? No, we in Echinus prefer to carry on the business of our forefathers. Look at what crawls up out of the water on its own! All we have to do is go out each morning and empty our little traps. Then, the rest of the day is ours to do with as we please. What could be an easier, happier life than that?"

"I became tired of the routine and decided to branch out on my own," confessed the young Yote. "But when I decide to marry and settle down, this will be what I do to make my living."

"We have all we need in the cove," expanded the grandfather. "This is the center for all varieties of crustaceans. We are the champion capturers of molluscs because of the countless generations of experience that we enjoy." An idea struck the mind of Uint and he expressed it at once. "Let me join your little party and lead you to points where many different sea forms can be seen."

Yote and the newly-weds instantly accepted this proposal, so that a group consisting of four now made its way along the arenaceous shore of Echinus.

The vacationers viewed pagurid clams, ostreans, homards, langostas, escargot, crevettes, asteroidals, squillas, bernicles, skate

CLEMENT S. MASLOFF

rays, squid, and whelks in traps where they had been caught. The wide variety of different species was astonishing.

"Who would have imagined so many kinds of catches in one place!" sighed Megaera.

Tugau thought of something. "Are there any chelonian about, like turtles or tortugas?"

A sudden silence fell over them. Neither Yote nor Uint was able to give an immediate reply.

Both honeymooners noted that something awkward had occurred, even when the boatman who had brought them there began to improvise an explanation of their reluctance to speak.

"It is extraordinary that you ask that, sir. That sort of creature has had an important role in the history of Echinus. Perhaps it will be clearer if my grandfather explains what happened long ago to the chelons of the cove. The story is a sad and tragic one, you will learn."

All eyes turned on Uint, who waited a time before saying anything.

"This has been passed on through the ages as a true history of how this place came to be settled. No one can measure how far back in the past it may have been. At that time, our portion of the sea coast was deserted. Fishermen in small boats could come hereabouts to fish and capture what was available. Our particular cove was known for its abundance of giant tortoises and tortues. Delicious, exquisite tortugas and terrapins came from this locale. They were in demand all the way to Diaema, the capital of Provincia. A great trade in these species developed here.

"The hunt for them grew to such dimensions that the inevitable came about: the population of chelonians fell into steep decline. Down and down it went till absolutely none of them were left. Only a few surviving examples managed to crawl away to what is called the wild coast, a short distance to the south. Only after the disappearance of turtles was Echinus settled by coastlanders. But the memory of what had once been here has remained with our people. But no tortugas ever return this way, as if the remembrance of what once happened has never been lost.

"It is an unfortunate historical event, isn't it?"

Megaera was the one who answered the old man.

"Yes, it certainly is. But if the chelonians still survive somewhere close by, why can't we sail there and have a look at the great creatures? I, for one, would find it most interesting. I have never seen any giant tortoises. How large do they grow over the many years of their long lives?"

"Surprisingly enormous and heavy, " replied Yote, looking at his grandfather. "It is a rare occurence for anyone to go into Calamary Bight. Would it be of value for the two of you to make a visit that far off the ordinary track?"

"Indeed, it would," said Megaera, turning to her spouse for seconding and confirmation.

"I believe that seeing the place will be worthwhile," he declared, looking at his mate with anticipation of the enjoyment and pleasure soon to come.

Yote gazed for a moment up into the sky.

"It is late to sail there today. How about tomorrow morning?"

"Fine," nodded Tugau.

"I can hardly wait," said his wife with a smile of satisfaction.

All at once, a proposal came from the mouth of Uint. "Would you let me go along as well?" he asked. "It will please me a great deal to have another look there."

The matter thus decided, the tour of Echinus continued.

Uint showed the tourists his favorite calamondin tree, from which he picked two small orange-skinned citruses for them to try. Their taste turned out to be a new satisfaction for the two tourists.

The group walked inland a short distance. Along the path, Yote pointed out an ant bear, a tamandua, and an earth pig. "We call them the toothless ones," he said with a laugh.

It was Megaera who spotted a marsupial thylacine with gray bands on its back.

"I know it from children's books as the zebra wolf," she gushed. "It is beautiful, isn't it?" she smiled with spontaneous pleasure.

Again it was she who noticed a spiny, ant-eating echidna hiding behind a thick bush. This increased her joy all the more. By the time they returned to the sailboat she was in a trance-like state, barely able to wait for their return the following day.

After taking leave of Uint, the grandson transported the happy pair back to where their excursion had started that morning.

The couple had a late supper at the Thyone's dining hall that evening. A clear sky presented a blanket of brightly blinking starlight. They sat by a large window looking out over Tortue Bay.

"Did you enjoy our little trip today?" inquired the grinning Tugau.

"Of course," she answered. "I can hardly wait for tomorrow. What do you think we will see out there in the coastal bight?"

"That remains to be seen, my dear," he told her in a dreamy mood. "What is to come must always be in a fog, whether thick or thin."

At that point, a tuxedoed waiter appeared and handed them menus. He stood at attention with stylus and pad waiting for each to make a choice. Tugau ventured first.

"I am considering the selachian selections: hammerhead or dogfish. It is impossible for me to make a rational choice, so I think it best to try one of the exotic dishes. How about the one that is called devil fish? What precisely is it?"

The waiter told him with a knowing smile. "It is a great manta ray from the ocean deep. The creature measures up to twenty feet in length. I highly recommend it to those unfamiliar with the dish."

All of a sudden, Megaera grew agitated and troubled. "What is the testudine casserole? Does it contain the flesh of a turtle? Is that what it means?"

"Yes, madam," answered the waiter, no longer smiling. "It is made from both the calipash and the calipee of the turtle. The former is taken from next to the upper shell and is a green gelatin. The latter borders the lower shell and has a yellow color to it. Each of these is a delicate jelly with a delicious flavor. Together, they are a heavenly gastronomic combination. I recommend it if you like new, adventurous foods. There is no question in my mind that you will like it. Everyone who tries it raves about its particular taste."

Megaera continued to question the man.

"Where are such substances found and obtained? I thought that the tortugas have become rare and are now under the protection of the law."

The face of their server reddened as he groped for a satisfactory answer to her.

"Yes, our system of protection makes all chelonians forbidden for private or public hunting. No question of that. But I believe that it remains legal to import giant turtles from elsewhere, beyond Provincia. Hunting for them may not be prohibited abroad, in other lands. I do not know for certain the origin or provenance of the tortuga on our menu, I am sorry to say. It would not be difficult to find out, though, should you be that interested in the matter. It is always possible that the law in Provincia will itself be changed or amended.

"Is it that item you wish to order, Madam?"

"No," asserted Megaera with force. "It was only my personal curiosity. I think that I will try the devil fish, as my husband is probably going to do."

Her wish now plain, the waiter turned and hurried away to fulfill it.

"You seem quite concerned about the tortugas, my dear," he commented with a grin, looking at her with curiosity in his eyes.

"I do not believe they should all become extinct," she said with a sigh.

"Neither do I," whispered Tugau, almost to himself.

Yote arrived with his sailboat as the daystar rose a burning yellow into the eastern sky. His two passengers, having come early, awaited him with anticipation. They were about to go to a place whose existence they had not suspected at all. What might they be lucky enough to see there?

The waters of the great bay were choppier than they had been the day before.

"There is some sort of storm out there on the sea," said the guide. "Nothing that we should worry about, though. It will pass quickly, as it always does."

Before long, the boat had rounded the cape and entered the cove of Echinus. Here they remained only long enough to pick up the grandfather, anxious to be on his way to the bight they were going to visit that day. The old man greeted each of the married couple with a hearty handshake and a beaming face.

"We are on our way to a place special to all persons who know it," he said as they sailed out of the cove. "I believe there is something of an enchanted character to that bight."

In a surprisingly short while, the small skiff arrived at the destination.

It was not a true cove, only a slightly bending inlet of the sea, an indenting in the straight coastline by a slight curving. There was nothing here to impress anyone.

"Let me ground the craft in the shallows," proposed Yote. "Then, we can wade the short distance up to the beach."

Tugau climbed out after the two locals, then helped his wife lift herself into the shallow water.

Hand in hand, the couple followed the other pair onto the fine-grained brown sand. Only small insects were scurrying about the smooth silicon surface. The scene seemed a thoroughly silent one.

It was Uint who led the others to a large stone shelf projecting out of the sand near the outer edge of the beach. The others followed his example when he sat down on the smooth sand.

From time to time, the members of the party of four exchanged glances. They were waiting for something, without the two vacationers knowing what it might turn out to be.

Minutes passed, but no one dared say a word. The right time had not come for that.

All of a sudden, Megaera spotted something dark emerging out of the water and pointed to it.

The three others turned and saw it, but no one said anything.

Megaera looked over for a time at her husband. He was watching the object slowly moving out of the water. As soon as she turned her eyes back on the mystery creature, Tugau was peering at her. They had missed an exchange of looks and visual connection by less than a second.

The realization that the great mass they were observing was moving ashore struck both husband and wife. These two understood somehow that the pair of coastal natives was not at all surprised at the phenomenon exiting out of the sea. It was what they had come there expecting. It was not something new for them. What was occurring had to be a clearly recognized pattern, one they were quite familiar with.

Neither spouse dared ask where the event was heading.

At last, though, the gigantic entity began to gain some identity.

It had to be a giant tortuga. What else was determinable?

A mighty carapace became visible, slowly making for the stone ledge the four sat on.

With no haste at all, the being was fulfilling its purpose of forward motion.

Before Megaera realized the fact, the black green testudo was six feet from the ledge. She had no doubt where the mass was headed. But as she turned her face to look at the old man, Uint, her eyes caught a sight that nearly made her melt.

CLEMENT S. MASLOFF

The grandfather was not sitting on the hard stone surface. Not only had he gone down onto the granular sand, but he had turned into another being, another form and shape.

No longer human, the appearance of Uint had become testudine.

He was a turtle reaching out to combine with another of his own kind.

Suddenly, the unavoidable conclusion descended into her mind from somewhere. She knew that she was a biform diploid, born to be a sylphine like her parents, ancestors, and brother.

Tugau was a feline chatan in his second form, with bipolarity built into his nature. Both of them would be defined as shapeshifters in many areas of the galaxy.

And this old man of the coast was a diploid being with two phases of existence, the secondary one taking a chelonian, testudine form. Just as she and Tugau could experience instant transformations, so could Uint. But he became a large, ancient turtle. That was his secundus form, it appeared.

She turned to where Yote had been lying, but he too had moved onto the sandy beach. And he also had metamorphosed into a tortugan being, a second giant turtle.

Grandfather and grandson both slowly advanced toward the stranger from out of the water. They both were exhibiting the secundus natural to their diploid category.

As she observed this, Megaera began to shake with stress. How was this going to end? She turned her head toward Tugau. What she now saw was incredible and shocked her mind.

He had remade himself into his own secundus, the chatan cat she had seen only a few times before that moment. Now her husband had become a large wildcat.

What was his intention? What was he up to?

Suddenly she understood. How better to meet the great sea turtle than as another non-human form? Two types of biform beings would be present now. They would be facing each other.

But what should be my own course? Megaera asked both sides of herself. The answer and the transformation came simultaneously to her.

As the two testudine diploids reached and contacted the visitor from the deep, they were watched by the two friendly secundi of the newly weds, the chatan and the sylphine.

Tactile communication between the three great turtles was indecipherable for the audience of the two different diploids still on the stone ledge. Within a minute, this contact was broken off. The visitor from the sea turned about and began to creep back the way it had come. So did the other two, returning to where they had transformed themselves into turtle secundi.

The pair on the rock looked on in wonder, not daring to move. This was something neither of them could have foreseen.

As soon as one of the turtles reached the ledge, it instantly became Yote again.

The other one followed, in a moment becoming Grandfather Uint. Both were human beings once more.

Where was the unknown, unidentified one, though? Back in the water from which it had emerged.

Tugau changed back, followed by Megaera. They exchanged long, steady looks.

There was a lot of explaining to do on all sides, by every one of the diploids.

Surprisingly, nothing was said by anyone while the four were still on the beach. Only after all had climbed aboard the sailboat and were on their way back to Echinus did Uint turn to the visitors from Diadema. He began with an apology.

"Forgive me for not telling you ahead of time what was going to happen today. My grandson and I both believed it was best for events to take their own course. Neither of us was certain whether there would be any emergence from the waters. It might have been all for nothing had we started with revelations and confessions on our part. It had to be this way, although there were risks involved in keeping the two of you in ignorance of what might occur."

Tugau took the opportunity to make a declaration.

"We recognize what diploid transformation is, because both my wife and I are capable of experiencing it, though not in the way that we witnessed back there on the beach. You see, we two do not have the turtle as our secundi, but entirely different forms which I can explain to the two of you in time.

"Neither of us is astonished, disoriented, or scandalized by what we saw. This tesudine character was new and unfamiliar to us, but thoroughly acceptable. There are still some questions in my mind, and I believe in my wife's as well. These can wait. But we both assure you that there is nothing to fear from us or our knowledge of what transpired.

"We are your true, sincere friends. You can completely trust us."

The smiles he gave the old man, then the grandson, were frank and deeply felt.

"I shall allow Yote to do the explaining," stated Uint. "He can say it much better than me."

The young boatman took a step forward and told his story.

"As soon as you climbed aboard the craft yesterday, I noticed that both of you were different, not like the ordinary tourists who come to Cape Ness. At once the suspicion arose that both of you possessed double forms of some sort. I had to conclude that neither of you had tortugan twins inside. You mentioned that your home was in Diaema. There are none like us so far from here. The diploids that resemble us stay near the sea, in the coastal region. This is the zone where we are able to survive.

"So, I reasoned that your form was different from ours. That was the only logical conclusion.

"But that does not matter at all. All doubled people can be of great use to us."

"In what way is that?" asked Megaera, her forehead furrowed a little.

Yote spoke with his face turned directly to her.

"We, the torugan doubles of this coast, have been the protectors of all chelonians, whether biform or not. There are people who wish to hunt and trap them without any legal limits. Generations ago we pushed for the laws that protect the lives of all great turtles in Provincia. Only imports from other lands are beyond the jurisdiction of our courts. But now a new danger has arisen, The national legislature of our country is considering proposals to abolish the age-old restrictions and prohibitions. The fishing industry and the restaurant businesses are agitating for making tortugas fair game for huntsmen. We need to stop that campaign. But how?"

Yote looked at his grandfather, who now took up the statement and argument on his own.

"Diploid people everywhere must be mobilized to fight this outrage. There are many of them, but how can they be reached in time? We, the testudines, are all here beside the coast. Greater numbers are needed to stop the harm and damage that would result from new laws.

"That is where the two of you come in, as well as many others. Your friends, relatives, and acquaintances can join and help. Not only diploids, but solidly human people need to be stirred up to oppose the lifting of the hunting ban. The law must remain the way it was written by our ancestors. Otherwise, a mass slaughter is going to happen. I can predict what the fate of doubles caught in tortugan form will be. Captured victims are doomed to being killed. That will become inevitable if the protections are lifted and abolished."

The newly weds looked at each other. They agreed on their course without a word being said.

Megaera took the initiative of making a solemn pledge and promise at that dramatic moment.

"I come from a family of sylphines. Have you heard of us?"

"Yes," said Yote. "You are fliers of the upper air."

"We can spread your message in all directions. Wherever there are sylphines, they shall learn of the danger to the coastal biforms like you. Other varieties of diploids will also learn what is going on. No species of bifold will be ignored or omitted. All of them shall be informed at the peril that your species faces."

When Uint climbed out of the boat on the cove of Echinus, he took leave of the couple by kissing each of them on the brow.

No one said anything, but all of them understood the meaning of the gesture.

VII
The Ursines

Xuthus was at a loss about what to do with the rest of his life after his cure from laudanum addiction. Several friends advised him to take a vacation, a long one if necessary, to straighten out his thinking and plans for the future. Very well, he decided, but where was he to go?

Perusing a number of tour manuals, he chose the Algid Peninsula as his destination. Far to the north and east of Diaema, it would take him a long distance away from the zone of his unhappy early years, the Zenithal Mountains. The climate there promised him a refreshing coolness, relief from the heat of the southern summer.

He made his reservations and said his good-byes, taking passage aboard a steamer carrying travelers to the tongue of land jutting into the cold waters of the Eastern Sea. An adventure to make him forget his recent years of despair, that was the goal. New places would hopefully distract him from personal thoughts and cares.

Xuthus spent his free hours on deck, looking out at the blue-white waves as the ship steamed forward. As the vessel neared the peninsula, more and more fishing craft, a few large and the rest small, became visible. These waters were the home of umber graylings, goldline spotfins, blue shiners, algid char, sculpin, and tuifish. The vacationer gazed into the sea for long periods, trying to catch sight of these rarities, passing away the empty time he had on his hands.

A sudden voice from behind him broke his concentration on the fish.

"You appear to be deeply interested in our waters," said a pleasant tenor.

Xuthus turned around to catch sight of a towering athletic figure. The man, in a checkered red and black paletot, extended his right arm and introduced himself.

"I am called Mazre. My business on the peninsula is bear hunting. It takes me over the whole territory. It keeps me always on the move in pursuit of the wild creatures. I am now returning home after a long rest in the southern climes."

The two shook hands as Xuthus introduced himself without giving out any trade or profession of his own.

The tall woodsman invited his new acquaintance to have a drink with him in the steamer's lounge. Xuthus accepted and the pair were soon seated at a window table in the long serving chamber. A waitress quickly appeared. Mazre ordered a pale nogg and his companion did the same.

As he eyed the dark face and shadowy eyes of the man, Xuthus had a feeling that the Algider hid some secret of immeasureable value. What could it be?

"Do you have accommodations reserved ahead of time?" inquired the hunter with audacity, as if this was an old friend he interrogated.

"No," admitted the visitor. "I will get for myself whatever I can find. Whatever may turn up will have to do."

A grin covered the mouth of the woodland venatic.

"I can save you from paying high rent if you wish. My wikiup lodge is large and comfortable. There is a spare room available for a guest. I can offer it for a low fee, for nothing at all," he said with a laugh.

Xuthus gave a start. "I do not wish to burden anyone, not at all. It would be necessary for me to help out in some way to provide recompense. What would I eat?"

Mazre smiled. "I have a full larder at home. And do not forget that I am always hunting. There is always some game about in the woods. Will you come and share my bounty with me?"

In an instant, a decision was made to accept the offer.

"Yes" said Xuthus. "I believe that what you propose is exactly what I need. My purpose in traveling to this peninsula is mainly to leave civilization as far behind as possible. So, I will go with you to your hunter's lodge and give myself time to rest and think."

In a jovial mood, the two conversed about the benefits of life alone in the forest.

They debarked at the harbor of Varden and began a long, difficult hike to the cabin of the hunter. Most of the talking on their trek came from Mazre.

"It's a good thing you thought to bring that heavy woolen dreadnaught with you. Many a tourist is shivering the first day on our peninsula. The weather is always either cold or cool hereabouts. A cheechako tenderfoot has to be ready for the surprises that we get from the changing conditions of nature. When a strong williwaw blows off the sea, the wind can reach a hundred miles an hour in velocity. That is not something for anybody to play around in, believe you me."

As they went on through the picean forest, the exhilarated hermit pointed to birds common at that latitude. The chat, wheatear, redbacked volean, blue grouse, wandering tatler, slate-colored junco, snowbird, and northern ringdove were identified by the native inhabitant of the peninsula. He also pointed out a scurrying sciurine, a white varine, a tree cavy. a first-year leveret. and a wild lutria. A large lagopus with brilliant white plumage fled up into the cerulean sky as the two men approached it.

"If I had my weapon here, that would be worth the time and effort," declared Mazre in a strong, singing voice. "That is a valuable bird to bring down, stuff, and display."

"What animals are present in these woods?" asked Xuthus with renewed curiosity.

"There are plenty of cervines and wapiti left around here, but I have to go into remote locations to find reindeer or rangifers. The most valuable game are less common and harder to track today. It takes more time and effort to take hold of them."

"How about the giant mammut? I have read that it is today extinct. Only the great bears are left of the beasts that once roamed about over the entire North."

Mazre did not have an opportunity to answer, for at that moment they crested a hillock and came out over a deep fold of valley. The hunter stopped in his tracks, pointing downward at a rough, log lodge he himself had long ago constructed to live in.

"That is my cabin," he told Xuthus. "Let's go down and take the heavy pack off your back. Then I will cook you a meal like you have never eaten before."

Pan-fried ardilla meat taken from a freeze box was the main course that the woodsman prepared, smothered in wild honger gathered in the valley forest. Desert consisted of lingonberries and crowberries, washed down with saxifrage tea.

"Were your parents people of the forest, Mazre?" suddenly said the guest.

The native of the peninsula stared at him for a time with his midnight eyes.

"Indeed," he replied. "As far as I know, all of my ancestors lived in this valley or else nearby. The forest goes back far into our past. It always has. Over countless generations, my people shot the game and battled against the conservators."

"Conservators?" questioned Xuthus, his curiosity aroused.

"The so-called keepers and protectors of our natural riches," explained the host. "Our ancient rulers set them down on the Algid Peninsula to guard the fauna of the land. Their duty is to preserve all animal life from extinction by hunters. Ages ago, though, the government stopped paying their salaries. Today, they live off the forest the same way that the ordinary woodsmen do. But they still claim the right to interfere in any hunting they consider in any way harmful."

"They can set limits to what others do?"

"Right. Those like me must pay them fees and penalties when they come and demand their exactions. The conservators are our only tax-collectors here."

"Are these heavy burdens?"

Mazre slyly grinned. "A share in all that they see us fell is claimed by them. These parasites depend on our catches to feed themselves and their progeny. Why should they hunt or do anything else? Custom has taught them that the woodsman will always be around to provide them with the means to survive and live well."

"You see them as oppressive exploiters, then?"

A nod of the head came from the forest nimrod.

"The more we shoot, the more they take. That has been their unending role here."

Mazre decided to change the subject. "I have an extra straw pallet you can sleep on tonight. Let me get it out and ready for sleeping, my friend."

In a couple more minutes, the two of them were resting in deep slumber.

The evergreen forest was shining with roseate auroral light when Xuthus rose and stepped out of the lodge. A flock of goldeneye ducks flew overhead, honking and squealing. Fresh morning dew shone brightly on leaves and plants, giving the scene a pleasant, friendly warmth. Xuthus was about to turn about and re-enter the lodge when his eyes caught sight of an upright figure on the edge of the thick valley wood.

It was a man of enormous size that he discerned. The stranger wore a dark ochroid paletot and had a flat, wide-brimmed petatus hat on his head. No movement was visible for a considerable time. The two stared at each other, each waiting on what the other might do next.

Who is this odd person? Xuthus asked himself. But he could come up with no answer or explanation. The shape was a puzzle to him.

All of a sudden, the voice of Mazre came from the opened door of the cabin.

"I see that you have come at the dawn hour, Metum. What is it that brings you to my valley so early in the morn? Do you want something from me? What can it be?"

The tall one at the perimeter of the forest slowly advanced until he stood only a few spans away from the bewildered, unsettled newcomer.

"Who is our visitor, Mazre?" asked the stranger. "Why is he staying in your cabin? Is he going to hunt in the area with you? What does he do and why is he with you?"

Xuthus felt the presence of his host as the latter moved forward till he stood directly behind him.

"You are a perceptive conservator, Metum. There is no one else as sharp as you. Yes, I have a guest on my place. His name is Xuthus, and he is vacationing on the peninsula after traveling from the South. You caught sight of him, I am sure."

"The South! Why would anyone from there want to come into our woodlands? It does not sound on the level to me. There is something doubtful in what you tell me. I wish you would explain what this person aims to accomplish here."

Mazre moved forward till he was parallel with his cabin guest.

"Metum is head of all the conservators in this region. He is Marshall of the Fauna for all the surrounding hills and valleys. I have known him for a length of years. It is best to get along with him as fully as one can."

Xuthus thought he heard a tinge of sarcasm in the voice and words of the hunter.

"There is good reason for my early appearance," announced the headman. "I am here to relate to you a serious warning about what you do out in the forest."

"What does that mean?" demanded Mazre, not concealing any of his anger. "What kind of warning are you talking about?"

Metum stepped forward until he was immediately in front of the two.

"I recently returned from a joint assembly of the conservators of this zone of the peninsula. A decision was reached that all huntsmen of our areas must be told to share every animal they bring down. There can be no secret hunting of game, no hidden meat supply. No mercy is to be shown to those who carry out unregulated killing, who fail to report and share what they shoot.

"So, I am here to inform you of the new commandment from all the conservators. It is a clear imperative to everyone in these forests. It shall apply with full force to you, Mazre. A word to the wise is what you now hear from my lips. Your future will depend on full, absolute obedience to this mandate placed on everyone in the forests."

With that, the large shape turned and walked away.

The pair who had listened to his commanding statement looked at each other, but neither of them said a word.

Back inside the cabin, Mazre busied himself preparing a breakfast of barley cakes. Only when both were finished eating did the woodsman reveal his plan for the day.

"I intended to go up into the heights and carry out some scouting and hunting. You would learn a lot if you came along with me. What do you say?"

Xuthus voiced his consent, so that the two went into the forest in a little while. Mazre was the one armed with a long, wide-caliber firelock. His unarmed companion was meant to be an observer without any weapon.

They walked along paths that took them ever higher, away from the valley lodge of Mazre.

An unfamiliar natural silence filled the ears of the surprised Xuthus.

How still and placid these woods are! he marveled to himself.

Is it real or only a result of my imagination? Xuthus asked himself.

The evergreen trees appeared to rise higher and thicker as they went upward and onward.

Several whistling marmots, attempting to hide, became visible despite their efforts. Then a red pine squirrel scampered away with speed. Mazre pointed a finger at these, but did not shoot with the weapon he carried over his shoulder.

A small massasauga snake slittered off the path ahead of them.

Xuthus spotted the tiny chipmonk know on the peninsula as a hackee. He learned this new name for that animal when his guide pointed to it and told him what it was called in the region.

In a little while, Mazre indicated a weighty creature fleeing them through the trees. "That is what we call a wejack, known as a woodchuck elsewhere."

At a bend of the trail, a fat grayish brown racoon with large black cheek patches came into view. It stood still gazing at them, petrified in absolute fright.

Both trekkers halted.

Mazre took his firelock and aimed it at the doomed animal, but then had a sudden change of mind.

"I think I will let the hand-scratcher go," he softly said. "They never taste good anyway."

The spared target used the opportunity to slink away as the hunter placed his weapon on his shoulder again. The march onward began once again. As they came to the edge of a grassy clearing, Mazre whispered to Xuthus.

"I want today to be a day for bigger game than what we have seen up to now. No reason to fire at small animals when more valuable ones are sure to appear. Just be patient, my friend."

They smiled at each other, then were about to start out once more when Xuthus glanced to the right. Something there, light blue in color, drew his attention.

His eyes were nailed to a tall, full shape in the distance.

What could it be? he tried to determine.

The vision of Xuthus focused on a sky blue splotch that was moving toward the two of them.

An animal it was, one that had no fear of human beings.

The huge creature stood on two fat legs and had two furry arms protruding away from its stocky torso. An idea seized hold of the mind of the spectator from far away. It had to be a bear. Not a black, brown, or white one. No, it was some sort of freakish variety with a cerulean pelt. A blue bear?

Could such a being exist in nature? Was it at all possible? What made it so different in hue from all the other varieties of bear?

Xuthus suddenly came to the realization that the animal could be game of priceless value to a hunter. He turned his head to the side where Mazre stood. His companion seemed to have solidified into unmoving rock. The eyes of the woodsman appeared glazed over, directed toward the bear in the distance.

A blue-colored bear!

Why didn't Mazre shoot it down?

When Xuthus turned his head to view the great bear again, it was no longer there at the same place as before. Where had it disappeared? What had happened to the unusual animal?

How could anyone believe what had just been experienced? wondered the vacationer. Should he question his own eyes and mental capabilities?

For a good fraction of a minute, neither man said anything.

Finally, Mazre turned to Xuthus.

"Let's go back to the cabin. There is no more to be done today. I will explain to you what we saw once we are back in my valley. Do not worry about what you believe that you just saw. I also witnessed the strange sight just as you did."

The return walk was a quick and silent one for both of them.

Mazre cooked a quantity of cervine numbles for an afternoon repast. He did not present an explanation of the strange event in the woods until they had both finished eating. Then he invited Xuthus to sit with him outside on a homemade bench in the shade of a tall fir. When they were comfortable, the hunter began to speak.

"I owe you an answer to why I did not attempt to shoot the blue bear that both of us saw. It is a long, complicated story. I was unable to carry out that task in the forest. And it was best for both of us to eat before I explained why I acted the way that I did. That is why I have not mentioned the incident until now."

Xuthus gave a nod of understanding to his host, signaling him to go on.

"The beginnings of all this go back to early history, when the conservators first came onto the peninsula. They settled down and claimed dominance over every native inhabitant. There was strife, but the conflicts ended with the complete victory of the invaders.

"Ordinances dealing with the fauna were established by the ruling stratum of conservators. One of the most important regulations had to do with bears, all varieties of them. Strict limits were imposed on the hunting of those species. The brown, black, and white bears could be taken as game, but under a set system of numerical quotas. So many of each kind in a particular zone each year, but no more. That was strictly enforced by the conservators. The penalties involved were very hard ones.

"The most severe prohibition was that pertaining to the blue bear, the rarest of all. None of them, under the threat of capital punishment, was ever to be felled. This type of bear was to remain untouchable, as if it were a sacred animal. Eating the meat of blue bears is a crime. Hunting it is wholly banned. No exception has ever been allowed.

The rule cannot be altered today or in the future. It is like something written in stone, meant to remain the law forever."

The pair exchanged searching, probing looks.

"I have never learned the reason for the limitation," continued Mazre. "There has never been any justification given by the conservators beyond that of preserving the blue ones from extinction. It seems that they fear the disappearance of the rare breed of bears. The truth is that it is infrequently we see them anywhere in the forests. Of all the ursine species, it is the least common kind on the Algid Peninsula. I myself have, over the years, seen but two others. Today was only my third sighting of that sort. Who knows when or if I shall view another one? The appearance of a blue bear is not an everyday occurrence."

Xuthus spoke next, in a subdued tone of voice.

"I have never heard or read of such a variety," he confessed to the woodsman in a cool, dispassionate tone.

"There has long existed a secrecy about the blue ones and the rules in regard to their special treatment. The situation has never been pubicized or written about."

"I see," muttered Xuthus. "I see," he repeated mutely.

In the moments before waking from sleep just before dawn, the young man from the Zenithals dreamed of blue bears. What was it that rang with familiar echoes in his unconscious thoughts? Some intuitive recall of his own almost forgotten origins? Everything that arose in his mind had an inpenetrable aura of mystery about it.

He slipped outside to observe the auroral splendor. His conscious mind concentrated on the sight he had seen the previous day. He could not erase the blue image from his mental storehouse of memory.

As a sylphine diploid, he sensed a propinquity of some sort.

Was there a form of doubleness unknown to him and other outsiders here in these forests? What was its nature?

His mind groped to understand the unique ursine creature he had seen. Was its inner nature as binary as his own? Were they both of the same kind, though also different as well? He wished that he had answers to the questions weighing on his mind's thoughts.

Pondering the puzzle, he failed to hear the first call from the cabin door.

"Breakfast will soon be ready, my boy," shouted the forester a second time. "Come and eat fast. I have a busy day planned for us."

Xuthus moved toward the one at the door. "What shall you and I be doing?"

"In a few days, the inhabitants of our zone will be celebrating the annual Ferine Festum. Have you ever heard of that holiday?"

"No," said Xuthus, approaching the doorway of the cabin.

"It is a joyeous occasion for all who attend. A lot of exchange and trading goes on amid the revelry. That is my personal interest there. I go to the Festum every year and sell what I can afford to part with. During the winter, I like to carve wood and animal bones. I can show you what I have available for me to sell at the festival. Then, the two of us can walk there so that I can reserve a convenient spot for the tent where my wares will be placed on display. Are you willing to come along and help me, Xuthus?"

"Of course," replied the latter. "I will be your assistant there, Mazre."

There would now be work to distract the visitor from his obsessive speculation about the blue bear.

The location for the scheduled celebration was an open, treeless alcove alongside the shore of the Algid Sea. Preparations for the coming holiday were aready well advanced when Mazre arrived with Xuthus at his side. The latter assisted the huntsman by carrying the pegs and canvas for a small tent where handicraft goods were to be brought later for sale. Counters, tables, and structures of boards were set up on the grass field in an irregular pattern. Seesaws, teeters, a whirligig, and a roundabout were constructed for the innocent amusement of the woodsmen and conservators expected for the roisterous celebration. Groups of forest dwellers hurried about, merrily busy with scores of preparatory projects.

It took the two new friends only a short time to erect the sheltering tent that Mazre was to use in his coming commerce at the event. When the work was completed, the hunter made a polite suggestion to his guest at the cabin.

"I have to talk with some of the people in charge of arrangements," he smiled. "Why don't you take a walk about and see what might be of interest to you when the Festum begins in a few days."

Xuthus readily accepted the suggestion, leaving his companion and heading for the ribbon of sand on the narrow rocky beach. Here he saw men and women spreading out baskets full of rockweeds and fucoids from the sea for drying out. He had not yet become used to eating seaweed vegetation, so popular on the strange peninsula where it seemed food was always scarce.

Standing with face and eyes toward the expanse of water, Xuthus failed to sense the approach of someone from his rear.

"Hello. visitor from the mainland," called out a strong male voice. "Are you prepared to have a merry time at our Ferine Feriae? It is an event unlike anything in other regions, that is for certain. I advise you to expect many surprises of all sorts. Experience with the unexpected is a prime attraction at our main zonal assembly. We all get together and have a wild time of it."

Turning about instantly, the astounded and overwhelmed traveler saw the giant shape of Metum, the conservator, a flat purple potatus hat with an enormous brim covering his head. This member of the peninsular elite had the smile of a satisfied, fully fed feline.

"Everything here is very new to me," gasped Xuthus. "I am still trying to reach full equilibrium, if that is possible."

The tall, large figure stopped grinning and became stone-faced. "I have some advice to give you. As the old saying goes: the wise need but a single word. What I want to say to you can be of great value if taken and followed. Do not stay any longer with your unbalanced chaser after game. Leave his cabin and go elsewhere as soon as you have a chance. It will not be lucky or pleasant for you to remain with that fellow. He can only cause harm and trouble to anyone associating with him. His peculiarity of character can mislead and bring evil to others. Do you understand what I mean?"

Xuthus wanted to tell him that he did not, but dared not raise the ire of the conservator.

"I do not intend to stay here much longer," he explained. "There will be a point in time when my departure will be inevitable. But first, my desire is to see your zonal festival."

"Do not remain too long beyond the holiday, if you know what is in your own best interest. No good can come from associating with a mad man, I guarantee you."

With that, the heavy conservator whirled about and strode away with large, speedy steps.

Confused and disoriented to a degree, Xuthus returned to the tent of his comrade, the huntsman.

That evening, after an early supper of roasted jackrabbit, the pair went to bed. Next morning was to see the start of the Ferine Festum and they planned to set out for it long before the first rays of dawning appeared in the sky.

Xuthus had moved his pallet near an open window through which light and fresh air could enter. Sleep did not arrive quickly for him that night. There was so much to think and worry about: the eerie warning of Metum, the sight of a blue bear, the sense he had of the presence of a wild, dangerous diploid with two forms in the peninsula woods. What was the meaning of all he had seen, of all he had heard? His previous experience with anthropotherions gave him pause. Must he stay away from the blue bear he had seen and from its human double? Or should he approach and try to address the ursine secundus somehow? He was unable to understand or cope with the profound sense of anticipation he felt. What might be coming next?

Thought followed thought, yet sleep stayed away from him. Xuthus could not compel himself into mental rest, though he knew he needed it for the great exertions of the morrow at the festival. His effort to fall asleep exhausted his strength and energy.

Sleep, sleep, he commanded. But no obedience to his injunction occurred. He grew more disgusted with himself.

The hoot of a barred strix owl went on and on. Was the forest bird in some kind of mating? he asked himself.

Other bird and animal sounds came, punctuating the persisent hooting. There was no moment without some sound.

How busy the forest is once day has fled, Xuthus speculated.

Why does the lighted up world sound so different, in contrast to the din of night?

Something deep inside and invisible impelled him to sit up suddenly and look outside through the window opening as if expecting something or someone. Was he waiting for something anticipated?

In actual fact, there was a living being far up on the nearest hillock to the valley. Through the starlit shadows he could discern an irregular object of light blue color. No question what it was. His eyes were set on the outline of the ursine diploid, the frightening blue bear he had viewed in the forest in the light of day.

I am observing a creature who is looking at the cabin, Xuthus told himself.

What does it want? What is the bear after?

It does not see me looking at it. What could be the object of its surveillance of this lodging?

His mind suddenly fixed on the threatening image of Metum the conservator, the grim face that had stared at him on the festival grounds that day.

The ugly giant had overflowed with loathing of Mazre. Was the silent watching by the blue one a result of poisonous animus, some complex based on vengeance? What could the huntsman have done to provoke the venom of a beast such as a bear? What buried emotion connected this ursine to Mazre? he wondered.

I must uncover what the cryptic nexus consists of, resolved Xuthus.

But not now, not tonight.

Much will be there to do tomorrow at the Festum. Will there be time to think out an answer to all of this?

He settled back onto the pallet, falling asleep enexpectedly fast.

The crowd already present in early morning constantly grew with new arrivals.

"Go around and see everything for yourself," Mazre instructed his friend. "I will take care of business here in the tent."

Frolickers, carousers, and roisterers flocked about the tables and boards where pale nogg was served by young maidens of the zone. The atmosphere was a spirited one.

Xuthus strolled by games of skittles, bowls, kegels, and quoits where lads and oldsters competed with fervor. On their knees, some played at taw with precious agates. Others threw dardos at targets nailed to short posts. A raree show had been set up and entranced spectators were glued to the box showing them a puppet drama.

Off to one side, musicians were providing melody and rhythm for rigadoon dancing on a grassless plot of ground. Feet and legs moved with abandon, yet never collided. The emotional atmosphere grew ever lighter, yet never fell out of order and control. Woodspeople and conservators seemed to forget differences of status in the special circumstance of heartiness and communion.

Are all the conservators the same? Are they copies of Metum, the one he had crossed paths with? Xuthus wondered. He did not know the answer to that question he asked himself.

All of a sudden, the outsider was drawn to a small curtained stage where titival puppets moved about, drawn from above by gossamer strings. A small group stood about gazing at the animal figures, one of which was a blue bear.

It attracted the attention of the newest viewer. Xuthus watched as the large beast tangled with enemies from distant lands: a panthera, then a mandrill, and finally a giant singeape. The fight between these puppets grew fierce.

He watched with fascination as the blue one defeated each foe in turn.

Did the exhibition hold some arcane meaning? he asked himself again and again.

No answer came. The drama was inexplicable for him.

The solution to this puzzle was not available, so he walked away from the small stage.

As the number of people in the crowd grew ever greater, the general mood became uninhibited and raucous. Much of this resulted from the continuous drinking of nogg and spirits by the participants in the festival.

Xuthus returned to the tent of Mazre to discover that his friend had sold most of the wooden wares he had brought. Yet his host did not appear at all happy or satisfied. On his own, the hunter gave the reason for his gloom.

"Wherever I go, whatever I do, that conservator follows me. He refuses to leave me alone, but insists on vexing me and whatever I am doing. This nemesis, this adversary pursues me wherever I am. Does he want to destroy me? The monster aims to take away my very right to exist. His goal is my destruction."

Xuthus, with no answer to provide him, tried to distract him from his worries and despair.

"I have heard people talking about the fireworks exhibition tonight. When will that begin, Mazre?"

The latter seemed to lose some of the stress he was under. "When the twilight begins. There are several hours until we arrive at that."

Xuthus excused himself and went back to the fairway of fun and revelry.

Teams and individuals took part in tugs-of-war, crack-the-whip, sack races, and human pyramiding. Amateur acrobatics were attempted, to the amusement of the crowd of spectators. Would-be wrestlers and pugilists fought a few rounds inside informally drawn rings on the dirt ground. They became quickly exhausted and worn out. Varied strains of music floated from different directions. Instruments of wood and string sounded. The scene was vigorous and full of movement. The pitch of activity rose ever higher.

Never had Xuthus witnessed such a madcap scene of exuberance and merriment. He absorbed the emotional currents that grew and widened.

The afternoon passed on imperceptively, until the twilight arrived. The finale had come. The noise of a petard rocketing upward announced that the pyrotechnics were commencing.

Xuthus decided to return to the tent of his companion to watch the exhibition with him.

From a safe distance in a vacant field, projectile after projectile flew out over the waters of the bay. A rainbow of colors illuminated the gathering dusk. Booming noises grew ever louder, rising into a magnificent crescendo of light and sound. Scampering boys set off an accompaniment of exploding triquitraques, older men fired pistols into the air. Boisterous ferment was near becoming riotous tumult, sensed Xuthus as he stood next to Mazre in front of the now empty tent where the woodsman had sold a year's worth of handiwork.

All at once, in the strange glow of the pyrotechnical lighting from over the sea, both observers simultaneously glanced down at a huge form advancing toward them.

It was the conservator named Metum who seemed to be staggering forward toward the tent. Is the giant sober? asked Xuthus. It might be that he was inebriatred and beyond the boundaries of self-control.

What would the man try to do in such a state? Xuthus asked himself.

Mazre, seeing the potential danger ahead, suddenly bolted forward. As if anticipating an attack, he struck the first blow of the foreseeable conflict.

Surprise gave the smaller hunter the advantage.

The conservator was unable to block the momentum of collision with the accelerating body of the other. He was bowled over, off his feet and onto the ground, by the speed of the lighter opponent.

Both of them fell to the ground. But it was unquestionable who the victor was.

People crowded about the place of battle. No more blows were hit. As the fireworks over the water ended, an expectant hush fell over the area around the two combatants.

Xuthus rushed forward, helping Mazre to his feet.

Two conservators in petatus hats did likewise for the other antagonist.

Without a word with the other side, both groups departed.

Metum stumbled off on his own.

Xuthus took down the tent while his host sat on a rock, resting and restoring control over himself.

Gradually. the celebrants left for home as night fell.

Since Mazre said nothing, his cabin guest also stayed silent.

The return to the valley was entirely a physical operation, without any talking at all.

An enraged diploid can share the same angry emotion in both phases and forms, Xuthus understood. What might the blue bear now attempt in retribution for the insulting humiliation of its double? That was the question now vexing the thought of the vacationer. For he had become certain that Metum was the primus to the bear's secundus. The two were linked forms of the same diploid.

The forest beast was surely more of a danger than its human counterpart. Xuthus decided he had to stay awake the entire night in order to protect Mazre from vengeance by the blue bear.

I can do it, he said to himself. I can stay on guard, avoiding falling asleep. Everything depends on my wakefulness. The responsibility for safety in the hours ahead is mine. Otherwise, my friend is helpless and vulnerable as he sleeps. Who can predict what the bear might do with its anger inflamed? What form of madness might its emotions take under those circumstances.

He decided to place his pallet beside the front window of the cabin. Nothing could come near without his seeing it. The host and his visitor said good night. Mazre went to the far corner of the front room and was soon asleep on his floor mattress. There was no sound from that quarter, no snoring or sound of breathing. But Xuthus could sense that the tired woodsman was fast asleep. Fatigue had knocked him unconscious.

Watch and wait, that was the watchword for the sentinel guarding at the window.

The sky outside was clear and unclouded. As time passed, the movement of the stars was perceptible to the nightwatcher. He knew intuitively that the attack of the blue bear was going to happen. An inner power that was instinctive told him so.

How had the feud with Metum begun? Who was responsible for initiating it? That was not the important consideration tonight, Xuthus decided. The climax of the conflict was near, that was what mattered for the present. Inescapable happenings were on the darkened horizon.

Nearly in a state of waking dream, he saw a fleck of blue on the periphery of the forest. Then the image disappeared. But then the blue reappeared and this time stayed visible.

He had seen what he expected to. What now, though? What sort of action would soon be called for?

In the next several moments there was a scene that astonished and dumbfounded him. It was something he found incredible at first. He could not understand what his senses informed him was occurring.

A second splotch of blue was there beside the original one. It stood still next to the first one, as if helping to survey the field and the cabin.

Then, to the left of this newcomer, stood another figure of light azure, similar to the first two.

Xuthus felt absolute confusion and incomprehension. How could this be? A configuration of three diploids in animal form? What outcome was there to be for outnumbered Mazre? What was there that he himself could do in this situation?

Xuthus thought of the firelock in the cabin. It might bring down a single attacker, but not all three in one group. The force of numbers would be too great to defeat in conflict. Complete salvation from the menace appeared to be unattainable.

At the same moment, the three shapes emerged out of the forest into the open field leading up to the cabin. At a slow, identical pace, they moved forward in the same direction. But now there were two additional blue bears immediately behind them and that pair appeared to be carrying a heavy load together. The two were bent over a long article they were transporting toward the cabin with all their combined strength. This twosome followed the advance guard of three bears ahead of them.

What can be happening? Xuthus pondered.

He had identified five separate animals. Was one of them was the secundus of Metum? Which one?

A little distance from the front door of the cabin, the procession of bears on two legs stopped. The three making up the front line suddenly turned around toward the pair hauling the heavy load.

Xuthus was now able to make out what they were carrying: a body of some sort. An inert, unmoving human torso, that was what the unseen watcher decided they were holding in their hands. But then these two porters lowered the body down onto the ground, laying it on the grass.

What is going to happen next? trembled Xuthus with apprehension. How is this strange configuration going to end?

When it came, it astounded him.

All five blue bears turned around and made a hasty retreat back the way they had first advanced. They very soon disappeared into the dark of the woods.

The five were gone. Only the strange cargo remained. Xuthus decided to go out of the cabin and examine what they had left there.

Mazre appeared to be still asleep in his corner, unaware of what had occurred.

What had the contingent of blue bears placed out there under the night sky?

It took him only a second to identify the ugly face of the human corpse. The mind of Xuthus whirled and reeled until the truth became clear to him.

This was a dead Metum, and he was a victim of diploid justice. That had to be the story of what had happened in the dark night.

What a colossal error I have made! he realized. How mistaken I have been!

Metum had been an evil foe of all blue bears, not just one of them, the huntsman's secundus.

What a misreading of reality he had committed!

Xuthus looked up at the star-covered zenith of the midnight sky. The patterns of light seemed just and correct to him.

Misinterpretation had blinded his eyes and confused his thought. Mazre, not the conservator, was a blue bear. The one he had seen with his host in the woods that first time happened to have crossed their path by accident. His error had been a total one. He had reversed what was true. His understanding had been backwards.

What was he to do now, though?

When the woodsman awoke and rose at dawn, there was an unexpected situation he faced.

His guest was gone, having packed his few items and started for the main harbor of the peninsula. All that he had left was a short farewell note lying on the cabin table.

"In front of the cabin you will find the dead body of your mortal foe, the conservator who persecuted you. In retaliation for what he did at the Festum, and also for previous harm and insult he forced you to suffer, a posse of blue bears attacked and punished him. They brought his body here as a sign of respect and sympathy for you. His terrible torture is at an end, forever.

"I must apologize for not understanding the true condition and situation about you. I was wholly wrong in what I believed. Due to the guilt I feel, it is no longer possible for me to stay. It is necessary that I leave. If I had only known who you were, perhaps I could have helped you.

"If only I had discovered the truth in time on my own."

Neither of them saw the other again.

VIII
The Ordinals

Xuthus, determined to become a practicing psychognostic, studied at the Institute of Psychopathy under the renowned Dr. Origo. He was given a free room by his brother-in-law Tugau in the residence behind the latter's botanic dispensary. His years of study were hard but happy ones as he became an adept of psychiatric therapy using the methods of psychognosis.

His sister, Megaera, was the one who had chosen the fishing port of Bonito as the place for her husband to open his natural pharmacy. She and Tugau had agreed on inviting Xuthus to join them in moving from the metropolis of Diaema to the smaller coastal community. All three of them saw Bonito as the beginning of a new stage of life. They were turning a page to a new chapter.

"Why do you choose to enter such a difficult profession?" his sister had asked Xuthus when he started his course work in the local university.

"Perhaps because I myself have suffered such profound difficulties," he told her with a sharp laugh.

It seemed obvious that psychognostics was an area of fascinating, intriguing interest for a sylphine diploid like himself. The mind of a single, monistic individual was difficult enough to understand. How much greater was the complexity of a bifold personality in a diploid condition?

Early psychological research had attempted to divide primus from secundus and analyze each one separately. But, in time, this was proven an ineffective method of exploration and treatment. A complete reversal became necessary. There began a conjoined attack on both halves of the diploid, a simultaneous advance on both fronts. Neither stage could be ignored. A holistic approach became the dominant one in the revised, renewed psychology that became one of the foundations of the science of psychognostics.

From the start of his academic studies, Xuthus found out that the problems of diploid patients were not amenable to compartmentalized treatment of a particular phase or form. Increased knowledge about either the primus or the secundus had major effects on understanding the mental operations of the other, parallel section of the biform pattern.

Year followed year of education and enlightenment for Xuthus. With each step forward, he came to know more about his own double nature as two in one.

In his final year, Dr. Origo summoned him to his office to discuss his future plans and direction. The large, heavy-set therapist sat behind a gigantic gopherwood desk, rising to shake hands and congratulate the student on his graduation.

"Do you have any specific plans as to where you will set up an office for practice?" he bluntly asked the industrious, ambitious Xuthus.

"No, sir. My future is still open and undecided. I have made no commitments at all. Whatever work I go into, though, I will always remain interested in extending the frontiers of our field and discovering more of the secrets of mind and personality. Research will be very important to me."

Origo radiated a smile of satisfaction. "I know of an open position right here in Bonito. The job became available only days ago. It would entail becoming a junior partner of someone already with a practice. The location is down in the harbor district where mostly fishing families live. They would provide the majority of the patients. Your partner would be an experienced woman, Dr. Choreia. Have you heard of her?"

"No, I can't say that I have."

"She was one of the best students I ever taught or advised," he said as if gazing into the distance. "Her mind was sharp and original. Only last year she wrote a study named 'The Undefinable and the Unnamable' for the Journal of Psychognostics. I have a copy of it that could help you in understanding the way she thinks. Let me get it for you."

The large doctor rose and walked to a shelf of folios from which he took one small volume. He brought it over and handed the book to Xuthus.

"What do you say? Are you going to fill the opening with Dr. Choreia, my boy? In a way, the two of you are very similar in character and personal interests, I believe."

What could he say? Acceptance was taken for granted, it appeared.

"When can I begin, sir?" inquired the neophyte.

"As soon as she agrees. Her patient load is heavy and you will be sharing it from the start. I will write down her address on Quay Street. It would be helpful to you to read some of her published studies before going to see her. She is extremely private and introverted, I must inform you. Her interest and strength is with patients, not with colleagues in psychopathy. That will become clear to you through daily personal contact."

Xuthus looked down at the cover of the folio book he now held. The title of the work was "An Exploration of the Unset and Unprobed Aspects of Human Personality".

Rising to make his exit, the new graduate gave a nod and strode off to the door.

It seemed to be good fortune for him that Dr. Choreia specialized in exactly the area that most interested and fascinated him: the unexplained, unconscious portions of the mind. The nature of diploid personality clearly fell there, it was clear to him.

My work in the dock district is not going to be dull, he told himself.

Xuthus had good news and a cruel decision to convey to Megaera and Tugau.

He found them in the living room of the apartment behind the botanic pharmacy. His brother-in-law was reading the Bonito

Ephemeris News, while his sister was busy knitting stockings. The new psychognostic, standing at the entrance to the room, got directly to the point.

"Dr. Origo found a good spot for me right here in town, down in the harbor district. So, I'll be looking for a flat near my place of work."

The two of them looked at him with sudden astonishment. "You are going to leave us, then?" said his sister. She already knew, though, what he was going to tell her.

"Yes. My first patients will be people who live near the office I'll have. It will be best to know how they live from first-hand experience. It should show them how deep is my interest in their mental and personal problems. My hope is to build up rapport with those who are ill. I believe that familiarity with their way of life will make me sensitive to their pain and inner conflicts."

He beamed a smile at Megaera, then at her husband, Tugau.

"We shall still be seeing you, won't we?" said the latter. "Our door will always be open for you. If there is anything we can do, don't fail to ask us, Xuthus."

The one who was leaving lowered his head and murmured a soft "Thank you." Then he went on to his immediate plans. "Tomorrow morning I go down to the dock district and meet my practice partner, a woman practitioner."

"What is her name?" inquired Megaera.

"Dr. Choreia. She is well-known in our field. Dr. Origo has a very high estimate of her abilities and thinks she will be a big help to me in settling into an active practice."

"Let's hope so, dear," said Megaera with a thoughtful grin.

In the harbor bay, one could see trawlers with fish lines, as well as jolly boats, smacks, and dandies. Small skiffs, dinghies, dories, sculls, and gigs slowed the speed of all water traffic. The larger barquentines, shipentines, and sloops dodged the smaller craft and the fishing vessels. Along the shore dockings, the fishermen who called themselves piscators repaired their seines and fish nets, their minds set on enlarging their harvest from the sea. The world of water was the arena where they fought every day for their income and sustenance.

The scene, decided Xuthus as he surveyed it, was one of unending motion and activity. No one relaxes, no one rests. Is there any wonder that stress and tension abound hereabout? he reasoned. There were pressures present that were potential sources of trouble, that could produce distress in the vulnerable. A therapist would face an unending file of potential patients in this sort of psychological environment.

He promised himself to spend his time alleviating the pain felt by harbor inhabitants. That would be the ultimate goal of all his professional efforts and labors.

With that vow in mind, the psychognostic strolled along the cobblestone, walking to his new office. The apartment he had leased was only a short distance from where he was going to work. His life now was to be surrounded by the struggles of the fishermen. He could look out at the boats going out on the clear waters of the Amphiscian Sea.

Xuthus made his way to the building where his future partner had practiced alone until now. This is our first meeting, he said to himself. Both of us are students of Dr. Origo and share his framework for understanding the mind. There should be no problem in our working together, thought the newly licensed therapist.

He knocked at the office and the door was opened by a tall, slim woman with slate blue eyes.

She possesses a bewitching body, the newcomer realized in the first few seconds. He saw that her hair fell in curly golden locks and tresses that approximated that rare metal.

It was an incredible fact: his new partner had the beauty of a legendary mermaid of the sea.

"Come in," she commanded in a melodious, cooing voice. "I recognize you from the description Dr. Origo gave me when he visited here."

Xuthus stepped in, closing the door behind him.

"He came to talk with you about me?" he asked her with surprise.

She smiled seraphically. "Yes. I learned much about you, though the two of us have never met each other before."

Dr. Choreia led him into her consultation chamber, a darkly furnished room lined with shelves of folios. She pointed to a sponge sofa where he sat down, while she found her place behind a tiny candlewood table she used as a desk when interviewing patients.

Did she see herself as one who had to analyze her new colleague? he wondered. Should he have such unfounded suspicions of her, though? There was no reason for him to fear what she might conclude about his diploid nature. Yet he did not plan to bring it up on his own. If she asked him, he would tell her the truth. If she did not do so, he did not intend to volunteer anything. That seemed logical and morally justifiable to the newest practitioner of psychognomy.

"Dr. Origo informed me that he gave you a copy of my treatise to read," she said in a level tone.

"Yes. It was of deep interest to me. May I admit that it was quite agreeable with my own perspective on psychognosis. There was much in it that I can make use of. Our theoretical agreement is nearly total. I discovered many of my own unconscious views brought to light and elucidated in your work. It served as a sort of preview to meeting you in person, I have to admit."

Her slate blue eyes seemed to dig into him like a mining excavator of some kind.

"Where exactly did you find something that did not match with your own thinking?" she suddenly inquired, presenting him with a momentary jolt of surprise.

Xuthus, a bit overwhelmed and taken aback, groped for an acceptable reply as best he could.

"Not any major point at all. I accept the division of the human personality into the three functional areas: the Imago of identity, the conscious Logos, and the unconscious Quid. That is clearly the best way to characterize and analyze the individual persona. But what if that individual happens to be half of a diploid with two forms to it? What is the effect of carrying an attached secundus upon the thought and the personality of the human primus? How does the condition of doubling affect possible problems? I can foresee the need for a wider perspective in the therapy of bifold diploids. A simple unit-by-unit approach cannot be enough or adequate. Does that make any sense to you?"

She remained silent a short time, considering how to reply to his unexpectedly firm attitude.

"Biforms are less than one-tenth of the total population in Provincia, I believe. How do they affect our psychognostic methods of treatment or theoretical understanding? I ask myself. Can't we treat our diploid patients with the same methods as all others?"

Xuthus came back with a new question. "Do you treat many of them in your own practice?"

"Only a few," she answered. "I doubt that many of them are attracted to the harbor district where the bulk of my patients live. The businesses and enterprises of this zone and region do not seem to attract any large number of such individuals, I fear."

"My own research plans include a study of how having a secundus affects the persona of a primus. It is an interesting question that, I believe, has never been studied scientifically to any great extent. Is it possible, Doctor, for me to take over the treatment of diploids already under your care as well as new biforms that may appear here in the future? I think that I could uncover and learn a great deal with those patients."

All at once, Choreia gave a sharp laugh. "Why not? You can take all of mine. There are only a few. And any new diploid patients will be yours as well. I can see no objections, if that is your wish. It can easily be arranged that way."

"Thank you," he told her. "Thank you, Dr. Choreia."

"Let me show you the rooms that I have set aside for your use," she said pleasantly, going on from what had just been settled between the two of them.

The first patient Xuthus saw was a type of diploid he had never met before and was therefore unfamiliar with. This was a fishing-boat captain named Loligo who claimed to be a variety new to the recently graduated and licensed psychognostic, whose knowledge and experience of the binary condition was not total or exhaustive.

The analyst sat in a soft chair opposite the one where the lanky piscator sat. The former wore a light summer suit of coastal silk, while the latter appeared in dark denim sailing clothes.

"Tell me what a ondinal is, Loligo. I am ignorant what that term means because I grew up inland. You are much more familiar with the diploids of the sea than I happen to be."

The patient made a sour grimace. "If you are a landlubber, then that can be the case. A lot of those who do not know the sea have never heard of ondinals. Let me explain them to you, Dr. Xuthus.

"Everyone knows, or should know, that fire, air, ground, and water are the four basics of this world of ours. Each of them has a special spirit who dwells within it and is acclimated to the conditions that dominate that basic.

"We, the ordinals, are the special biforms whose realm is the water of the sea. Our origins and character are located there. We have an affinity to everything nautical and tend to be marine creatures. There is nothing tied to a human that is anything like us. We are unique and different. That is our fate, to which we are destined by our nature.

"Under usual conditions, our lives are happy ones. Since that has always been true, why do I myself suffer such inner pain and misery? Why can I not straighten out the nets that surround me every day and night? Evil dreams torture my sleep. Merciless thoughts bedevil me at all hours. There is no port, harbor, or refuge anywhere. On and on this malady attacks me. No relief, no solace ever comes to me. I try this, I try that, but nothing can cure or rescue me from my shadows and troubles. My situation, like that of my brother and sister ondinals, appears to be an absolutely hopeless one. I myself am unable to do anything about it by myself, and that is the reason that I have come to you seeking help.

"What can you do for me, Dr. Xuthus?"

"When does the secundus appear within you, Loligo?"

"That is the strange thing: almost always when I am on the water. Hardly at all on the land. Why should that be so, sir? Why is my other self always present at sea?"

The new psychognostic thought for a moment. He had never foreseen anyone asking him any such thing.

"That is an important question to which I have no answer to give. Why is it that the upland areas or the mountains are the homes of unique kinds of bifolds suited to those regions? Is it something in the surrounding conditions or in the particular secundus that creates such correlations? There must be much more study of the matter before even the beginning of an answer becomes possible. I would not dare reach any conclusion today with all that remains to be learned."

Loligo grew grave and thoughtful.

"I can only say this: peace and happiness only appear to me when I am an ordinal out in the deep waters. My attacks of painful melancholy occur here on land, in my present human form. Do others of us ondinals suffer in the same manner? Tell me the truth, if you know it."

Xuthus said nothing in reply, because his knowledge on that subject was a complete void.

For a short while, neither analyst nor patient spoke, as if dreading the possible consequences.

"What can I do for alleviation, sir", asked the piscator with evident anxiety.

"When are you going out on your fishing vessel again?"

Loligo looked surprised. "In three days time. Why do you wish to know?"

Xuthus drew a deep breath before answering. "I would greatly like to accompany you. It would permit me to observe your secundus form in its familiar, most frequent setting. Can I do that?"

The fisherman gaped in astonishment. "Why...yes. I see no reason not to. There will be no objection from my three-man crew that I can foresee. I am certain of that."

Xuthus grinned at him. "I will obtain the proper clothing for going with you on the fishing craft. My presence, I hope, will not disturb the work that goes on aboard."

"I only have two assistants on my smack who help with the dragnets. There will be no trouble from them, I assure you. That pair are used to my transformations, because both of them are also ondinals like me. You are not going to be any sort of problem for either me or for them."

He seemed to give a slight wink of the eye.

"Let me set up my arrangements to be away, then," said the doctor, reaching for a note pad.

Xuthus pondered all that evening about what he was after on the coming sea voyage.

What changes in Loligo would he have to be on the lookout for beyond those in his physical form?

There was certainly going to be a transforming of the self-image, the mental Imago of the fisherman. How would the secundus see itself, and how might that affect the personality of the primus, Loligo himself?

How much of the instinctive, intuitive unconscious of the primus still continued within the mind of the secundus? Xuthus wanted to find out. How much of Loligo's original human nature was shared with the secundus and how much was changed into something different from what it originally was? What did the primitive, wild Quid become within the newly shaped body of the second self?

The consciously thinking, rational Logos also presented problems and questions, like the other components of the personality did. How did the ondinal secundus think and cogitate? Was it similar to human mental activity? Or was its thought uniquely ondinal?

There was no answer to these questions in the existing psychognostic literature when Xuthus searched them. His own biography and experience as a sylphine was not adequate to permit generalization on such a wide scale.

As he contemplated the many aspects of these three elements of the mind, Xuthus grew worried and anxious. What was he about to discover on board the fishing smack? Why had no one succeeded in applying the psychognostic method and framework on any of the many diploid varieties yet? Was there serious fear of what the findings and conclusions might include?

Less than a tenth of the human population of Provincia would qualify as biform. Their psychological functioning was still a profound mystery.

A sudden question struck Xuthus. He had not yet informed his partner, Dr. Choreia, of his plan to sail for several days with his patient on the fishing boat. Should he tell her of his plan to study a diploid's double nature? How much should be revealed before he left for the sea?

If he began to describe any portion of his plans, all of it was certain to eventually coming out. No, it did not seem possible to open only a part of it to her.

Xuthus concluded it was best to keep everything completely secret from his partner. When the study was completed and his questions answered, the results could then be shared and spread about to many more individuals.

Until then, he would tell Choreia that he needed rest and planned a modest sea excursion. The details of the voyage need not concern anyone but himself. His trip was to be a private activity.

If things went smoothly, there would be brilliant success to report.

Loligo came to the apartment of Xuthus in the evening and invited him to accompany him to a dockside eatery called the Abyssal Depths.

"We can discuss our plan over lobscous stew. That is a dish that all seamen love to eat. Have you ever tried it before?"

"No," said the doctor. "But I have heard that it described as exceptional."

"You must judge for yourself, then. Come, it's on to the Abyssal for us."

They had only a short stroll along Quay Street and they were there. A quiet, secluded booth in a far corner satisfied their desire to talk in private. Loligo ordered for both of them, then turned to his therapist. "Do you know how I began in this profession of piscator? My father made me work on his smack as soon as I was old enough to do anything. He was what is still called a neritic boatman, staying in the shallow waters along the coast of Provincia. What were we after? Small things, like snails, mussels, oysters, clams, gobies and cuttlefish. I learned to deal with them as a very young lad.

"I spent my teenage years on my uncle's crab boat hunting for king, horseshoe, and hermit crabs. But there was no promising future for me in neritic, shallow water fishing. I wanted to advance out into the thallasic and pelagic zones of the sea. First, the Amphiscian Sea, then into the Chasmal Ocean. What greater dream could any young mariner have? I worked hard and seized every opportunity, and in time my ambitions were realized. But it was a hard, difficult course I plowed for many years.

"You name it, I fished for it with nets and seine lines of every sort.

"At first, I was on ships that were after flatfish, jackfish, and rosefish. I became acquainted with everything in the sea, then in the ocean. Just name it, and I helped catch it. Cero and pintado, pikefish and gar, scomber, solea, and flounder, gadus and perch, pilchard and arengus, shad and alesa. I came to know them all from experience on the water.

"I took part in adventurous voyages for beluga and sturgeon, octopus and manta. All the different menhaden fell at my feet: the pegy and the fatback, the hardhead and the mossbunker. I came to know the common piscaries where almost all the boats congregated, as well as the secret sites where our prey hid. In a word, I became expert in all kinds of sea harvesting."

"And what will be the prize catch of the coming voyage, Liligo?" asked Xuthus with interest.

The seaman gave a deep, hearty laugh.

"Why, my own namesake is the game we seek out there."

"Namesake?" puzzled Xuthus.

"Let me explain. Our target is the loligo squid. Anyone can find calamary squid, but only the truly adept know the haunts of the loligo. I am one of those who possess that knowledge." The piscator beamed from ear-to-ear.

The waiter, an old former fisherman with rheumatism, arrived with their hot sailor's stew. Both customers ate with gusto and relish, saying little more about their planned voyage.

Xuthus was intent on telling Choreia only the absolute minimum necessary in order to justify his sudden, early taking off several days of vacation.

He entered her chamber and spoke from a standing position.

"I must be gone for a little while," he bluntly announced.

She sent him a look of startlement. Her slate blue eyes turned sharply upon him.

"Is it an emergency of some sort, Xuthus?"

"I do not dare to be too specific, but the matter is very important to me. There is another person involved whom I have given my word I shall not identify. At least until I return here from my trip."

She looked away for a second, then turned and focused directly on her partner.

"Never mind. I think I understand. There is no reason, no justification for anyone prying into the areas of privacy that all of us, even I, claim for ourselves. Will your patients be told in time to change their appointments?"

"So far, I have only four patients. All of them are being informed by post of the cancellation of their sessions in time so as to not inconvenience any of them."

"Good," she said with a blank expression. "When is it that you leave?"

"In three days. There is much for me to do in preparation. Please excuse me for my haste."

With that over, he made a quick exit out of her office.

The sky was clear and cloudless the morning that Xuthus climbed aboard the fishing smack. Its sails were cleanly white, shining in the early brilliant light. The two workers who were to accompany them labored hard, preparing to cast off out of the bay. Already, trawlers and smaller craft were sailing into the Amphiscian Sea, ready to begin their hunt for the daily catch. Work lay ahead for every hand.

Reaching the location that Loligo knew to be full of squid, the owner of the vessel ordered his crew of two to stabilize their position by lowering sails and letting out the nets carried on board. Xuthus watched from the built-in bench in the stern. After a time, Loligo moved back there and sat down beside him.

"What we use are drift nets that do not approach fish directly, as trawl nets and seines do. But they are not the same as stationary nets, because they are attached to the floating smack. The wind and the tide move the drifting buoys that hold them upright. Each of my nets is fifty span long. They have depth of about fourteen span. The nets are set up in the fleets we have formed by circling around. I now have a wall of netting hanging perpendicularly in the water. The buoys are connected by a headline with hanging strops. Our catch

CLEMENT S. MASLOFF

will be caught securely as it moves within the nets through the open spaces that I have left there for them."

"You have a lot of experience using drift nets?" inquired Xuthus with curiosity.

"Indeed, I have," confidently said the other. "What haven't I gone after? Here in the warm waters of the Amphiscian Sea I have caught pompanos, crevailles, spearfish, pilotfish, swordfish, amberjacks, scads, sourels, leatherjacks, moonfish, and horsefish. Far from any shore, I have netted marlin, sailish, blue shark, skipjack, bonito, and the strange globefish and swellfish that can blow up like balloons."

"The last two you mentioned are rare delicacies in Provincia," interceded Xuthus. "Their popular name is blowfish, and they are very expensive to buy."

Loligo gave a slight wink. "I have, like most veteran piscators, hunted the sea for the hard-to-find varieties: blackfish, lancet fish, lizard fish, glassfish, cutlass fish, pomfrets, and the phosphorescent lantern fish. Finding them kept me awake and on my toes, no doubt of that."

"You stayed in deep waters, then?"

"Not always. I went to tropical areas when I needed quick money. There I found squirrelfish, silversides, mullets, croakers, snappers, groupers, grunts, goatfish, and threadfish. There is demand for almost everything the the water, even dangerous poisonfish and scorpion fish. I was able to find buyers for greenlings, sablefish, lumpfish, mousefish, seapoachers, rockfish, and lionfish. The weever can attack and cause major injuries, but I have caught and sold it. I have also handled toadfish, jawfish, and stargazers."

"You must have come across and seen some very curious varieties indeed, Loligo."

The latter nodded yes with satisfaction.

"The wolffish has sharp teeth so powerful that it can crush shellfish with them. For beauty of color, there are paradise fish, angel and butterfly fish, and moray eels to see. There is the mutton fish, which tastes exactly like the meat of a lamb. And for size, the

Chasmal Ocean is home to the giant tunny, which can weigh over a thousand pounds, as well as the daystar fish, which is two thousand pounds heavy."

"Have you tried to catch such monsters of the sea?"

"No, but I once tangled with a devilfish that stretched over twenty span across. The cursed beast got away, but I was fortunate to have escaped alive from my contact with it."

"The sea holds some enormous leviathans, then?"

"In the Chasmal Ocean, for the most part. Our own Amphiscian Sea is a much more placid location in terms of such giants of the waters."

Without another word, the tired captain closed his eyes and began to snooze. Having no alternative, Xuthus tried to do the same. His efforts failed, the psychognostic soon discovered.

A loud shout of terror shot through the torrid, still air.

Xuthus instantly opened his eyes and realized that something was disastrously wrong. He could feel the smack rising from below on the port side. What was this?

One of the work hands, his face a terrified yellow, ran toward where Xuthus lay. His arm was outstretched, pointing to a place in the water behind the vessel.

Loligo managed to rise to his feet before Xuthus did. Turning his whole body around, he stood there transformed, electrified by what he saw. The lower part of his jaw began to tremble, but suddenly stopped as he named the threat rocking his sea craft.

"A cachalot! A cachalot is entangled in the nets and capsizing the smack!"

Xuthus did not, at first, understand what was happening. He stood up and looked back at the cause of the swaying and jouncing. His eyes bulged with surprise and wonder.

A huge walfish, what could be identified as a spermatic baleine. All the various names of the great leviathan came into his mind simultaneously. He recalled the balaena and the phalaina described in the ancient texts of Provincia as sea legends. This was no myth, but a towering monster over a hundred span in length, trying to remove the net encumbering its gigantic tail.

The enormous gray form threw itself against the back of the smack.

Everyone in the vessel now knew that there was no safety aboard for them. There was nowhere else to go but the Ampiscian Sea.

All at once, Xuthus felt something on his forearm. It was the strong, solid hand of Loligo. A hollow voice came to his ears.

"The water," it whispered. "Only it can save us."

As if the captain had taken control of his body, Xuthus moved with speed to the bowside with the other. The two leaped over, almost simultaneously.

What a warm embrace the water was giving him! the overwhelmed landlubber realized. But can I swim? I have never tried to in my entire life.

A rising calescence, an increasing warmth surrounded and enveloped him. The only visible shape near to him was Loligo.

"Give me your hand," said the captain. "Do as I am doing, and the water will not harm you."

Xuthus, extending his arm, clung to the hand of the ondinal.

All of a sudden, it became clear to the new swimmer that his partner was now in a secundine stage.

There is nothing to fear, Xuthus told himself, for I am under the protection of a ondinal who can easily traverse the sea of water.

At that moment, though, a strange noise rent the air.

Both swimmers turned toward the smack. The sperm whale had broken it in two with the might of its tail. At last, it was liberated from the encumbrance of the drift net. Its war with it was ended. There was no more for the cachalot to accomplish hereabouts. It gracefully sped away.

Xuthus looked into the face of his companion. He could discern its fishlike contours. The two arms resembled nautical fins. For the first time in his life, the psychognostic was looking at a ondinal.

Loligo was now a merman natator with the swimming instincts of a fish.

What can I learn about his mind and self-concept in this form of a secundus? wondered Xuthus.

He took hold of one fin of the ondinal and was guided through the waves of the sea.

All of a sudden, words began to stream out of the mouth of the swimmer beside Xuthus. It seemed as if the two of them were in the office back in Bonito, delving into the patient's unconscious mind from the vantage point of the ondinal rather than the human aspect. The secundus was the form that was speaking.

"He thinks you can save the unity of his being, but no one can do that but his own self. I myself am more than willing to conciliate and weld ourselves together. The trouble he faces is not from me, but inside him. How can I describe it?

"Loligo lives only in the surge of his conscious thought. The spectrum of his inner self has been narrowed and constricted. He lacks the breadth needed to become a happy man. He is a piscator and nothing more beyond that. I myself exist on a wider scale than he does. I see and feel more, though he calls me his secundus on a subordinate level below his own.

"In reality, I am more a primus than he is or has been. Loligo censors and inhibits himself with tight restrictions on what he thinks or does. As a result, he unknowingly burys and represses many thoughts and feelings that drift over to me and cause pain. I should not be secundus to him. He should be secondary to me and I should be the only primus..."

Xuthus began to have new insight into the biform situation. Primus and secundus can become fierce rivals, competitors who battle for supremacy. There is nothing that compels them to exist in harmony or unity. The friction between them can disturb the development of both. The result can be terrible pain and suffering.

On and on the two swam, only the merman ondinal talking, revealing the nature of its form.

After a considerable time, the secundus spotted something on the distant horizon.

"A vessel, a big ship!" he announced with joy. "I believe we can make it there. Let us try for the craft, you and Loligo will find refuge on board."

By the time ropes were lowered to haul up the pair of swimmers, the human face and shape of the fisherman were again visible. The rescued pair were immediately assigned to a vacant cabin aboard the vacation steamer named 'The Periapt'. The vessel's nurse saw to it that they received warm blankets and hot parsnip tea.

"Do you know what this giant boat is?" muttered Loligo. "A hazard cruiser for gamblers. The passengers have no specific destination. They are aboard to gamble at cards and other games of chance. The ship is moving further into the sea, away from the coast of Provincia. I think they will be steaming about and around for a considerable time."

Xuthus looked down at the expensive carpeting. It looked as if there could be plenty of time to study his patient.

A knock, heavy and loud, sounded on the cabin door.

"Come in," called out Loligo. Both men were uncertain what to expect.

A tall individual in a cream-colored formal cutaway coat and black pants entered. His beard was long and narrow, his face pale and serious. A small dark moustache decorated the area above his thin lips. Leaden gray eyes looked at the piscator, then at Xuthus.

"My name is Gagne," he said slowly. "I own this ship. It was fortunate for you that we found the two of you. Your luck saved your hides."

Loligo posed a question. "This is a luxury gambler, then?"

The stranger grinned. "Yes, you might characterize it as that. But there is first the matter of what to do with two men rescued out of the Amphiscian Sea. We won't be docking anywhere for a very long time. Taking on unknown strays can be costly. Are the two of you willing to work off the expenses involved with saving and maintaining you?"

"Of course," replied Loligo with reluctance, foreseeing trouble ahead.

"Certainly," answered Xuthus with spirit. "I have some familiarity with games of chance. Specifically, with cards and dice. Can your ship use one more dealer?"

Gagne examined him closely. "Why not, if you can perform as required?"

The psychognostic grinned. "I assure you, I can satisfy any of your needs."

"Very well," replied the owner. "You can start tomorrow. But proper dress will be necessary. I think that can be provided from our wardrobe of employee suits. Our purser will arrange to fit you out. Are you familiar with a wide range of games?"

"I believe that I have sufficient experience as a multifaceted player, sir."

"We shall soon see for ourselves whether that is the truth."

Finished speaking, Gagne turned and left the cabin.

When the rescued pair turned to each other, it was Loligo who spoke first.

"Did you catch the signs?" he whispered.

"Signs? What signs?"

The piscator stepped nearer. "Our new employer is a ondinal, however much he strives to hide the fact. I identified him at once,"

The two stared back and forth, attempting to understand what that might mean for them.

CLEMENT S. MASLOFF

Loligo was given a waiter's uniform and became a dispenser of strong drinks to passengers lounging outside the main casino of the steamer.

Xuthus, in a cutaway similar to that of Gagne, served as a baccara dealer, dealing out cards to crazed patrons around a long green table. Winning was decided by everyone comparing the cards that they held with those the dealer gave to himself last of all.

Non-players congregated about the table, eager to experience the thrills of the card combinations indirectly, vicariously. Excitement never flagged as hand followed hand in endless gambling.

A little way from the table of Xuthus, there was the sound of rotating roulette wheels. Further on, silence reigned as cardplayers concentrated their minds upon hands of monte, all fours, old sledge, seven-up, faro, pitch, cinch, bezique, penuchle, brag, and a variety of old, almost forgotten card games.

Gagne walked about, his sharp eyes taking in the action and non-action about the long, spacious hall of games. The atmosphere of exuberance captured Xuthus thoroughly. The gambling passengers revealed hidden traits of themselves to the observant card-dealer. He believed that he detected a small number of diploids among the players and watchers.

His eyes observed avarice, frenzy, jealousy , lust, and a series of emotions well hidden in everyday life, only exposed here at sea.

The diploids whom he uncovered were mostly ondinals, but not entirely. Some were sylphines, like himself. Others were rare types he was not familiar with or had never seen before.

He discussed his experiences with his companion, Loligo, after work as they rested in their cabin.

"These characters are fascinating to me. I wish I understood them better. What draws them to make this kind of expensive voyage, from Bonito into the Amphiscian Sea, and even into the Chasmal Ocean, then back again? What are they getting out of it? What actual satisfaction results from taking the risks involved in the gambling?"

Loligo made a sweet grimace. "It may be a lot like what fishermen do. It is not only the catch that draws us, but the emotions of the hunt, the chase. Do you understand what I mean? Something deep inside craves adventure. It can turn out to be a fatal chance, a deadly risk, but the player is driven to seek and accept it"

"Yes," agreed Xuthus. "It is a quest rooted in the shadowy depths of a person, both for ondinals and all the other biforms, as well."

"What do you doctors call the unseen, unknown part of a human being?" asked Loligo.

"The spectrum, for its wide range of imagined but unrealized possibilities."

"When I fall into the secundine stage, I sense that there is an unlighted darkness inside. One exactly like that inside all the other ondinals. But everything there is invisible to me."

Xuthus became hypnotically interested in what had just been revealed.

"When you are like you are now, in the form of the secundus, is there inward perception into the unconscious area of the mind?"

"Yes, it seems so. Why should there not be?"

Xuthus slept very little that night. He devised in his mind a new term for the unconscious spectrum of a diploid secundus.He named it the umbra, a shadowy region shared in common by both phases of the bifold being. The primus and the secundus possessed and were themselves possessed by the dark, deep umbra. They shared it as an overlapping unconscious, not perfectly identical for both of them.

That was his conclusion from all his observations of the many types of diploids.

A hyaline glassiness characterized the surfaces of the walls, ceiling, and furniture in the private office of the owner of the casino ship. Gagne used it as a retreat where private conferences could go on in security. He had told the head waiter to tell Xuthus to report

CLEMENT S. MASLOFF

there after his work as a baccara banker was over several hours after midnight.

Gagne sat in a glass wool soft chair. He pointed to another one facing him for his employee to take.

"How are things progressing for you?" asked the gambling entrepreneur.

"Quite well, sir. I have learned a lot about our business. The players are interesting to watch. Yes, I have picked up useful knowledge here."

"We are now in the Chasmal Ocean. In another week, we shall have to turn around and head back to Bonito. Are you happy about that? I have something I want to ask you. It is this: would you consider staying on as a permanent dealer? That includes your taking a percentage share of the casino's winnings at your table. It is my main reason for having you come to this office.

"I want to start training you in our secret methods for augmenting the odds in favor of the house. Do you understand? We have ways of reading what the cards are as they are dealt out. There are nearly invisible markings that enable those of us in the know to predict with total accuracy how the numbers and faces will come out. That is a valuable capability that raises the take of both the house and the gifted dealer. It is not unprecedented, may I say. There is a long history behind our means of improving our odds."

Xuthus felt a rising gorge of anger, but managed to stifle and conceal it.

"Are you saying to me that fleecing the passengers is alright in your estimation?"

The owner of the ship smiled like a cat. "Those are your words, not mine. I would rather call it evening out and adjusting the odds. After all, they climb aboard for an enjoyable experience. To them, it is an adventure not available anywhere on land. Our fares and rates are not exorbitant. Why shouldn't I make an acceptable profit out of the excitement I bring to otherwise drab lives? Every one of my customers gets their money's worth."

"I see," reluctantly said the psychognostic.

"We can start you in the daytime, after you have the sleep and rest coming to you. Do not forget: all professions have their artifices. There is nothing new in that. I want you to master our tradition of methods so that you enjoy maximum success as a dealer. Let me confess: I hope to make you my head banker in time, when my present one retires to the land. How does that sound? Your take will be phenomenal then."

"I must think over what you told me," mumbled Xuthus, his mind already made up. He rose, excused himself, and left the hideaway office, determined to escape the evil ship as soon as he could, in any possible way.

But first he had to discuss their future with Loligo.

"We have to jump ship and escape as soon as possible," concluded the piscator when he had heard the complete narrative of the offer of the owner to Xuthus. "There can be nothing but tragedy for us if we remain on this devilish ship. We must flee off of it."

"But where to?" asked the psychiatrist-baccara dealer desperately. "We are stranded in the vast waters of the Chasmal Ocean. There are no islands anywhere nearby. Little traffic crosses the area we are now in. What hope do we have of rescue out there?"

Loligo pondered for a couple of moments.

"I have heard other waiters talk about Retroversion Night. That will be in the near future. The entire ship will be in masquerade costumes for the occasion."

"What exactly is it?" asked the puzzled Xuthus.

"During that night, the vessel turns around and starts back to Bonito. It marks the beginning of the return voyage. There will be much celebration and imbibing of intoxicants. Do you see what I am getting at? Everyone's guard will be down. No one will be too aware of what is going on in the surrounding waters in the dark."

"What, then, do you propose that we do?"

Loligo lowered his voice to a murmur. "There are the emergency rescue rafts. If we cut one away, it could get us a good distance away under the cover of darkness. No one would be too watchful. Do you have a better idea than that?"

Xuthus was unable to think of one.

"We will make our move on Retroversion Night, then," he decided.

Ribbons, tapes, wreaths, and festoonery decorated the ship's main hall. The casino tables and gambling equipment had been removed for the occasion. Long tables covered with delicacies gave off an inviting general aroma to the spacious place. Everything was ready for high celebration.

Passengers entered dressed in masks and costumes they had brought from Provincia. Familiar figures of folklore and literature were visible strolling about. Comic arlequinic characters were in multi-colored spangled tights and slanted masks. Women wore peasant camisia and smocks. Clowns and pranksters appeared in piebald rags. The place looked like a convention of the mad.

The passengers in mask and costume were assembled when Gagne and his crew of employees marched in. Their cloaks were black with folded wings attached to them. Crimson masks concealed the identities of those behind the vizards. Xuthus and Loligo were part of the eerie company that Gagne had put together and costumed for Retroversion Night, the high point of the entire voyage.

The shipowner had been explicit in his orders to his new workers, among whom were the two who had been rescued from the sea.

"Every year, I dress my employees up as fallen Numens. You know what they were? Folk legend in Provincia tells of how these angelic beings came down from the outer cosmos and mated with human beings, taking wives and husbands from our ancestral population. They are supposed to have taught us many useful arts and skills, laying the foundation for modern science. So, I have all my workers impersonate these celestial rebels and pioneers who left the skies to dwell among the human race. There are costumes for all of you tonight."

Gagne, as leader of the Fallen Ones, took the prehistoric name of Azazel. The purser posed as Semiaz. Others dressed as Tamel, Ramel, Asel, Ezequel, Baraqyal, and Ananel. Xuthus was given the costume of Zaqeal, while Loligo became the Numen called Turel.

The ship's orchestra played zarzuela music. Many couples danced to its mercurial beat. The great hall became filled with wild gyrations.

The two fugitives sat alone at a small circular table near the kitchen door. There was to be no food that evening, so that all the cooks and waiters could put on masks and participate. Xuthus had decided that he and his comrade would depart for the lower deck through the empty cookery. They waited patiently for a moment when the crowded conditions would cover and hide their disappearance.

Xuthus stared at his partner in preparation for the coming maneuver. The maxixe being played by the musicians came to an end and the dancers swept away to empty chairs.

Their waiting ended as Xuthus signaled to Loligo, first with his eyes, then by rising from the circular table. The piscator started up instantly. The crushing rush of the dancers to their chairs and tables prevented Gagne noticing their movement opposite to the general current. Only as the two passed through the swing-doors leading to the kitchen did the owner of the ship catch sight of the escaping employees. For a time he remained still, uncertain what was going on. But once the pair had disappeared into the cookery, Gagne bolted to hs feet.

"Get those troublemakers trying to run off!" he shouted loud enough to be heard over much of he large hall. After a moment of startled confusion, several cooks, waiters, and card dealers followed their boss toward the kitchen door. The stream of withdrawing dancers impeded all these pursuers of the pair, making their forward advance slow and interrupted. Chaotic disorder reigned over the dance floor of the hall.

Meanwhile, Xuthus and Loligo had reached the darkness of the outer deck. They went to a rescue dinghy and swiftly unloosened its holding ropes, releasing the craft to fall into the water below with a loud, jarring splash.

"Now, jump with me down to the boat," commanded Loligo.

Holding hands together, they simultaneously leaped into the void of night. Just as Gagne came out of the door to the deck, the two disappeared off of that level, falling downward toward the sea.

Both struck the water at the same moment. One was on the right side of the boat, the other on the left.

Gagne came to the deck railing and looked down through the ship's shadow. He peered as if thunderstruck. Several of the crew joined him in the next several moments. Only the stars of the galactic circle furnished them any light.

On board the escape canot, Loligo untied a small oar and began sculling away from the cruise ship.

A waiter asked the petrified Gagne an important question.

"Shall we chase them, sir?"

The owner seemed to shake himself back to consciousness.

"No. Those two tricksters are not worth the effort of a chase after them. I will have to write off the cost of the dinghy they stole. At least I got some work out of them, though."

He turned away from the ocean and went back through the kitchen to the Retroversion Night celebration that had been interrupted and spoiled.

Fortunately, the fugitives had succeeded in stowing away stolen food supplies on their little boat. They used a tarpaulin cover for protection from the burning rays of the daystar during the hours of light. Day after day of rowing eastward gave them endless opportunity to talk about their past, present, and potential future, when they succeeded in reaching land.

Xuthus voiced his speculations. "I think that there is a possible explanation of the genesis of diploids in what we saw onboard the Periapt."

"What are you thinking of?" asked Loligo, lying across from him.

"The Fallen Numens. What if they visited our planet away back in prehistorical times? If, by chance, they mated with human beings, what would the resulting progeny turn out to be? What if the mixed heritage came out a new sort of creature, able to move itself back-and-forth between two different forms, a primus and a secundus that we now see in our bifold population? It is pure speculation on my part, but almost all sciences begin with such thoughts rooted in something else like legend or fantasy. But this theory of mine can provide a lean, tidy explanation: all the diploids are descended from both human and Numen ancestors."

Loligo gave a start. "You are one of us diploids?"

Xuthus took time to explain his sylphine nature based in the Zenithal Mountains of Provincia.

"Can you fly through the atmosphere? That is what I have heard your type do," said the fisherman.

Xuthus looked downward into the water. "I have not tried any flight in years. There has long existed a fear in me that the ability may have been lost. Therefore I have not even tried it, perhaps out of doubt I could accomplish it."

The piscator leaned his body forward. "Could you rise up and over the water when we enter the Amphiscian Sea? I am asking myself whether you might be able to locate one of the islands there."

A lengthy period of silence followed before there was an answer from Xuthus.

"Yes, but I will have to overcome the unfounded fear that has plagued me for so long. The time has come when it is essential that I attempt to fly again. There is really nothing for me to dread. I can handle the risks involved, that is plain and clear."

CLEMENT S. MASLOFF

"In a few days, we will have entered Amphiscian waters. That will be the appropriate moment for you to attempt a survey from the air," said Loligo with confidence in his voice.

After several days of rowing and mental preparation, the pair decided they were in position for the first air flight by the sylphine diploid.

Xuthus stood upright at the end of the rescue boat. Lifting his arms upright over his head, his mind entered a state of near self-hypnosis. He sensed the inner rotation of invisible gyres of his mind. The human body of the psychognostic had a final feeling of abandonment as it transformed into a winged sylphine form.

Primus turned into secundus. The new form of the bifold began to rise upward, taking to the air.

Success! the sylphine form of Xuthus told itself as it proved it could still fly.

I have not lost my aerial capability. Now the object is to find an inhabited island that can furnish us transport to the mainland.

Xuthus returned from his flight with the good news of having found a long, large tropical island not too far to the east. He described it as best he could to his partner.

"Monkey Island!" reacted Loligo. "That's what it must be. It sounds as if you flew over that isle. I have never been there. It is the primary source for the importation of pets and monkey meat. It is called a strange and uncanny place."

"Are we going to aim for that island?" asked the human form of his partner.

"That appears our best bet, since there are no alternatives anywhere near where we are in the sea."

"Our destination must then be Monkey Island," said Xuthus with a long sigh.

IX
The Knuckle-Walkers

The small spot of green grew wider and larger, until the headland of Monkey Island clearly became a lush tropical forest. The two voyagers were increasingly excited. They rowed with determination, approaching a small, indented estuary. Neither of them was sure what they were going to find on this unfamiliar ocean isle.

Towering trees were soon identifiable: satinwood, fiddlewood, kingwood, gumwood, featherwood, and the great deodars. The sounds of live jungle creatures became audible. Here at last was an environment where human beings had a chance to survive.

The pair soon learned they were being observed by several young men. Figures rushed about on the narrow sandy shore, in anticipation of the landing of their dinghy. The closer they rowed, the larger the crowd and louder the din they made. Neither fugitive knew for sure where on Monkey Island they might be. They had arrived from the west, that was all they could say. Both of them realized that they were about to meet human beings that would probably be different from those they were used to.

A welcoming gang waded into the shallow water and dragged their boat ashore. The attitude of the strangers was neither warm nor cold. No emotion beyond surprise was shown by anyone. There was no way to predict what might be happening to them in this unknown environment.

All at once, an older man with an aura of authority about him appeared from a copse of trees.

Xuthus and Loligo, by then lying on a grassy area between the beach and the forest, gazed with caution and curiosity at the hulking figure of an athletic middle-aged man wearing a large pith hat. Dark eyes of slate blue bulged with nervous force.

The stranger spoke in a baritone to the new arrivals from the sea.

"Where have you come from?" he curtly demanded to know.

Loligo gave an explanation he invented at that moment.

"We were passengers on an excursion ship that sank in the Chasmal Ocean. There were few survivors. We were fortunate to take a boat and row ourselves here. For all that we know, we may have been the only persons to have survived the sea disaster."

The questioner moved closer to the two on the grass. "What was the name of the vessel you were on?"

"The Periapt," answered Xuthus. "It was based in the port of Bonito."

"I see," said the man of undefined authority, eyeing them coolly. "The boys will take you both to my villa when you feel yourselves able to walk. For the time being, you can stay with me. I shall try to arrange your return to the mainland." He paused a moment. "My name is Temo. I am Dr. Temo and manage an experimental station here near the shore. Do not be surprised when you see and hear wild monkeys about the plantation. They are part of the work we carry out, the center of our scientific activities."

His statement finished, the man turned and departed up a narrow path.

The cry of a forest turacou shook the evening air as Xuthus awakened, strengthened and refreshed.

He shared a room containing two beds with Loligo, who was already up and dressed.

"You were terribly tired," smiled the piscator. "I let you sleep as long as you had to. A gosoon brought some camellia tea for us. I've already had a cup. Would you like some too?"

Xuthus rose, put on his clothes, and sat down at a small table on which a demijohn rested. He poured out a cup of red liquid and drank it. Only when he was finished did he say anything.

"I don't understand at all what these people are up to, do you? They don't make any sense to me in how they talk and act."

Loligo, seated across from him, shook his head. "There is something unusual going on here. I have never heard of anyone raising monkeys before. What is the doctor we met getting out of this plantation of his? What is the angle behind all this nonsense? I wish I could answer all these questions that are troubling my mind."

"He claims to be involved in a scientific enterprise, that much is clear. His objective may only be increased knowledge of the animals," mused the psychognostic aloud.

"How does the man pay for all this, though?"

Xuthus shrugged his shoulders. "That I cannot say. The activities hereabouts are a mystery to me too. Their business is not self-explanatory." He gave his companion a friendly grin.

In a short while, a knock came on the door to the room.

"Come in," called Loligo.

A white-haired domestic opened the door. "The Doctor wishes to see both of you in the dinette. The meal will not be a formal one," he sneeringly said, looking down at the ragged pants of both Xuthus and Loligo.

The pair followed the servant down a lengthy hallway. The latter stopped at the end of it and opened a door for them. Xuthus entered first, then his companion.

Dr. Temo sat at the head of a small table, indicating that he usually ate here alone. He pointed to the two toonwood chairs prepared for them. The pair cautiously sat down.

"I am dining on conger eel tonight," said the host. "I hope that the two of you are able to handle it after your ordeal at sea."

Another door to the dinette opened and a servitor all in white slipped in carrying a large covered tray. Placing the load before the doctor, he removed the lid, revealing three platters containing boiled conger, camote yams, and haricot salad.

The hungry refugees began to eat with ravenous appetites.

Dr. Temo ate slowly and sparingly, often glancing at one or the other guest at the table. He did not attempt to hide his burning curiosity about them.

As the outsiders finished, the servitor appeared, as if on cue, with desert. This consisted of bowls of pompelmous and pomelo fruit swimming in hesperidium syrup. The still hungry visitors quickly downed the special combination.

Their host decided it was time to talk seriously with them.

"I have not inquired what you were doing so far from any shore, nor what your occupations might be." He first stared at Xuthus, then at Loligo. The latter answered him first.

"I am a fisherman by trade. The excusion ship we were on was capsized by a gigantic walfish. It was a frightening experience that I never want to repeat. The event is very difficult to describe or talk about."

Dr. Temo looked toward Xuthus, waiting to hear what he had to say.

"My profession is that of psychognosis. As a therapist I attempt to discover the causes of internal conflict and alleviate the pain that results from deep problems. My aim is to become able to read the innermost thoughts and feelings of patients."

The eyes of the host took on a bluish glow, as if afire.

"That is interesting," he noted. "My one child, a daughter, is in the same field of work. In fact, she has her practice in Bonito, the seaport."

Xuthus grew excited. "I may know her. What is her name?"

"She is called Dr. Choreia."

The other was shaken upon hearing she the name of his partner. "We share a close connection, then," beamed the overjoyed Xuthus. "She is my associate in practice. We share the same office. I certainly know who she is."

"I must write and inform my girl. In fact, she has made plans to visit me very shortly. Such an item of news will certainly interest her. She will be eager to learn you are safe and to see you. What an amazing coincidence. Who would have imagined such a coming together as that between the two of you and me, the father of your professional partner?"

The dinner proceeded to its end in a jovial atmosphere. Temo spoke glowingly, with sincere pride, of his daughter, the successful psychognostic in Bonito on the mainland.

"I am a primatologist, but her area of the human mind and personality is much more complex. Perhaps it was growing up on our plantation that gave her the burning scientific interest she has. I have great hopes for what she will be able to achieve in years to come. Her talents and potential are rich. She holds my dreams for what our family is going to contribute to the progress of science."

"Yes," agreed Xuthus. "She has a brilliantly creative mind."

"I often recall how bright and curious she was as a small child. Growing up here on Monkey Island, she became acquainted with many varieties of small primates at an early age. They became her first friends and took to her. She was always attentive to their feelings. I can remember many instances when she nursed and cared for sick monkeys. Her sympathy knew no limits. That was when she first manifested her kindness of character. It was her drive to help the ill and the suffering that brought her into the field of mental therapy and psychiatry."

"I agree," said Xuthus. "She is an amazing human being. There are not many about like her."

The dinner soon ended and the guests left in a hopeful mood. Xuthus had something to look forward to, for he was going to see his partner in a short time.

The next morning, Dr. Temo took the two on a tour of his breeding stations."We sell the babies to zoological gardens and to individuals so they can be raised in monkey colonies or as personal pets. My creatures have found new homes all over Provincia and other countries."

"I imagine that many varieties are native to this island," said Xuthus."Did you acquire the rest elsewhere on our planet?"

The breeder smiled with deep personal satisfaction.

"I have searched everywhere for new types of monkeys," he explained. "Also, I have carried out interbreeding of closely related stocks, with notable success, may I say."

As the trio moved about the compounds and stations, Temo named and described each variety of monkey behind the wire fence.

"Those are the ones indigenous to the island.The ones with the short beard and the hair cap are the hanuman and the entellus. Notice their extremely long tails. Those are their distinctive marks. They are animals with a lot of pride and ready to fight to uphold their reputation in the forests and jungles."

The three men walked on to a second station.

"This area is given over to the guenon monkeys that I brought from the Taggery Islands. Those small ones there are talapoins that gang up together for mutual protection. Now, look at that long-legged one with olive-green hair. Notice its black face. I found it on the island of Circe. The people there call it the green monkey. But only a few hundred miles away on the island of Nisus, I bought several wild vervets. They can be seen over on the left, grayish green with large black speckles all over. It's a sight, isn't it?" he said with an odd grin about his mouth.

Temo guided them along a central path to another fenced-in compound. "Here are the nocturnal varieties that live in high trees. I obtained most of them by hunting in the land of Drusera. These grivets have very soft fur and a face that resembles that of a fox. Notice their large eyes and pointed nose. The Druserians believe that they are the spirits of the dead wandering about after dark. Legend has it that they originated in a land that sank into the Chasmal Ocean.

"Next, we come to the black macaco. Beside it is the jungle macaque with a short tail and big cheek pouches. That brownish yellow monkey sitting by itself is a rhesus macaque from the Isle of Ramace. They are useful in laboratory research. It is beautiful, isn't it? Nature has granted each species its unique characteristics and personality. No two of them are identical, each one is different and original."

They continued outward, reaching what Temo called his Loris Station. Here they viewed slow-moving lemurs and other lethargic nocturnals.

"That is a potto, with large, long hands and feet. It hardly has any tail. The all-black animal is called an indri. Those with shaggy brown fur, large ears, and long, bushy tails are aye-ayes. Up in those trees are colugos from the land of Curcuma. They are also called flying lemurs. I see them as my best acrobats."

Temo ended up showing his awantibo, galago, and avahi lemurs, then took the guests back to his residence for a short lunch.

"Are you impressed with the wide range of my monkeys?" he asked the pair.

Both nodded their heads and answered in the affirmative.

Their host suddenly frowned. "If only my daughter would give up her work in Bonito and come home to take part in my experimentation. We could accomplish so much together in monkey research and breeding. Such wonders might result!"

Neither of the outsiders said anything more for a short time after that.

That afternoon, Temo led the two to a new station and pointed to a monkey with a white face and a hooded crown of black hair. "On the island of Cimcifuga, it is called a sajou, while on the mainland it is known as a capuchin. The next one there is the ateles from the land of Pulsatilla. It has such long, spiderly limbs that popular tradition names it the spider monkey. Isn't that interesting?"

They walked past a station of tiny marmosets with tails as long as the rest of their bodies. Then they stopped to look at a silky-furred relative of the former.

"That is a tamarin and it closely resembles a squirrel," said Temo. "Next is a monkey from faraway Boraga called a ouistiti, with the strangely tufted ears and the banded tail. Elsewhere, it has the name of callithrix."

Entering the last of the stations, their guide pointed out the saki, the titi, the dourcouli, the hocheur, and the mangaboy that had startling white eyelids.

"Isn't that a shocking face for a monkey?" laughed Temo. "My late wife loved to cook these tasty rascals. She was an experienced gourmet, and epicure of monkey cuisine." His face turned serious. "My daughter, Choreia, never developed a taste for those dishes. From childhood, she felt sorry for the monkeys on the dinner plates. The girl had deep love and sympathy for all the creatures in the forest and on our plantation. She had a natural revulsion toward the exploitation of monkeys for food."

An abstracted, distant look came over his face.

Loligo spoke up next. "I understand that there is frequent use of monkey meat here on the island, and there is a flow of such exports to the mainland, to Provincia and all the other countries."

"That is a traditional business for us," muttered the primatologist as they entered his house. "It is one of the main economic bastions of our island economy."

Loligo rose before dawn, while Xuthus still lay asleep. Going out the exterior door for a breath of air, he saw an unexpected sight in the dim gray light from the sky.

Two mules were pulling a large wooden wagon hauling a load of cages. In the latter lay monkeys that appeared to be completely inert and unconscious.

What was this strange cargo for? Where were the two drivers taking their primate passengers?

In a fenzied spell of curiosity, Loligo decided to follow the vehicle at a distance from which he would not be spotted.

The wagon took a path along the coast to a long promontory sticking out into the Amphiscian Sea. Its destination was a two-storey stucco building where work was going on in the brightening daylight of morning.

What sort of enterprise could this be? wondered the fisherman. Vague suspicions started to arise in the back of his mind.

The investigating newcomer to the island decided to approach close enough to see what a crew of workers were doing inside. He first saw how the monkey cages were being emptied of the sleeping animals. Teams of two strong men carried the creatures inside in large metal tubs.

What is going on inside the structure? the observer asked himself. He crept slowly along the sandy beach of the cape, until he reached a large, glassless opening. No one was about to catch sight of him as he came near and peered through. He was able to see what was being done inside.

A scene of ghastly slaughter presented itself. The monkeys, one by one, were being killed and butchered. Their necks were cut with long, thick knives. Then the blood was drained out. It was a horrid, terrible sight for Loligo to witness. His reaction was one of disgust and revulsion to this horrendous sight.

The place was an abattoir, a butchery for monkey meat. He could see workmen cutting up dead animals on enormous tables of jacarauda wood. The smell rising from the shambles filled his nose.

The reason for the massacre of drugged primates was instantly clear to him. The scene was one of unending, single-minded carnage. There was no interruption or let-up in the gruesome business that was going on.

What an activity Dr. Temo was engaged in!

In the full light of day, Loligo slinked away, prepared to describe to his traveling companion what he had seen for himself.

After listening to what had happened, Xuthus took time to think over what all of it might mean.

It was a situation no one could have foreseen. His mind focused on the daughter of Temo, his psychognostic partner. She was soon to be on the island, available to tell him more. That would provide him the opportunity to inquire more deeply into the ugly industry of her father.

"Let's not ask Dr. Temo anything till I have spoken with Choreia," he proposed to his friend. "She is the one who can enlighten us the best. Then, we will know much more."

Loligo nodded his head yes. He could see no alternative to what his companion was proposing that they do.

At their noonday lunch, Xuthus made a request of their host.

"Can I travel to Caiman Harbor on the coach that will bring your daughter home?" he asked the father at the end of the meal.

"Of course," replied Temo. "I myself cannot go to town because of business here. Yes, she will be glad to see you come to fetch her. You can use one of the buckboards that she always liked riding in. That should please her a lot."

Loligo explained that he would not be going because of a painful headache he had dreamed up ahead of time as an excuse. His intention was to remain where he was and rest so as to conserve his strength and energy.

So it was Xuthus who drove a two-horse buckboard to Caiman to meet the steamer bringing Dr. Choreia back to Monkey Island. He started from the plantation very early, providing him time in the town before the arrival of the ship from Bonito. Tying up the wagon and horses at a post near the docks, he searched the commercial center for a store that sold meat. That was the item of trade he was interested in investigating. The subject had captured the full attention of his conscious mind.

Xuthus found a shop with a sign in front reading "Comestibles". He quickly entered the food store, scanning about till he found the ice locker that held meat. A short man dressed in butcher's white walked away from it after closing the glass door. The psychognostic went up to him and spoke.

"Excuse me, but I need some help. I am completely new in Caiman. Would you be kind enough to assist me?"

The small figure in white stopped, looking Xuthus in the face . "What is it that you desire, sir?"

"It may sound like an odd request, but it has to be made. I am hungry for the meat of an entellus or hanuman. I know they are part of the natural fauna of Monkey Island. Could you sell me some cuts of them, or advise me where I can get myself what I am after? Otherwise, I feel as if I am completely lost here."

A shadow seemed to fall over the face of the other. Instead of an answer, he presented a question of his own.

"Are you one of us? I mean a knuckle-walker?"

What was Xuthus to say to that? Uncertain what the little man was talking about, he merely nodded his head in an affirmative way.

The short one led him to a corner of the food store to make sure they were alone.

"I have nothing today but what was ordered by regular customers. It is not possible for me to spare any of the meat for you. I'm sorry, but I can order more monkey cuts for next week and include whatever you want to order. What specifically do you desire? I am able to satisfy the most demanding taste because I am located here on Monkey Island. Just name it and I know where it can be bought. My specialties are cebus and presbytis meat. Do you recognize those terms? They are technical terms for the capuchin and hanuman monkeys."

Xuthus invented a request for lean cuts of monkey flesh for a roast, not too certain what precisely he was talking about.

"I shall remember to include you in my next order to the plantation that supplys me. The station where they are bred and raised is not too far from here. You can come in and pick up what you want in five or six days. I shall be happy to serve you as my newest knuckle-walker customer, sir."

The investigator turned around and exited as hastily as he was able to with some degree of decorum.

A long horn toot announced the approach of the packet ship. Within minutes of its being tied up at the weir, the passengers began walking down an angled gangway onto the dock.

The slender form of Choreia was the first to descend. She wore a dress of gray blue velour that matched her slate eyes to a remarkable degree. A gleaming white bandeau held her golden hair in place. She broke into a beaming smile the moment that she spied Xuthus standing at the base of the gangway leading to the land level. The young woman was obviously thrilled and glad to see him safely in one piece.

"I am here to welcome you and drive you back to the plantation, Choreia," he explained once she stood before him. "What happened on the sea is a very long story. I can tell you the main incidents we experienced as we drive home. A buckboard is waiting up street, tied up and ready to go."

"How is my father?" she asked as they walked away from the steamer.

"He appears to be well. Why do you ask? Has he been ill?"

She made no response. Soon they reached the two horses and the vehicle. Xuthus held her by the arm as she climbed aboard, then circled around to the other side and himself boarded. In seconds they were on their way out of Caiman Harbor.

As they traversed the trail though the tropical forest the driver gave a general description of what happened to him and Loligo on the sea. The collision with the leviathan sperm whale, their rescue and adventure aboard the steamer, how the pair escaped and their voyage to Monkey Island. He made no mention of diploids or their role in the events he talked of. His narrative was a highly selective one.

All of a sudden, she became the one who raised the topic of bifold natures.

"Didn't you learn that Loligo is a ondinal? I should have told you that he is a diploid with an oceanic type of double."

Xuthus smiled a little. What dared he tell her at this particular moment? He was unsure how he should proceed.

"I uncovered that fact at once, but it did not affect our relationship or what happened to us at sea." He decided to try to divert her attention from the subject of biform diploids toward actual events that had recently occurred.

"I may not return to psychognostic practice and analysis. Your father has invited me to become a member of the staff on the plantation. What do you think I should do, Choreia?"

"You have interest in primatology?" she said, surprising him with the question.

He did not answer her directly. "I understand that your father had his heart set on your joining his work with monkeys. Why did you choose to go into psychognostics instead?"

The passenger beside him blushed. "What irony, if you should take the position offered to me to fill!"

Xuthus fell silent and pondered. He decided that he had to be truthful and candid with her. He could no longer keep certain personal matters hidden from her.

"I cannot be a part of his way of treating the animals he breeds. It is something unacceptable to me. Primates are too close to us biologically to justify the cruelty and abuse that occurs here. I feel profound revulsion against the actions and practices that I have witnessed since arriving on this island."

She turned her head toward him as he spelled out the brutality he had seen and learned about in relation to the animal population, specifically the monkeys.

"That is why I myself was unable to remain and work on the plantation," revealed Choreia. 'My conscience was too outraged to accept such merciless treatment of animals. The monkeys should never be used as a means of achieving diploid pleasure, as a source for biform gluttonly."

Xuthus looked puzzled and confused. "I cannot understand what you are talking about," he said in a halting voice. "How are diploids involved in the outrageous treatment of monkeys?"

She did not answer his questions at once. Only when the gate to her father's plantation came into view did she tell him what she had meant by her puzzling statement about diploids on Monkey Island.

"This all has to do with the knuckle-walkers. My father accepts the idea of theirs that only monkey flesh can satisfy their ravenous carnivorous appetite. His theory is that every member of the diploid species of knucklers has an instinctive drive toward primate cannibalism. The larger ape must feed on the smaller monkeys to fulfill its endless craving. That, for him, is a natural process that cannot be changed or reversed.

"Are you familiar with the knuckle-walker secundus and how it looks and acts?" she inquired of the partner sitting beside her.

"No," he answered. "I come from the Zenithal Mountains and we have no such diploids there. That is a part of the general picture with which I am ignorant and unfamiliar."

She was silent for a moment, then made a surprising revelation to him.

"Both my father and I are knucklers by heredity. I think I have dropped all desire to feast on the monkeys. But he believes it is an instinctive drive that cannot be erased. I will give you some secret literature about the type and we will talk about it. You must become aware of the monkey problem that plagues the knuckle-walkers as a biform grouping. It haunts them from their earliest years until the final moment of their lives."

They both became silent as they came near to the plantation residence.

Temo and his daughter sat at opposite ends of the table while the two male guests occupied the sides. Limited small talk occurred during the appetizer bowls of smallage and figs. But when the main course was served, a swift reaction came forth from Choreia.

"I can tell at once what this roast consists of," she declared, darting knives at her father. "Why do you have to do this my first day back home? What possible purpose can it serve you to make me eat what I loath to accept as acceptable food for humans? You know what I think and believe about this murder and atrocity committed against the helpless little monkeys."

Temo made an effort to look surprised at her sudden behavioral and emotional outburst.

"I can't understand you, Choreia. There is no compulsion involved here at my table. One eats what one pleases. There is no authority capable of commanding that anyone act contrary to inner feelings. Control yourself and do whatever you please, or refuse to eat whatever displeases you. There is nothing that anyone can do to change the thoughts in your mind. Likewise, you cannot compel anyone else not to eat a food that you will not accept. It goes in both directions. All of us must be granted the same, equal freedom."

He gave her a stern, victorious look that included a slight smile at the end.

"I will stay here," she asserted, "but eat something else."

"You refuse to try this specially raised, extremely tender bush baby?" he cynically asked her.

She pursed her lower lip. "Anything but such a slaughtered primate," she said through her teeth.

At that moment, the gosson entered with a tray of cheese ramequin. Everyone looked up and gazed at what he carried.

"I'll have some of that, please," she announced sharply. "At least it will help me fill my travel-weary stomach and not compel me to vomit an odious food."

All of a sudden, Xuthus spoke up. "I will have the same," he told the servant. Then he turned to Choreia. "It is best for me to skip the main dish. That will be in line with my usual dietary practice. I am not used to some of the food eaten on Monkey Island. It is best for me to avoid food that I am unfamiliar with and might have unforeseen consequences."

"Give me the ramequin, too," chimed in Loligo. "I know I can digest that."

A sullen mood prevailed for a time. When dessert time arrived, the gossoon brought in a gigantic tray with four dishes of spiceberry marmalade. As they finished this off, Dr. Temo started to make comments in a low, subdued tone.

"With so much food available on Monkey Island, there is no need to be restrictive or limiting. What I mean to say is that there should be no offense taken when people have varied tastes in food. Variety is the spice of the lives we lead, so that no one has the right to criticize or censor the food that others consume. That's how I see it."

A frigid chill arose from the plantation owner. Everyone present could feel the coldness.

Without a word, Choreia jumped up and fled from the room.

The three males watched her go, then themselves departed without speaking a word to each other.

Choreia sent a short booklet that described the knuckle-walker diploid through a servant to the bedroom shared by the two men. Xuthus read it rapidly and then related the contents to Loligo.

"It says here that the primate called the knuckler was not a direct ancestor of the human race, nor even a close relative, but a completely different genetic line. It has a bent posture and drags its fingers on the ground like the chimpanzee and the gorilla do. The body is extremely hairy and the head and the brain are smaller than that of modern human beings. Isn't that something?"

"It doesn't stand up straight when it walks?" said a surprised Loligo.

"The walk is defined as quadrupedal. The two forelimbs hold their fingers in a partially flexed position that allow the body weight to press down on the ground through the knuckles touching it. This study claims that our human ancestors possessed what it calls arboreality, so that their life in the trees made them move about upright on two legs. The knucklers, like the gorillas and chimps, were mostly confined to ground movement about. Their digits are curled inward and always flexed because of this method of locomotion. Human beings supposedly began as forest dwellers, while the knuckle-walkers of all species were inhabitants of the plains and prairies of grass. They took a different path of development and evolution from ours, this author says."

"I guess all of that is hard to believe until you see one of those biforms for oneself," mused Loligo.

"The hands of the knuckler has little ridges and concavities that grew there to prevent overburdening the long, columnar arms. They are long-armed but short-legged creatures, recognized at first glance as non-human. The arms are commonly kept rigid and there are ledges and notches in the wrist bones that never appear in any of the early hominids or today's human beings. They are vastly different from us, lacking the power of speech and language."

"It's too bad that the booklet gives no picture of the knuckle-walker," sighed the fisherman.

"From all that I read, I think that I would know one when I saw it," grinned Xuthus.

That night, Xuthus had a phantasmal dream that was rich in cryptic significance. On awakening the following morning, he recalled every detail of the arcane vision and described it to Loligo.

"I was on the wharf in Caiman Harbor, that much was recognizable. Even my single trip there for Choreia impressed the setting into my memory. I saw groups of men and women strolling about on the dockside, but there was one particular aspect that stood out at once. Each person had a small monkey on his or her shoulder. Isn't that odd and curious? I could tell that some of these creatures were tarsiers, others were tiny guenons and guerzas. I caught sight of a mangabey on the shoulder of one bulky, huge man. There was wide variance in the range covered, but there was not a single individual without a pet of this particular kind."

"A pet?" asked Loligo, as if mesmerized by what he was hearing.

"These animals were not on chains or leashes. They were as tame and well-behaved as can be. I had the impression that the monkeys were happy and well-treated. Not one of them seemed unhappy. They were pleased to be carried about by a human being who might be their owner or master. It was an uncanny scene to watch in a dream.

"A large packet steamer was moving into the dock. When I scanned its upper deck, I was astounded to see a familiar figure standing at the railing. It was Dr. Temo, and he was looking down at the throng of people with the monkeys on their shoulders. His gaze was inclined down toward the wharf and he was staring at one specific individual. It was his daughter Choreia, that's who it was. And she was looking up at him, a happy grin on her face. Her father was coming home from a long voyage to the mainland.

"But his face appeared angry and resentful. It was clear that the multitude of shouldered monkeys had sparked his emotions. His own daughter was carrying a small bush baby that weighed little and was no heavy burden.

"It appeared to me that Choreia had bested him in their quarrel concerning the monkeys. He was the loser and she the winner. His mind festered with resentent. But then I saw the unexpected. Dr. Temo transformed before the eyes of the crowd below. He turned into a primitive primate knuckle-walker on all fours. His dumb face and eyes gazed at Choreia with the hatred of a beast, with the ire of a wild animal. He was no longer the person we two have seen.

"There, in my dream, he had changed from a primus to a secundus. A naked knuckler stood on his four limbs, his forefingers balancing on the wooden deck of the steamer. That was the end, for my dream was over. I awakened in a sweat, the memory of what I had seen imprinted forever in my brain. What did it mean? What did it foretell, if anything? Help me, Loligo."

The latter looked at his companion with sympathy. "That is one of those night visions that only the dreamer himself can unlock. It concerns the monkeys and the diploid knuckle-walkers, so it must touch upon both Temo and Choreia. If you reveal what you saw to her, there is a good chance that she can unravel its meaning for you,

Xuthus. I would ask her for help in solving the mystery of what your dream was signifying."

The psychognostic thought all morning on the advice from his friend. Just before noon, he found Choreia on the veranda of the residence building, returned the booklet on knuckle-walkers, and told her the details of his dream of monkey pets. She appeared to understand it immediately. An uncanny excitement seized hold of her mind. This resulted in a flushing of her face.

"That fits in perfectly with what I have been considering in the back of my mind!" she asserted with spirited enthusiasm. "I have been imagining how a monkey can replace the secundus of a knuckler on a permanent basis, always present to hold the primate form of a human being. You have discovered the solution, Xuthus. A pet monkey can be made to embody the secundus of a knuckle-walker. That would surely cure the diploid species of its habit of consuming monkey flesh."

He thought on the complicated matter for a short while, the two of them staring at each other.

"I consider your idea worth trying," he finally told her. "We will need some monkeys to train and transform into substitutes for the secundi of knuckle-walkers."

"They can be taken from one of the stations tonight," she decided with determination. "Do not forget, I myself was born a knuckle-walker, child of a father who is one. I have not transformed into my secundus for several years because of the ability I learned to suppress my double form. But I can still attempt a projection of the secundus lodged within my mind into another body, that of a monkey. That may succeed or it may fail, but it will be a useful experiment for us to undertake. If we succeed, that victory will be historic and momentous.

"But this cannot wait. We must act at once, tonight at the latest," noted the partner of Xuthus in an urgent tone.

It was nearly midnight when two men entered the station where the hanumans and entelluses lived and were now sleeping. Loligo carried two small cages he had found in a tool barn. Xuthus carried a third one. It proved easy for them to kidnap the animals needed by Choreia for what she intended to accomplish. Only while they were being carried away in the cages did two of the monkeys awaken. Soon the situation became a bedlam of noisy disorder. Howling and screaming grew louder. The entire station awoke and panicked into wild madness. This then spread to neighboring monkey communities. The two raiders managed to reach the entrance gate to the station where they appeared in the nick of time.

With their three prisoners in cages, the two humans entered the tool barn where Choreia awaited her fellow conspirators.

"They should, perhaps, have been made comatose before bringing them here," she said to her fellow conspirators. "But what is done cannot be undone. We have to go on to the projective transformation at once."

"Each individual hanuman and the entellus must become acquainted with the human who is to become its primus," suggested Xuthus, looking directly at her. "How long do you think that will take to accomplish?"

She appeared to frown. "Only a few days, perhaps a week. Do we have that much time available before what we are doing is uncovered and becomes known?"

Xuthus thought a moment before responding to her fears.

"We can hide these three cages in our bedroom. Loligo and I will take turns minding and feeding the creatures. They will come to know us, and we can do the same with them. No outsider, only you, will be allowed to enter, not even the cleaners."

"I think that I can escape notice and be with the two of you for the projection experiments." said Choreia. "Our course is set and we are going to learn what is possible between humans and monkeys."

The pair gazed at each other with searching looks.

In three days, Choreia succeeded in completing a complete secundus transfer into the chosen entellus. The proof of the projection and relocation was in the new behavior of the monkey converted into a tame pet. It kept its eyes glued to her whenever she was present. The power over it by the primus in their relationship was total and supreme. If Choreia released it, the animal did not run away. It seemed tied to her for life, as if in permanent hypnosis. It loved being cuddled and carressed by its mistress. The monkey had been transformed into her ever present secundus.

Choreia had lost much of the knuckler character she had been born with. And an indestructible link between primus and secundus had been forged with a pet monkey. The two had become inseparable and were permanently bonded to each other from now on.

Xuthus and Loligo marveled at her victory, but theirs was not far behind.

First, the two confessed their diploid natures to their partner. Xuthus acknowledged he qualified as a sylphine, Loligo that he was ondinal. What would be the result if they attempted transpositions similar to that of Choreia? Would it be as easily attained as in her special case?

In only a few days, identical success came to Xuthus. At first he felt an absence inside himself, then a link replaced the loss of what had been there within him. A new tie that he had never had before now came into existence.

"I no longer can sense the sylphine one within me. My ties to my pet monkey has taken over the place where my double was before. I feel that I now have a new, different secundus as part of my existence," he explained to the other two.

He was astounded by what had happened to him.

A new satisfaction, heady and exuberant, entered the life of the psychognostic. His general orientation and attitude had been transformed by something as wild and primitive as a little monkey.

Last of all, Loligo experienced a secundus projection of his ondine double. His monkey became as cuddly and affectionate as the first two. It displayed tenderness and devotion that matched that of the ones that were transformed into secundi before it. He too was surprised and amazed by this experience of his.

Each of the three human beings were able to feel the adoration and the worship of the primate that now shared in the unconscious of its primus. A permanent, unbreakable bond held them in a coherent union.

None of the three need fear the loss of their former sylphine, ondinal, or knuckle-walker self. There was now a primus with a new tie and relation to a monkey secundus.

They had attained a condition that no previous diploid of any kind had ever created before in the history of the planet. Each was now united to an independent being, a separate creature.

Who would have believed such a breakthrough possible?

Degree by degree, apprehension was rising in the mind of Dr. Temo.

Why was his daughter spending many hours in the room of the two guests?

What was she engaged in with the strangers who had washed up on the shore? Why did none of the three return to the mainland and their duties there? What was keeping each of them on Monkey Island? he asked himself.

These questions ate away at the tranquility of his mental state. He paid attention to every word and movement of each of them, especially his daughter. She had always been distant, but now Choreia had become silently hostile to him. But she came to him late one evening as he worked on business accounts in his office suite at the rear of the residence.

"I am leaving for Caiman tomorrow morning, father. My aim is to catch the packet steamer for Bonito. Because my departure will come before dawn, I thought it best to say good-bye tonight."

"This is a sudden decision, then? And are you leaving with your partner and his friend?"

Was she hiding her slate blue eyes? Yes, he decided, she looked aside as she answered. His daughter was concealing something important from him.

"Yes, it is better that we depart together. There is no longer any purpose to any of us remaining behind. I shall be taking with me a pet I recently acquired. It will not be missed in the station where I found it."

She now gazed squarely into the face of her father.

"What species is this pet of yours?" asked Temo, his curiosity and suspicion aroused.

"A hanuman. The two of us took to each other and cannot separate."

His face burned crimson as he gazed at his one, his only child. He seemed dismayed.

"A missing monkey complicates my accounting," he muttered. "I shall have to put it down as a gift charge. I guess that you deserve a present from me as you go away. Who can say when we will see each other again? That is what it will be, a gift from your father."

His smile had something forced and cynical about it, she thought. There were some complicated thoughts that he was engaged with, she suddenly realized.

Choreia had been about to kiss his brow, but decided not to do so. She realized how little the two of them truly meant to each other. The time for genuine love had long passed. It was never going to return as it had been when she was a child growing up on the island.

As she silently shuffled out of the office, her father made a decision to have a look at the monkey she was taking to Bonito with her. Why not personally evaluate what it would cost him? He had a perfect right to inspect the gift he was making to his one and only child.

Until their departure for Caiman Harbor in the morning, the three who were leaving on the steamer decided to store the three cages holding their monkeys in a safe place. Their choice was the tool barn, where no one was expected to enter during their last night on the island.

Xuthus and Loligo carried the cages there. Choreia insisted that she must go along, her wish being to stay near her beloved secundus as long as possible When the trio reached the barn, she came up with a surprising proposal to her co-conspirators.

"Why don't I remain here with our three friends until it's time to depart? They won't be all to themselves and I won't have to be lonely till dawn. It seems a good solution for all of us."

Xuthus and Loligo exchanged glances, then the former voiced their decision. "Yes, if that is what you wish, Choreia. I see a lot of good sense in your idea."

The two men quickly exited,leaving her with the three caged primates.

Dr. Temo saw the outlines of something unknown but dangerous to him.

Why was his daughter secretly meeting with the suspicious guests?

What treacherous project was being hatched in the corners of his plantation? he wondered with increasing alarm.

Every evening he began to roam about, on the lookout for evidence of an invisible conspiracy. There was no doubt in his mind that there was an unseen, unknown plot afoot somewhere. But what could it be concerned about?

Was his own Choreia involved in these affairs? He had suspicions that she was connected somehow. It was important that he find out what she may have been dragged into by her strange professional partner.

He was unable to name or describe what was happening, making it all the more horrible and frightening. His fight was with something unseen and unidentified. He had to learn the extent of the danger involved.

There was not the slightest clue of the nature of the overhanging threat. Not until he wandered into the supply barn, having heard a screech of some kind coming from inside. Had one of his monkeys escaped and hidden itself in the structure? Was that what had happened?

Temo, carrying a small whale oil lantern in his hand, opened the door and entered the barn. His eyes at once caught sight of Choreia sitting beside cages that contained hanumans. The latter, awakened by his light, started to make noises of alarm.

Looking up at her father, Choreia gaped with a widely opened mouth.

"Father!" was all she was able to say in her sudden terror.

He moved closer, the little lantern's rays focused on the three cages where the fearful monkeys writhed and shook in consternation. What possible peril did they face?

"You have three of the monkeys in here," barked Temo at his daughter. "What are you planning to do with them? His eyes fell on several of her packed trunks and bags. "Are you going to take these animals with you? Why are you here with these cages? I have to know what is happening to you, my dear."

All at once, Choreia rose to her feet, boldly staring at him with defiance. "I plan to go to the mainland with Xuthus and Loligo. There is no possible alternative. And I am taking these three monkeys with me. That has been decided upon and is scheduled to occur soon."

"So, my property can be stolen from me while I am supposed to be asleep. Is that the strange game that the three of you have devised? I call that treachery and deceit."

"Father, you do not understand," she called out desperately. "You are mistaken."

"Oh, I understand quite well. I can comprehend the entire design being carried out by the evil gang that you have joined up with."

The shrill shreiking of the encaged primates, reaching as far as the residence, began to wake up all those asleep, including both Xuthus and Loligo.

Dr. Temo, his eyes swollen with insane anger, stepped close to the nearest cage, the one that held his daughter's pet monkey.

When he was only a foot away, he roared and shouted madly at the bewildered hanuman.

"You traitor! You stupid beast! Don't you know who has fed and sheltered you? Betrayer! Evil monstrosity! Is this how you repay me for all I have provided for you?"

The unexpected movement of the monkey occurred with lightening speed, faster than the eyes of either the father or the daughter could follow or understand.

No human being could have perceived or comprehended what the new secundus accomplished in only a few moments.

With its long arm and whipping tail it dislodged the lantern in the left hand of Temo. Before the latter was able to react, the isinglass protector was smashed and the illuminating fire had flamed up.

The shirt and coat of the screeching man now blazed red and yellow. The oil fire shot out in all directions. It grew fierce and unstoppable.

There was nothing the burning plantation-owner could do to save himself.

Choreia gazed in a trance of helpless passivity. The man on fire was doomed and was about to perish.

Xuthus and Loligo rushed in soon, but too late to change the outcome for her father.

Three pairs of human eyes and three pairs of monkey eyes watched in stunned fascination as the life of Temo came to a rapid end.

Within two years, primate pets like monkeys became common pets and companions among diploids of all stripes in Provincia and the adjacent islands.

The psychognostic profession became the champions of this therapy for patients. Diploids were in the forefront, led by the knuckle-walkers following the example of Dr. Choreia. She and Xuthus became renowned as the married couple in the vanguard of the movement for biform transformation and metamorphosis. Their innovative therapy for troubled diploids as well as the healthy caught on with millions of individuals.

The changed diploids no longer had primus and secundus phases through and over time, but were able to have simultaneous life and existence with a pet on the same level as themselves. Each of them was separate, with its own conscious mind and identity.

Diploids were never the same as they had been before. Their monkey pets had opened a new world for their divided existence. Their personal secundus had migrated into a creature they could live with and share love with.

A new mode of living now opened up for all the diploids who would accept and follow it.

The End

www.ingramcontent.com/pod-product-compliance
Lightning Source LLC
Chambersburg PA
CBHW020623110726

47899CB00002B/631